# PRAISE FOR

# THE MAN FROM THE BRAZOS

by

## Ermal Walden Williamson

"I like **The Man From the Brazos** because the plot was well done and makes you think as you read. So many westerns are fun to read, but they don't stick in your memory very long. This book will stay with you. Ermal is developing into an excellent western writer."
**Judge Roy Bean, SASS #1 Single Action Shooting Society**

"When abolitionists and slavers clash for control of the Kansas territory just before it was to achieve statehood, Matt Jorgenson found himself caught up in their bloody, brutal conflict. Matt was fast and fatal when handling a pistol, but being an accomplished gunhand with a widening reputation is no defense against falling in love with another man's woman or being able to stop the murder of his best friend in a time when pre-Civil War politics was setting neighbor against neighbor. Highly recommended for all western buffs, **The Man From The Brazos** is an entertaining and vivid read."
**Midwest Book Review (see more about me) from Oregon, WI USA**

"I found I really liked reading about the younger version of Matt Jorgenson and how he became known as a quick draw. It is obvious that Mr. Williamson is more comfortable with the pen in this story as it flows along quite well and the story always keeps the reader interested in what is going to happen next. The characterization is wonderful and the evolution of Matt into a quick draw is a pleasure to absorb. A lot of westerns don't really delve into much historical relevance, but The Man from the Brazos is rich with historical importance. You won't regret picking up this book and letting it take you back Kansas almost 150 years ago."
**Conan Tigard**
**http://www.bookbrowser.com/Reviews** .html

In
Sval
Good wishes
Belgium

John Wayne

Williamson
2008
Browny

# PROLOGUE

## THE DESTINY OF A FAST GUN

February 2, 1871

A person's destiny is next to impossible to see at the beginning of one's life, for certainly no one can ascertain what he will become as it is not a person's privilege to see. A "fastgun" was a euphemism that had not yet been established. To become a fast gun would certainly be a turning point in Matt Andersen's career, a career he had not chosen and for which he had not prepared himself, and as a man on the run, he called himself, Matt Jorgensen.

He would find out that his destiny was determined by a set of circumstances, none of which were under his control. But once he had attained the mastery of his calling, his destiny was sealed and his life took on a totally new meaning.

For two men to come together under the umbrella of similar circumstances and forge a relationship together in time and space would be an act of God no one could understand or envision. Such was the case with Matt who became famously known as "The Brazos Kid", and Rod Best, Marshal of Abilene. How they met and became the best of friends, in spite of their fierce competitiveness in a business that called for guts and glory, would plum the depths of their exciting and romantic adventures which they shared together as two of the bravest gunfighters in the history of America's West.

One of the most infamous of days in the annals of Western folk-lore happened February 1, '71. Matt Jorgensen and his friend Steve Andrews rode into Waco, Texas where they were bent on spending the night earning some extra spending money playing that famous game of fortune, poker. Matt grew up in Montana and, with his brother Lukas, learned the game well enough to make some spending money.

Matt was now a professional hired gunman who, with Steve, his Civil War friend and companion, ran the Brazos Bar M Ranch south of Waco across the Brazos River. Both men were in their thirties. Matt stood six-feet four inches, with broad shoulders. His eyes were steely blue, and he had a gentle smile, which befriended him to the ladies. He wore denim pants, a dark blue woolen shirt and a tanned leather vest. A loose bandanna covered his throat, and a gray Stetson fit his head real nice. Tonight he just wanted to play cards.

Steve was a good-looking man with a bushy moustache and a full head of light brown hair hidden under his well-worn Stetson. His dimples let people around him know that he was also a gentle man like Matt, but firm. He was six-foot two straight up and down. He, too, wore a leather vest, but he wore his bandanna a lot looser than Matt, and his Stetson was black.

The men found themselves an active table towards the rear of the Green Slipper Saloon, and offered to join in as soon as a certain chair became vacant. The chair the dealer was sitting in was Matt's favorite seat. He chose never to sit anywhere else, as an early acquaintance warned him to beware of card cheats and killers who walk behind unsuspecting players. Besides, he enjoyed having the wall to lean on from time to time.

"You can sit in right now, men," the dealer offered as he shuffled the cards. "Sit down."

"No rush," Matt replied, standing at the bar instead. "Two whis-keys!" he ordered.

"Suit yourself," the dealer continued. "Might not get another chance with all the cowpokes pouring in this time of night."

"The Red Garter's down the street," Matt replied. "They can go there."

"That one's filled up already. What are you two waitin' for, if I might ask?" The dealer started dealing the cards to the other two gentlemen.

"You're sittin' in my chair."

"Your chair?  Your name's on it?"

"Nope," Matt answered as he paid for the drinks.  "Thanks."

"Then why d'ya say it's your chair?"

"I never sit in any other."

"Never seen you in town before."

"I come in once or twice a month," Matt answered, swigging down his drink.  "You're new in town."

"Been here a few weeks," the dealer replied, filling out the hands of his two players.  "You won't play unless you sit in my chair, right?"

Matt turned and stood with his back to the dealer, but watched his actions through the long mirror that hung behind the bar.  Steve sipped his drink as he walked around the table watching the men play.

"You're superstitious, I'll bet," the dealer suggested, watching his two counterparts throwing down cards for a draw.  "All right, mister," the dealer continued.  "After this hand, I'll take the other chair."

The dealer gathered his winnings from the two gentlemen players and moved to the other side of the table, taking his money and cards with him.

"I've never heard anyone being so superstitious in my life," a player said as he watched Matt walk over to the table.

Steve sat in the chair next to him.  "He's superstitious."

"I have," a tenor voice came from the far end of the bar.  "I met a man up in Abilene that did.  A marshal.  Always sat with his back to the wall.  Nothing superstitious about it.  Just didn't want anyone to take advantage of him behind his back."

"That it?" the dealer asked, tossing a double eagle into the pot for the ante.

Without a reply, Matt sat down, threw in his ante, and then took a cigar from his leather vest.

"You don't say much," the dealer said as he began dealing out the cards.  "What about your friend?"

"Let's play," Matt said, lighting his cigar.

"Sure, mister," the dealer replied, finishing up the deal.  "Mind telling us your names?"

"Steve Andrews," Steve answered, peeking at his cards.

"Matt Jorgensen."

"Matt Jor . . ." the man at the far end of the bar said, almost spilling his drink.  He was short, rather stout, sported a thin moustache and a goatee, and wore a black derby that suggested he wasn't a cowboy.

"The Brazos Kid?" he asked, looking at Matt.

"Sometimes called in my younger days," Matt responded with his eyes leveled to the man's hands dangling at his sides. He could see he didn't wear any guns. "Brazos to most, now."

"I hear you're one of the fastest guns alive."

"I'm a mite slower," Steve mused and tilted his hat forward.

"My name's Kelly Williams, reporter for the *Waco Gazette*," the man said as he started to walk over to Matt's table.

"Who's faster?" the dealer asked.

"The marshal this man met in Abilene," Matt answered, letting out a ring of cigar smoke while he examined his cards.

"Not any more, "Kelly said.

Matt took out his cigar, tilted back his hat, and looked straight into the little man's eyes.

"What do you mean, Mr. Williams?" the dealer asked, holding the deck of cards in both hands.

"He was killed in a saloon a few days ago. News just came in from the *Abilene Journal*, ready for the morning edition."

"Who was killed?" the dealer asked again.

Kelly watched Matt's face grow in anger. He shut up fast, and walked back to his seat at the bar.

Matt threw his hand down on the table, rose and walked over to the little man. "What's his name?"

"You know who I'm talking about," Kelly said, taking a nervous sip of his beer.

"Who?" Matt demanded.

"Rod Best! The Marshal in Abilene."

"The hell he did!" Matt yelled at the little man, turning him around and picking him up by his lapels, almost hiding Kelly's face inside his coat.

"Here," Kelly said, "I've got my notes right here."

Matt turned loose of Kelly's coat, and allowed him to reach into his pocket. His hand came out with a note pad, which he quickly handed to Matt. The notes were scribbled in Kelly's own shorthand, so he had to read them for Matt. Putting on his spectacles, he took the pad back, and read aloud. "1 February '71, about 10 o'clock p.m., Rod Best entered Jason's Saloon ... Abilene, Kansas ... became drunk ... involved with man's wife ... husband shot Best before he could draw."

The notes were scribbled in Kelly's own shorthand, so he had to read them for Matt. Putting on his spectacles, he took the pad back, and read aloud, "1 February '71, about 10 o'clock p.m., Rod Best entered

Jason's Saloon ... Abilene, Kansas ... became drunk ... involved with man's wife ... husband shot Best before he could draw."

Matt stood silent.

"I know you were good friends, everyone knows, I suppose. What are you going to do, Brazos?"

The Waco and Northwestern Railroad left early the next morning from Waco, and Matt was on it heading for Abilene, Kansas to pay his respects to his old friend.

As the heavy black engine chugged along leaving a plume of smoke and ashes strewn across the land abutting the tracks, his mind raced back to the time he had to leave his home in Bozeman, Montana just thirteen years earlier. It was the same year he met Rod Best.

It was a cold February evening, 1858, as chilled winds whipped through the Montana hills.

Matt turned from just having a serious conversation with his father, walked over to his mother, Annie and said, "I love ya, Ma."

His mother knew he had made his decision to leave.

Matt walked into the house for a last look at his brother, Lukas' body was draped on the floor with that of another man, Jeff Daniels, a killer.

Matt's father Wil, and Anse Peterson followed him in. Anse was the bartender at the Golden Eagle Saloon in town, and Wil's best friend. Having known Wil for many years, he watched the wild antics of Matt and Lukas as they grew up and often visited the saloon.

Matt knelt down and touched his brother's uncovered hand, and asked, "Can I help bury my brother?"

Anse answered him. "Best not, Matt. Sooner you leave, the better."

"He's right, son," Wil concurred.

His mother sobbed.

"Wish I hadn't shot that horse, now," Anse said.

"Where's the carcass?" Wil asked.

"I pulled it off to the side, and partially buried it with some weeds. Jeff said he'd finish it. Guess he never did."

Jeff was the no-good varmint who had talked Lukas into joining him in robbing the local bank in town. The scheme failed, and Jeff and Lukas were killed. The town minister, riding by in his carriage at the wrong time, was also killed. Because Jeff was dressed in Matt's clothes at the time, the town folk mistook his shot-up carcass to be Matt.

Anse had shot Jeff's horse earlier because of a broken leg, and in town, Jeff took Matt's horse. This added to the evidence that it must have been Matt who was the second man killed in the robbery. If the horse's carcass was seen, it would have given rise that a third man was involved, and an investigation into who that third man was could have led to Matt, who was still alive and hiding.

"Damn," Wil said. "Can't take a chance. At light, you and Matt backtrack, and make sure it's buried deep."

"Yes, sir."

"And you, son. When that's done, you're gonna head out South."

Matt stood up and felt Annie's warm embrace.

Annie looked over her son's shoulders towards Wil. "Why?" she asked quietly.

Wil put his big hand on Matt's shoulders and wrapped his other arm around Annie. "Cause, I love ya, Matt. That mean anything to you? One son's dead. I don't want both my sons killed."

Tears fell from Annie's cheeks.

Matt's tired body finally felt the pangs of weariness from running scared, the drink, and the beating from Wil's fists earlier when he first found out Lukas was dead. Wil's quick temper led to a beating Wil forgot for the moment that Matt had nothing to do with the botched-up robbery, and that he could be implicated in it as well if he were caught. Matt was in town only to stop Lukas, but failed, and in all the excitement and gunfire, escaped unseen.

Still sobbing, Matt collapsed in his father's arms as Anse helped keep him from falling.

Anse helped Wil carry Matt to the back of the house, and put him down on the bed where he slipped into a deep sleep.

Wil lingered over him for a while to assure his safety, and then he returned to the arms of Annie. Together, they kept awake. Anse sat on the porch and kept watch through the night.

Daylight was slow to come to the ranch that day, but before the winter sun had peaked its head over the nearest rise, Wil was on a hill digging the graves.

Matt and Anse rode down the road that led to town, as the sun had just broken the sheet of night.

Annie, dressed heavily with a long brown coat and scarf around her head, climbed the hill to join her husband. Looking out, she watched the shadowy figures of Matt and Anse ride away.

"He'll be back, Annie. Soon."

"I know."

Annie watched Wil. They were burying one son, and watching another ride away, and she never before felt that much pain in her heart.

"The cowhands shoulda gotten up by now. They can help you."

"I'd rather do it myself."

Annie stood there, watching Matt and Anse as they disappeared down the road. Wil stopped digging, grabbed her cold hand and held it tight as they watched the two men ride away.

A hard rancher, Wil bred and raised cattle as well as horses that earned him a decent living. His desire was for his sons to follow suit. He felt somehow now that he had failed them.

The first of the wranglers crawled out of the bunkhouse. Seeing Wil and Annie on the hillside, they quickly dressed and joined up with them. They had heard about the botched-up robbery before while putting the bodies in the front room. They were not aware of Matt's return, or of his having left. They believed that the two bodies being buried were those of Matt and Lucas.

Now, they carried the draped bodies in a buggy to the northern slope of the hill. The men helped finish the digging, in spite of Wil's resistance. Once the holes were deep enough, the men lowered the bodies gently into each of them, one at a time.

"They were shooting at Matt, too," Wil said softly to Annie as he held his arm around her. "If we tell the townsfolk it was Matt, they'd lynch him. This way, two graves, two crosses. Matt and Lukas. No one will know the better." He paused on the hillside and looked down the road one last time. "He tried to stop Lukas. That's good enough for me."

With the last clump of dirt on the graves, he whispered to himself, "I wish he could have stayed." Then he cried loudly, "Hell!" and threw the spade as far as he could.

Annie grasped Wil's hand and squeezed hard. "Ready, Wil?"

"Yeah." Wil nodded, and returned to the freshly dug mounds. Taking off his hat and bowing his head, he said slowly, "Lord, bless our children. And forgive them their deeds. Both are in Your hands, now. Amen."

One son rested there in the grave, and the other was riding away.

The couple left the wranglers and walked down the hill together. At the bottom, they stopped, turned, and looked back at the hill.

"They'll always be with us, Annie, Wil said hoarsely, "sharing a cup of coffee in the morning. We'll still see them ridin' the range. They'll always be with us."

Annie leaned against Wil, wiped her face with her apron, and looked into the morning sunlight.

"I know that, Wil." She sobbed and wiped her tears with her handkerchief.

Wil caressed her gently. "You can bet on it."

He looked again at the hill where two crosses stood, and thought, "If there was only another way."

The snow began to fall gently to the ground.

# PART ONE

# THE DAKOTA TERRITORY

# CHAPTER 1

## A COWBOY RIDES ALONE

February, 1858

A cowboy's life can be lonesome on a trail drive, even with five thousand or more head of cattle and a hefty bunch of cowhands surrounding him for company. Once Matt had the pleasure of riding with his pa and brother on such a trail ride, but now it was a lot lonelier for a cowboy without any family or friends.

Matt had always wanted to be a successful rancher following in his pa's footsteps. He had no aspirations of doing anything else, and certainly no yearning to explore other regions of the country. He thought about his having to leave the ranch because of being implicated in a killing, one that he only became involved in while trying to save his brother's life. His brother was killed, but he escaped, and now he was on the run for something he didn't do and he had no particular place to go. He thought about it that day, then and often, and wondered how it all came about. He headed his horse Skeeter towards Texas.

The way south was a wilderness to be explored for any man. Matt had to avoid nearby ranches or farmhouses where he would be recognized. After all, he was a man who was supposed to be dead. If he were found to still be alive, he would be wanted for murder. Instead, he rode the high country and skirted the plains for miles and miles. He rode until he could ride no longer, and he slept in the saddle when his eyes refused to stay open.

Feeling confident that no one knew him this far south, he reined up early on a cold morning at a ranch house in Dakota Territory. From what he'd seen as he'd ridden toward the plume of chimney smoke rising straight up from top of the house, the ranch was a pretty big spread with what appeared to be as many horses as they had cattle.

Bone-chilled and weather-beaten, Matt knew he must be scrubby looking with a week's beard growth as well. He'd take the chance no one would turn him away. His stomach growled, reminding him it had been days since he'd had a good hot meal.

A stout woman who looked to be in her sixties stepped out onto the porch wringing a rag dry before she threw it over a porch rail. "Saw you ride up, stranger."

Matt stayed in his saddle, feeling cold, and weary, but hearing her voice, he oddly felt welcomed.

"Could you use another hand, Ma'am?"

"Got more help than I need right now, son," she said gently, as she swept the loose strands of steel gray hair out of her eyes. She examined Matt's weakened condition as he hung in his saddle. "You look mighty tired. And hungry, I'd bet my last nickel."

"You'd win that bet, Ma'am. Haven't had a hot meal since -- well, I can't remember."

"Then, you gonna crawl outta that saddle, or do you want me to feed you sittin' up there?"

Matt didn't need a second invitation. He lifted himself out of the saddle and slid down to the ground with a groan he couldn't contain. He hitched his horse to a rail that stretched in front of the porch.

The woman watched him shiver as he rubbed Skeeter on his neck.

"Gotta feed m'horse first."

"Take him 'round back to the barn. I'll bring you some hot water, and you'll find some feed for your horse there, too," she said with her hand on the door. "I'll have you something to eat right shortly. Reckon I could find something for you to do to pay for it."

While the bacon fried and the eggs popped in the pan, Matt found an ax and a pile of sow-covered wood to use it on. A few chops were enough to prove he was less capable of performing the simple chore than he thought, although he did manage to split a few blocks into kindling. Hungrier than a full-grown bear coming out of a winter's hibernation, he was more than glad to quit when the woman called him to the table. Somewhere between second and third helpings, he decided to talk.

"Any more of that coffee, Ma'am? Ain't had any coffee for days."

Now, a cowboy can go without buttermilk for weeks. And he can go without bacon for weeks. But he has to have his makings and a good strong cup of black coffee and it's got to be hot. When she poured it into a cup and handed it to him, he grabbed hold, ran the cup beneath his nose, closed his eyes and savored the aroma.

"That sure do smell sweet." He chugged it down ignoring the scalding heat of it, and then grinned and held out the cup for more. "Ma'am, you sure are an angel."

She poured more coffee for him, put the pot back on the stove, and sat down at the table across from him. "What's your name?"

"Matt," he answered, stopping short of giving his real last name of Andersen. "Matt Jorgensen." It was a simple enough name, he thought.

"Pleased to meet you, Matt Jorgensen. I'm Margaret Daily, but everybody calls me Ma. You can, too. This is my place now that my husband's passed on." She watched him scrape every last drop of egg yolk from his plate with the last of a biscuit. "I won't ask any more questions now, son, till you feel more up to talkin'. Bunkhouse is out past the smokehouse. When you're ready, you can stow your gear in there. Jerry's our foreman. He and the boys are all out on a round-up. When they get in, and it'll be late, I'll introduce you. Meanwhile, you get some rest."

"I'm okay." Matt pushed away from the table and carried his dishes to the sideboard. "Thank you a lot for the meal. I'll just go on out and finish that log pile."

The day wore on and Matt found himself a home for the time being. Ma walked out to the porch an hour before sunset and looked towards the west as her men rode fast and furious, driving a hundred head of horses to the corral.

Her foreman, Jerry, rode up to the corral and made certain the gate was opened. Once they got the horses settled inside, the cowboys rode around the ranch shaking a day's work from their horses. Afterwards, they dismounted and walked them to cool them off.

Jerry hitched his horse on the rail and bounced up on the porch. Ma greeted him with a hug and a smile.

"The weather started actin' up on us, but we got at least a hundred head, Ma," Jerry said. "Whose pony in the barn, Ma?" he asked as he looked around to see who was on the ranch. "I happened to see it as I rode by the barn."

"A drifter. He came looking for work," she answered, hoping to find sight of him.

"Name's, Matt," a voice answered from the other side of the house. He came walking up with a pail of milk in both hands. "Been milking your cow."

Pushing his Stetson to the back of his head, Jerry looked sternly at Matt. "Well, now, sonny," he said, sizing up Matt prematurely to be a sissy because of him holding a pail of milk in both hands. "Who be you?"

"Name's Matt Jorgensen."

Some of the other cowboys with their reins in their hands came over to see the "sissy".

"What cha got, Jerry?" one of them asked, looking at Matt walking up to the porch with the milk.

"Is it a man or a lady?" another asked.

"Well, boy. Which are ya?" Jerry asked.

"If you're thinkin' milkin' a cow is a sissy's job, you ain't tried Bossy over there. I done lost a pail jest tryin' to get her use to me," Matt said with a big grin.

"He's lookin' for work, Jerry," Ma said, interrupting their fun. "Guess he didn't know milkin' was a mornin' thing."

"We can't use another hand," Jerry shot back. 'Sides, he don't look too good."

"Should have seen him earlier," she replied. "Take him on. You know I'll not turn a good man away."

"What can you do?" Jerry asked, as he watched Matt enter the kitchen and set the buckets on the table.

"Jest about anything," Matt replied.

"Can you break a horse?" one of the cowboys asked.

"Yep."

Matt was weaned on a horse and learned the hard way from his pa who rode with him. He broke his first bronc when he was still in puberty. This was his way of showing off, confident after a meal, with his muscles toned-up from use of the ax.

"Let him be, boys," Ma said. "He's all in. Rode all night, and worked all day. 'Sides, soup's on."

14

"First thing in the mornin' then, cowboy," Jerry said sarcastically as he and the rest of his crew headed for the washbasins.

It was not the most pleasant evening for Matt. He worked while the rest of the men ate. After supper Ma found extra bedding and gave it to him.

"Find the boy a bunk Jerry, and don't go fussin' over him," she ordered, standing outside the bunkhouse while the men bedded down for the night. "He's been workin' hard all day, and he'll be needin' a good night's sleep for what you've got in mind for him come mornin'."

Matt was the first up the next morning. He saddled Skeeter and took him out to the corral for some warm-up exercises. It had snowed that night, and putting Skeeter through his paces packed some of the snow down where horse tailings had become part of the landscape. He rode figure eights and danced with her by putting her into swift gallops, turning her, and trotting her back.

The rest of the cowboys joined in watching him before grabbing their first cup of coffee. Some of them were still wrapped in their blankets wearing only their union underwear, boots, and hats. For the most part, the group was a friendly bunch of cowboys out having a good time. They simply wanted to get the fun over with so they could settle down to another of Ma's good breakfasts.

Jerry stomped out of the bunkhouse fully dressed in heavy clothing with a scarf around his neck.

"Let's see ya," Jerry yelled out as he watched Matt put Skeeter through his paces.

Matt cleared Skeeter from the corral, and after hitching him to the hitching rail in front of the house, returned and paused for a moment to get a good look at some of the meanest cowboys he had seen since leaving Bozeman. At least they pretended to be the meanest. They were really good old cowboys taking advantage of the opportunity to have a little fun at Matt's expense. And besides that, they were freezing.

"You got one?" he asked, meaning an unbroken horse ready for him to ride. "Those you jest brought in look too tired to give me a good ride."

"Not one of them," Jerry answered. "We've got ol' Bellyacher. He's never been rode."

At that moment, a couple of cowboys brought in an Appaloosa gelding with their ropes on him. He was snorting frost from his nostrils, and stomping the tailings into fine dust as one of the cowboys wrestled him around the ring post to settle him down.

"Why'd ya name him 'Bellyacher'?" Matt asked, as he sidled Jerry to the corral. "Eat too many green apples?"

Jerry got the saddle on him while another wrangler fitted him with a hackamore. "You'll find out soon enough," he answered," biting down on Bellyacher's ear to keep him settled. "Get on him, boy," he mumbled with his teeth dug deep into the horse's ear.

When he heard Jerry's muffled bark, Matt mounted the Appy, aiming to stay the ten. Bellyacher snorted and Jerry let loose as Matt's hands gripped the reins. The gelding arched his back, went up off the ground and came down hard. The impact was jolting, and Matt like felt his back would break.

Two seconds into the ride, Matt thought about hitting the icy dirt and staying there. Four seconds, and he found the rhythm. He knew he could stay the ten without any trouble now. Six seconds slipped by into seven and eight, and he was enjoying the ride for all it was worth. He knew the next two seconds would be up and the cowhands would be cheering him on.

Then it happened. Matt seemed to be filled with confidence, something he hadn't felt since he left home. He could ride this horse, that was for damned sure, and he'd show this bunch of candy-ass cowpunchers a thing or two about bronc riding.

Bellyacher went for the rails and slipped on a pocket of ice that had been hidden by some tailings. Matt reined up a little too strong, causing Bellyacher to rear backwards out of control. Matt let go of the reins and grabbed for dirt. The Appy came down and hit his head hard against the wooden pole with his full body. As the Appy fell on his head and rolled out onto the corral ground, Matt scampered to safety, and quickly got up.

Bellyacher didn't.

"Damn you to hell!" Jerry cursed from his angered lips. He ran to the horse's aid. Bellyacher lay there in pain. With the help of the other wranglers, Jerry slipped the saddle off and eased the Appy as well he could into a comfortable position.

Ma had witnessed the ride, and the fall, and ran over to Bellyacher's side. Kneeling at his head, she cradled his head in her hands, looked into his painful brown eyes, and kissed him. He had been part of the family, even though no man had ever ridden him. Matt had come the closest to riding him.

"Bellyacher, sweet thing," was all she could muffle in her tears.

"We'll take care of him, Ma," Jerry said, lifting her up and away from the Appy.

He walked Ma slowly out of the corral as Matt looked on. A gunshot sent a chill down Ma's back as she momentarily stopped, and stood in her tracks, her body shivering in the cold. She had lost her favorite horse only a short while after the drifter rode in.

Matt ran to catch up with her.

"I didn't mean for this to happen," Matt said. "Ma'am, you don't know how sorry I am. I sure didn't mean this to happen."

Jerry let go of Ma for the moment, reeled around and slammed a haymaker to Matt's jaw, sending him to the dirt. "You pulled up on him and made him go over. Get the hell out of here before I kill you."

Matt scrambled upright and adjusted his jaw. He looked back at Ma, and knew the deepest pain he'd ever known. Everything that had happened to him in the past few weeks slammed together in his gut. He took Ma's shoulders and stared into her eyes. "I'm sorry."

Jerry's fists clenched. Matt dropped his hands and backed slowly.

"I'm leavin', but I'll make up for Ma's loss some way. You can count on that."

Matt knew he had done wrong in pulling up on the reins, It became another lesson he would never repeat again. He walked to the edge of the corral and mounted Skeeter, his only friend for the moment, and rode away.

The morning sun stretched Matt's shadow riding away from the Daily Ranch. He had earned his meals by doing his chores, and he got to sleep on a soft cot for one night. Now it would be another long night on the cold hard ground.

Three more days in the saddle brought Matt through a snowstorm, and into a two-bit town in the Dakota Territory, the only town around where many cowboys enjoyed their earnings on a Saturday night. The saloon was warm and inviting for a tired and cold cowboy, and Matt had enough money for either a meal or a hand of poker that night, but not both. He opted for poker, knowing that if he ate his supper money, it would be his last for a while to come. He prided himself on his card playing, he was a little bit better than the average cowboy, but not good enough against a real sharp dealer.

That night, he found a table at the Broken Spur Saloon where a fourth player had just left. If the player was a winner, Matt knew it would be bad luck to take his seat. However, as it turned out, the man was a loser, so Matt asked to sit in.

"Where you from, stranger?" the man asked, keeping his eyes on the deck he was shuffling.

"Mind if I warm my hands up a bit? M'name's, Matt Jorgensen. I'm headin' for Texas."

"Didn't ask you your name, just where you from?" the man repeated as he started dealing out the five cards.

"Upper Dakota Territory some," he answered. "Snowing like hell outside."

Matt watched the dealer as he dealt the cards. "And up there it's customary for the man on the left to cut the deck."

"It's a friendly game, mister," the dealer came back still dealing. "We know each other, but you we don't know."

"Goes both ways, mister." Matt watched the eyes of the other players as he removed his Stetson. "I'd prefer to have that gentleman cut the deck, if you don't mind."

"Well, all right," the dealer replied, picking up the cards. "Whatever suits ya." He gave the deck to the man to his left who cut them and returned the deck.

The dealer began to sweat, feeling a little uneasy with Matt sitting in. He was skinny man who Matt sized up to be in his thirties, and his well-manicured hands told Matt he was probably more into gambling than cattle. He was not a real smart gambler in Matt's book, but a professional. Even though the dealer said it was a friendly game, Matt knew he needed to watch him closely.

Matt's intent was to play a few hands to get to know which side of the deck the man was dealing. If he sized up that he might lose his supper money, he would make an excuse and leave the game.

As each player picked up his cards, Matt left his alone, watching the other players throw back the cards for new ones.

When it was Matt's turn for fresh cards, he finally picked his hand up and quickly said, "Two."

"You just picked up your cards and without time to look at them said 'two'. How d'ya know how many you'd need?" the dealer asked.

"It's my style," Matt answered. "I always draw two in my first hand. Kinda lucky at that. Usually win, too."

True enough, after a couple of raises, Matt was called, and he won the hand. He drew into a full house, having three deuces to begin with.

The man sitting to Matt's right, who had cut the deck, watched Matt pick up the deal. "You won a sizeable pot with a full house. Not a bad start."

"Thanks," Matt answered. "You gonna ante?"

"Wouldn't miss it for anything," he answered, and threw in his ante.

Matt finished the deal, watching the professional gambler carefully while flipping out each card. When it was the gambler's turn to take cards, he stood pat. Matt frowned a little.

"You better take at least two," Matt paused for the gambler's reaction.

"I'm good," the gambler replied as he took out a cigar and lit it.

He was good, but not good enough. Matt had him beat and raked in another pot.

The gambler looked at Matt intently, inhaled on his cigar, and said, "You've got a lucky streak going. Want to see how lucky?"

"I thought this was a friendly game," Matt answered, shuffling the cards for a fresh deal. "No thanks."

Matt dealt his second hand. The gambler was the last to check, and decided to stay.

"Last chance," he reminded Matt.

"How many?" Matt asked.

"I'll stand pat."

The pot was small, but the gambler won the hand, and once more took the deal. The game lasted another hour and Matt and the other two players were ever so slightly ahead of the gambler.

It was then that Matt finally figured out the gambler's ploy. Because Matt had thought he was competing with him, he was not aware that he was building the other two players' confidence. They were betting higher stakes because of his constant losing on smaller winnings. Eventually he would close in for the kill and win all of it, including Matt's winnings.

It would have worked, had it not been for Jerry and his wranglers walking in to wash down a week's worth of trail dust, and warm their innards with Red Eye.

"Yahoo!" was heard from one end of the saloon to the other when the cowboys let it out, shaking the snow from their clothing. Then Jerry stood still in his tracks as he eyed Matt sitting at a table.

"Boys! I see a low-down polecat whose smelling up the saloon."

*What a hell of a time to run into a gunfight,* Matt thought. *Miles from home. I don't know anyone. Hell, I ain't even fast.* Then as a last reminder he thought, *Empty.* It had always been his policy never to carry a loaded gun unless he expected to use it. This was not one of those times. *Maybe*, he thought quickly, *I can pull a bluff*. Either way, he figured he was going to get killed. He figured it best to die fighting.

He slid back in his chair to expose his .36 still strapped down tight to his thigh. He kept it strapped down to keep it from bouncing on him while riding.

"Where d'ya think you're goin', mister?" the gambler asked, taking hold of Matt's right hand.

Matt jerked his hand free and looked strong into the gambler's eyes. "Do that again, Mister Gamblin' Man, and you'll wish you hadn't met me."

"Mister," the gambler said, looking Matt straight on, "we've got some serious gambling to do. Nobody leaves this game unless I tell 'em to."

"Didn't hear you tell that to the gent that left," Matt came back.

"He ran out of money," the gambler retorted. "You've got mine."

"And I aim to keep it."

"You're playin' with a polecat, Bennie," one of the wranglers said.

"That right, Polecat?" Jerry asked Matt.

"I'm sorry about your horse, Jerry," Matt apologized, waiting for someone to make his play. "I can make good for him now." Matt showed the cowboys his winnings on the table.

Bennie began dealing the cards, and Matt kept his eyes on Jerry and his cowboys.

"Think you're fast with a gun?" one of the cowboys asked. His name was "Toothless", for obvious reasons. His age-old body slumping, he scratched his scraggly scalp under his Stetson, "You think you're a fast draw?"

"Don't know," Matt replied, hoping he wouldn't have to prove it.

"I saw a fast-draw man once. Fast. Never saw one faster. He was awfully fast," Toothless smiled showing his gums.

"The hell you did," Jerry said. "The day you quit making up stories . . ."

"I did, I tell ya. I ain't a lyin'."

"I want an answer, mister," Jerry said,

"Let him, be," Bennie said, holding the deck of cards in his right hand and a cigar in his left. "We're playing a friendly game of poker."

He winked at Jerry as if to let him know the next hand would be his. "Besides, we're friends."

"Can't be your friend," Jerry surmised, pointing to Matt. "He jest got into the area. Rode Ma's good horse into the ground. We had to shoot it. He ain't got no friends, Bennie, no friends at all. Right, mister?" He continued to ride Matt. "No one to drink with?"

Toothless and the other cowboys sided Jerry at the bar and ordered drinks. When the drinks arrived, Jerry downed his shot quickly, wiping the excess from his lips.

Toothless grabbed the bottle and walked back to the table where Matt was sitting. "Think you can beat Jerry here?" he asked.

Matt looked at Jerry with his steely blue eyes and said, "Your horse tried to kill me. It was an accident. I'm just glad I didn't get killed, the way he came crashing down on that rail."

"That's not the way we saw it. Right, men?" Jerry held his glass up as Toothless poured another drink.

"Right, Jerry," some of the men chimed in. Some of the others saw it the way Matt did, but kept quiet about it.

That was the moment Matt was waiting for, a time when the men's attention shifted from him to Jerry. As Toothless' body shielded his gun hand at the table, Matt slid his Colt part way out and rested the heavy piece of iron in the cradle of his holster, hoping no one would see him do it.

"That's how it were," Toothless added. "You had no right riding that poor critter into the rails like that."

"I couldn't do anything in front of Ma, stranger," Jerry said, taking his second swig of whiskey. "But I can kill you right here. Now, draw."

Matt put his hands innocently on the table to keep the men's eyes on them and not his holster. He then concentrated mainly on what Jerry was going to do. His focus was on Jerry. If anyone else joined in, well, it would be a chance he had to take.

"I ain't gonna draw on you, Jerry. You're too good a man for Ma to lose."

"You think you can beat him, don't cha, mister?" Toothless ribbed Matt with his wicked grin from ear to ear, hoping Matt would draw.

"Nope," Matt replied.

"Now, he's a sensible man," Toothless said, taking the bottle and pouring Matt a drink, and one for himself.

"Gettin' me liquored up ain't gonna prove anything either," Matt shot daggers into Toothless' eyes.

"Stop it, Toothless," Jerry ordered in a loud voice. "Can't cha see he's yella, and he ain't no excuse for a man." His hand went lazily to his gun grip. "Hell, I could shoot him right now before he'd clear his holster. Nice and easy like." He pulled out his Colt and just cleared leather when Matt stood up and pushed his chair away from the table with his boot. With his right hand, Matt whipped his Navy .36 from its holster and cracked it over Jerry's head, slamming him to the floor, and brought the barrel to the point of Toothless' nose, cocking the hammer.

"In answer to your question, old man, I know I can beat him," Matt said as he emptied Toothless' holster of its pistol and aimed it and his own .36 at the other cowboys while he motioned Toothless away.

Ernie, the bartender watched, but was afraid to say anything. He had never seen a fast draw like that before.

Slowly Jerry gained consciousness and pulled himself up into a chair at Bennie's table.

Matt motioned for Toothless to move out of the way. Quickly Toothless went to Jerry's aid with his bandanna and, using some of the whiskey from the bottle on the table, cleaned the blood away.

"Is he all right?" Ernie came around the bar with a wet bar towel.

"Hell no!" Toothless answered wiping the blood from top of Jerry's head. "Where the hell's the sheriff?"

"What for?" Ernie asked. "You men started it. Looks like you'd be needin' ol' Doc, Jerry."

"That wasn't fair," one of the cowboys said from the bar. "Hittin' him with the gun like that."

"I don't have time to play fair," Matt answered as he took the bottle away from Toothless and poured himself another drink. "You want a fight, fight! Don't jest stand there flappin' your damn gums."

Then, looking at the gambler, Matt asked, "We through playin' for the night?"

The gambler sat back in his chair and threw up his hands.

"Good. I'll take my winnings and leave," Matt pocketed his well-earned money. Plopping two eagles down on the bar for the drinks, he turned and walked away backwards with his guns aimed at the cowboys while flinging the swinging doors as he left.

Toothless was proud that night. Even though his boss got gun whipped by a stranger, he was delighted to have witnessed one of the fastest draws he had ever seen.

Toothless could hardly restrain himself afterwards when he sat at the fireplace with Ma. "His gun came out of its holster like greased lightnin', I'm a-tellin' ya," he said grinning from ear to ear. "Jerry had his gun half way out and already cocked, and a standin', mind ya. And … and this fella drew and conked him on the head. Faster than any man I knowed."

It was his favorite story to tell, which showed how proud he was of witnessing his first gunfight, although no shots were fired, and no one was killed.

Jerry got patched up, and survived his headache by sleeping the night away, while the rest of the wranglers continued playing poker in their bunkhouse.

Matt sat Skeeter out in the shadows, and waited for the lights to go out in the bunkhouse. When they did, he rode up softly to the house and saw Toothless alone in the kitchen with Ma.

After dismounting and tying up his horse, Matt walked softly in the snow up to the front door. After feeling confident that no one saw or heard him, he slipped inside. Quietly, he eased himself to the kitchen door that was closed off by a calico curtain, which, when opened, allowed a light into the dining area of the house. Once inside the dining area, he stayed in the shadows as he inched his way into the kitchen, keeping his body low.

"Evenin'" he greeted Ma and Toothless, pointing his .36 in Toothless' direction. With his free hand, he placed some double eagles on the kitchen table.

"That's for Bellyacher, Ma'am, and for the inconvenience I caused you. Damn fine hospitality. Didn't mean to abuse it."

Toothless started for his gun, but when he realized it was Matt, he stopped and kept his arms up high.

"Put 'em down," Matt ordered. "And keep your voice down unless you want to get shot."

"You don't have to keep a gun on us, son," Ma said, with a little smile on her face. "I'm glad you came back, though. I didn't think you would, after giving Jerry a beating like you did."

"Couldn't be helped, Ma'am," Matt said. "He was ready to shoot me." Then he pointed to the coins on the table. "Hope that helps. Gambler in town donated them."

"He won it," Toothless interrupted with his arms still up in the air. "Fair and square."

"Put your hands down," Matt ordered again, "before someone sees you looking like a bird."

Toothless put his arms down and with a grin the size of the territory said, "He was fast, faster than I ever saw. Yes, Ma'am."

"Gotta go, Ma'am," Matt backed into the dining area disappeared into the darkness. "Thanks again for the hospitality."

"I'd like to keep you on, son," Ma called after him.

"Kinda think I wore out my welcome with Jerry. 'Bye Ma'am." Matt went out the same door he came from and rode off.

"Ride easy, son," Ma said, watching him ride as the snow fell upon the moonlit roadway. She sat down at the table with a sigh. "Now there goes a man I wouldn't mind a-knowin'."

"I gotta go, too," Toothless said as he shook Ma's hand. "Jest somethin' about that dern cowboy that makes me think he needs my help."

With his spurs jingling, Toothless ran through the house after Matt who was on his horse and quietly riding away in the shadows of the moonlit trees. In the stable, Toothless saddled his horse quickly and rode after Matt.

A wrangler who'd heard the commotion walked outside into the night air catching Toothless riding away.

"What is it?" Jerry asked from inside, sitting on his bunk in his union suit nursing his head.

"Jest Toothless ridin' like the wind," the wrangler answered as he stepped back inside the bunkhouse.

"Where the hell is he riding to this time of night in the dead of winter?" another asked.

As the wrangler started to close the door, he caught sight of Ma with the light from the window silhouetting her as she walked towards the bunkhouse.

Ma saw the door open, and one of the wranglers standing in his union suit. "How's Jerry?"

The wrangler opened the door wider and Ma kept walking right into the bunkhouse without stopping.

"No better, Ma'am", the wrangler said as he stood there holding the door and freezing.

"Ma!" Jerry exclaimed, jumping up and covering himself with a bed sheet from his bunk.

"Oh, heck, Jerry," Ma said as she looked around the bunk. "It's not like there's anything to hide from me."

"Where's Toothless headin' this late at night?" Jerry asked, easing himself back onto his cot.

"After the man who gave me these," she answered, showing off a handful of double eagles.

"Who gave those to ya, Ma?" Jerry counted at least twenty that she poured from one hand to the other.

"The sissy you thought couldn't ride Bellyacher," Ma said.

"He's out there?" Jerry asked, nearly losing the bed sheet, while he and the other wranglers started for the door.

"No need getting into a dither, boys," she said holding her palms out in front of her. "He's paid for my horse. Anyway, no one could ride him, so I'm not complainin' none. What you got is what you asked for. Next time, don't go pointin' a gun at somebody lessen' you knowed a little more about him."

Jerry and the boys smiled sheepishly at Ma, and she grinned back at them.

"Also, jest wanted to tell ya. Toothless rode out to join him," she added, as she started out the door.

"Toothless?" Jerry shouted. "What the hell for?"

"He's old. Set in his way. Wants to have a little excitement 'fore he kicks the bucket, I suppose," she answered, and walked out the door.

"I'll be damned," Jerry said.

Hearing the roar of laughter from the bunkhouse as she walked back to the house, Ma smiled a little. Although she had lost her horse, she was well paid for him. Losing Toothless was harder to get over. She hoped somewhere, somehow, he would have his last thrill, and maybe, just maybe, return to be buried on her ranch.

Toothless was familiar with the area. With a full moon and the fallen snow illuminating Matt's tracks, he found him riding slow and easy.

"Wait up, Mr. Jorgensen," Toothless yelled as he neared Matt. His boots were pointed straight out and upwards in their stirrups and he leaned back into the saddle waving his arms.

Reining up, Matt turned in his saddle and watched the crazy cowpoke ride towards him.

"You plannin' on leavin' this world real soon?" Matt asked, pointing his Colt in Toothless' direction.

Stopping short of crashing into Matt, Toothless raised one hand high in the air while pulling on his reins with the other.

"Got room for some company, Mr. Jorgensen?" Toothless asked with a grin.

"What?" Matt responded, looking at his gummy grin. Realizing Toothless was harmless, Matt motioned for him to put his arms down. "Oh, hell," Matt exclaimed as he holstered his Colt. "You keep lookin' like a scarecrow with your arms flappin' over your head. Put 'em down."

Matt turned Skeeter back around and walked him down the dim-lit roadway, "D'ya know where I'm headed?"

"Don't matter none, do it?" Toothless asked, siding Matt. "You need company. And I'm company."

Matt smiled, "Jest always figure on keepin' in front of me. I'll feel a little more easy about it. And call me, Matt. I don't cotton to the 'Mister' bit."

Toothless agreed and the two rode together for the next two days. The fear of someone like Jerry and his cowboys catching up to them didn't set easy on Matt's mind, so their stops were kept short.

*Now I'm being labeled a fast gun*, Matt thought. Damn. *And now, I'm gonna havta learn how to use this damn thing.* He pulled out his Colt and pointed it in front of him.

Toothless watched him and just smiled. He had done found his fast gun.

"Now, you take Jerry," Toothless said, as he held the bacon pan low over the morning fire. "He's not one to harbor a grudge too long. He's got a round-up to tend ta, and that's gonna take all his attention away from us 'cause of this here heavy snow."

"Still, I have a feelin' we're bein' followed", Matt said, sitting on a rock and enjoying his first cup of coffee for the day. "And I'm still not too sure what side you'd be on if he did ride in here."

"Neither," Toothless said. "And he'd a knowed that, too." Taking out his pistol, and watching Matt duck, he dropped it out of fright of Matt hitting him, shooting him. "It ain't loaded. Even if it were, can't fire it. Darn thing's too rusty."

Then a shot rang out and a bullet ricocheted off the tree behind Matt's head, causing him to jump for cover behind the closest rock. "Put that darn thing away before you kill me," he ordered pulling his own Colt out of its holster.

"T'weren't me," Toothless said, examining his rusty piece. "That came from up there." Quickly he found cover for himself and pointed to the rocks above them.

"Stand where you are, Mr. Jorgensen," Bennie said, aiming his rifle at Matt. "Toss your gun in the fire."

Matt saw Bennie the gambler holding a direct bead on him, threw his .36 in the fire and stood up with his hands over his head.

Bennie skirted down from the rocks and walked over to Matt and Toothless. Toothless was getting good at keeping his hands high in the air.

"Now, we're not so big, are we?" Bennie suggested, pointing the rifle close to Matt's face. "Where's my money?"

"If you're referrin' to the money I won beatin' you at poker, part of it's in the saddle bags on my horse," Matt said.

Toothless kept looking at Matt, figuring that any moment Matt was going to come down hard on Bennie. He kept looking at Matt and winking his eye, knowing Matt would tell him what to do any second now.

Bennie went to the saddlebags, opened them up, and seeing the money inside, tied them back up.

Realizing he was going to take Skeeter, Matt said, "Not my horse."

"Turn around so's I can search you for the rest," Bennie said, patting Matt's pockets. Feeling a wad of money inside Matt's vest pocket, he relieved him of it.

"Not all of it, Bennie," Matt suggested.

Toothless was still waiting for Matt's arms to come down on top of Bennie's head and knock him to the ground. He knew once he made his move, he would have to join in to make sure Bennie would not get away.

"This is more'n I lost," Bennie said, stuffing the money into the saddlebags. "Sorry, gentlemen, but you lose, and I win."

He backed away to the horses, untied them, stepped up on Skeeter, and spurred him away, firing a shot in the air to scare away Toothless' horse at the same time. Without saying a word, Bennie simply waved his rifle and rode away.

Toothless was still hopeful for he had no doubt that Matt had a good plan up his sleeve for getting the horses back and the money, too. He ran over to the fire and kicked Matt's pistol over to him.

"Go get 'em, Matt," he yelled.

Matt handled his pistol carefully with his bandanna, and wiped it clean. He slipped it back into its holster once it cooled off.

Toothless stood there with a sorrowful look on his face as he saw his new idol giving in to a cheap gambler.

Matt whistled once, and that was all that Skeeter needed. He reared up, threw Bennie from his back, saddlebags and rifle with him, and came running back to Matt.

Mounting Skeeter, Matt rode after Bennie who was scampering up the snow-covered rocks towards his horse. Matt caught up with Bennie and urged Skeeter to knock him to the ground.

With his pistol aimed at Bennie, Matt ordered him, "Sit down, Bennie. Hand up your rifle, butt first."

Taking the rifle, Matt emptied the cartridge and pocketed it. "Now hand me the Derringer inside your vest pocket."

"How'd ya know I had a Derringer?" Bennie asked, handing it to Matt.

"Never saw a gambler who didn't. And now, my saddlebags. Hand 'em up to me."

He wasn't in any position to argue, so Bennie complied and gave them back to Matt.

Toothless rounded the corner in time to take the rifle from Matt and level it on Bennie.

"It's empty," Matt showed him the cartridge.

"What we gonna do now, Matt?" He smiled from ear to ear while holding the rifle on Bennie.

"How's your horse?" Matt asked.

"You know how he is, broken down," Toothless replied. "But what are ya gonna do with this cheap, no-good-for-nothin' gambler, who tried to steal our money?" Toothless thought for a moment, looked at his horse, and then up the hill at Bennie's fine mount, with a good saddle. "Now that you mention it, Matt, my horse would make a pretty good swap, if that's what ya figured on doin',"

"Not my horse, Matt," Bennie said, sitting on the ground. "The saddle alone is worth what you won from me."

"Well, Bennie," Matt said, "to teach you a lesson, we're goin' to take your horse and saddle. But, to show you that we have feelins', we're gonna let you have Toothless' good lookin' mare. We wouldn't want you to freeze out here without a good horse to take you home. Is that okay with you, Toothless?"

Toothless grinned and looked down at Bennie. "Okay with me, Mr. Jorgensen. "Thank you, Bennie, for bein' so generous."

"Jest one thing, Bennie," Matt said as he watched Toothless go after Bennie's horse and saddle. "Hope you don't mind, but we're gonna borrow your 'brand new' horse for a while to keep you from followin' us. We'll leave him a mile up the road. The rifle will be in the boot. I always figure a man needs protection."

Matt threw a canteen of water at Bennie's feet and, with Toothless, rode off with three horses. True to his word, Matt left Toothless' old filly less than a mile up a rugged hill and off the main road.

They sat their horses on a distant hill just out of Bennie's sight and watched as Bennie found Toothless' old horse. Once in the saddle, Bennie turned her around and headed back to town, a good fifteen-mile ride.

"Well, Matt," Toothless said, wiping the snow from his face with the back of his sleeve, "he's headin' for town. Now what are we gonna do?"

Toothless was satisfied with Matt's plan to get the better of Bennie. His cackle echoed throughout the canyon and on into the Dakota Territory.

Matt said nothing, but turned Skeeter south.

The next morning, just before mounting Skeeter, Matt took his .36 out of its holster and spun its empty chamber in front of Toothless.

"Well, Toothless," he said, "had they only known." He filled the chamber with five bullets from his belt, spun the chamber and flipped it back into its holster. Matt never had a good enough reason to keep his .36 loaded and in his holster. He had always figured someone could take it away from him and use it on him. And now, he kept his gun loaded.

Toothless stood next to his horse with his jaw dropped at what he saw. "What would you've done had someone else drawn down on ya?"

"Thrown up my hands-like you," Matt answered. "Or else took the bullet."

"I'll be hornswaggled," Toothless said, throwing his hat on the ground.

"Didn't you wonder why the bullets didn't go off when the gun was in the fire?" Matt asked.

"Come to think of it, yeah, yeah," Toothless said, rubbing his chin. "Never gave that a thought. But back thar in the saloony, you outdrew him. Heh. Heh. You were good."

"Had my gun resting half way out of its holster," Matt said. "Made it easy when I kicked the chair away from me, scaring everyone."

Toothless never got over hearing Matt's story. He mumbled about it while riding, and groaned about it in his sleep. He already saw action, any way anybody wanted to look at it.

For Matt, he took a chance, and it worked. He figured the next time he might not be so lucky, especially if word ever got out how fast people thought he was, and started gunning for him to prove that they were faster.

The idea of a fast gun had just started around the campfires and had never really settled as yet on any one individual. It could very well happen that Matt could be one of the first – and having a sidekick like Toothless as his spokesman could only help him.

Matt and Toothless rode south out of the Dakota Territory through Nebraska and into Kansas. Although Matt never fired his gun, one Bennie LaBeau from Canada quickly branded him a fast gun, and the tag trailed him from then on.

Matt and Toothless rode for days with little rest. When they did stop, Matt took advantage of the time and began practicing on his draw. He still thought he was too slow, and very inaccurate. He eventually got better with accuracy, but his draw still lacked something. He just couldn't figure what it was.

Toothless sat around watching him improve, and marveled at how well he had defended himself against Jerry and his whole band of cowboys. By the time they reached Kansas, the story had gotten so out of proportion that the cowboys figured to be over two-dozen men, and all mean cusses with drawn pistols aimed at Matt. Of course, Toothless made it known to everyone he met, that Matt outdrew them all. It was never short of amazing how one story could get bolder and bolder because of an old codger's exaggeration, and Toothless never told the story the same way twice in a row.

# CHAPTER 2

## A TOWN CALLED MUD CREEK

March, 1858

t was not the kindest time of year for Matt to start south across the country, but It helped having a companion like Toothless along.

Toothless was up in years, and had witnessed the evolution of the Sharps rifle from the long gun, and of Samuel Colt's pistols. A resident of the Dakota Territory for more years than Matt had birthdays, he was truly a man of the West.

He saw the Indian Wars, and watched men die for a pan of gold dust. He rode the trail drives for many months till he and his saddle were as one. He knew every tree and rock across the prairies, it seemed. He was as big an asset to Matt as a trail guide as Matt was to him as a guardian angel against would-be bandits and killers.

He heard the rumors spreading from border to border about an impending war between the States, some being Pro-slavery, while others were against it. Toothless had filled Matt in on the rumors each time he heard more tidbits from the towns they hit.

The most turbulent bit of news came when they crossed over into the Kansas territory that spring. The uneasiness that erupted in the state began in 1854, with the Kansas-Nebraska Act, which opened the territory to legalized settlements. The states could decide by vote, which were to be free states or slave states. In Kansas, it seemed the rich were Pro-slavery, while the farmers were for a free state.

It was a highly volatile issue when Matt and Toothless rode through the state. Fighting and killing raged among a diversity of people in Kansas on the issue of slavery. This led to election fraud, fights over land claims, and the once gentle Kansas became known as "Bleeding Kansas".

April brought with it the rains, and Matt and Toothless headed for shelter in a nearby town called Mud Creek, it lived up to its name. They found no one in the streets as the rain came down hard that night. They wore rain gear over their clothes, but their hats were so soaked that even the tops of their heads were wet.

They headed for a nearby livery stable. From Skeeter's back, Matt pounded on the door with his rifle. A well-built smithy opened the doors slowly, and let the two riders in.

Matt and Toothless dismounted and walked their horses to the stalls. They immediately began to wipe down the horses and bed them down for the night.

"Where ya from, stranger?" the smithy asked, giving the horses some oats and hay. The smithy was a stout man with muscles that seemed to run the length of his body. He was especially burly in his arms and chest. He wore a leather apron over his clothes, tied up in front.

"Dakota Territory, Wyomin'," Matt answered as he brushed Skeeter.

"Where ya headed?"

"Texas."

"You're a far piece from there. So you figure on stayin' in town a while, till the weather blows over?"

"Looks like. M'name's Matt. This here is Toothless."

"Glad to meet ya. Mine's Dan'l." The smithy shook hands with a vice-like grip.

"Got a place for us to sleep for the night?" Matt asked.

"Up the street, Mud Creek Hotel. Nice place. Rent's high. Good food, though," Dan'l added.

"Take care of our horses, and we'll be back," Matt picked up his saddlebags and handed Dan'l a gold piece. "Figure we'll be stayin' a few days."

"You got credit here for a week with this, mister," Dan'l said. He closed the doors on the gents as they walked back out into the rain.

The town was fairly developed. Two saloons stood right in the heart of town, flanked by a bank, a general store, a Chinese laundry, the livery, a freight company, and the Mud Creek Hotel.

"Let's make a run for the saloon, Toothless," Matt said, attempting to run across some half-sunken wooden planks stretched across the street.

The sound of horses and men yelling through the rain hastened Matt's retreat back to the stable doors.

The leader reined up and shouted out to the other men to stop. In all, there appeared to be at least a dozen hard-ridden men, grubby with beards, and wet from top to bottom. A few wore slickers, including the leader.

"You a greenhorn, walkin' out in the middle of the road like that?" the leader yelled down at Matt and Toothless.

"No one was around 'til you men came along," Toothless answered, wiping mud out of his eyes.

"You're not from around here," the leader recognized quickly. "Where ya from?"

"Rode in from Wyomin'," Matt answered, peering at the leader through the driving rain. "Jest got into town. Figured on a bite to eat, and a room for the night."

"What's in the saddlebags?" the leader asked, urging his horse over to Matt.

"Nothing that would interest you any," Matt returned, slipping his hand over his gun grip.

"Now, sonny," the leader quipped, "you let me be the judge of that." Flipping back his hat, he reached out to grab the saddlebags.

Matt's Colt came out of its holster lightning fast. What was in the saddlebags, plus in his shirt pocket was going to take him to Texas.

Toothless pulled out his rusty iron and pointed it at the men, feeling confident that Matt was completely in charge. At least, he hoped he was. If Toothless had to fire his piece, he figured it might just go off in his face, so he held it at arm's length. He hoped that his bluff would give the other men the impression that he knew how to handle a weapon.

The feeling didn't last too long, as the men behind the leader all drew their weapons and aimed at them.

"Now why in the hell would you want to draw up against fourteen of the toughest cowboys in all of Kansas, in the rain?" the leader asked, bringing his Colt out. "Put 'em away. Now!"

It was a standoff, and Matt knew it.

Toothless began to quiver. He whispered to Matt, "Your gun's loaded, ain't it?"

"Yep,"

"Then shoot the bastard!"

A shot rang out from the leader's gun, and Matt felt the pangs of a burning bullet hit his left shoulder throwing him into the mire.

Toothless threw away his weapon and ran to Matt's aid.

"We don't trade words here in Kansas, stranger." The leader dismounted.

He quickly went through Matt's pockets and relieved him of his money, then slipped the saddlebags over his arms. He heard the livery stable door opening and mounted up. "Next time, tell him that. Let's wet our innards, men. The drinks are on me."

The gang rode over to the saloon farthest down the street, dismounted, hitched their horses to the rail and walked in.

Toothless watched where they went, and kept his eye on them until he couldn't see them anymore. Their laughter rang through Toothless' head as he lifted Matt's head up out of the mire and yelled for help.

Dan'l opened the doors and walked out with a shotgun in his hands.

"Heard a shootin," he said, running to Matt's side.

"Where were ya when we needed you, dadburn it," Toothless spat. "Help me take him inside before he bleeds to death."

Once inside, the men laid Matt on a straw-strewn area. Tearing Matt's wet shirt was a job, so Dan'l had to use a pair of shears while Toothless kept the bleeding to a minimum with his bandanna.

"You keep him here while I go for Doc Parker," Dan'l said, slipping on his slicker and heading out a side door.

"How 'bout a dad burn sheriff while you're at it?"

Within minutes, Doc was in the livery, patching Matt's shoulder. "The bullet lodged against the shoulder bone," he said, feeling for it with his retriever. "Got it."

"I've got some horse liniment, Doc," Dan'l said, handing him the bottle. "Will that help?"

"Good lord, man," Toothless replied. "He ain't a horse."

"I've got some whiskey in my bag here," Doc pulled a small flask out of his case.

"He took the full blast, Doc," Toothless said. "Will he live?"

"Will know by morning," Doc answered, pouring the whiskey into the wound. "Good thing you got me here. Mrs. Berry is due to give birth any day now, and she lives outside of town."

"Well," Dan'l said, scratching his slightly baldhead, "how do you know when you're supposed to go out there?"

"They would have come and got me. I'll ride out in the morning, after I look in on this fella." Doc finished bandaging the wound, and slipped Matt's arm into a sling. "When he comes to, give him a swig of this laudanum and let him sleep the night," Doc continued. "Like I said, I'll check in on him in the morning."

"How 'bout the sheriff, Dan'l? Doc?" Toothless asked. "The guys who done it are down at the saloon. I saw them go in."

"You willin' to point them out to the sheriff?" Doc asked.

"Well, sure," Toothless answered.

"I ain't got the time to stay here and patch you up, and get over to Mrs. Berry," Doc said, picking up his bag. "Besides, I'd be willing to bet you that the sheriff is drinking with them right now. So you going in there would only make him furious, it wouldn't surprise me if he arrested you instead."

When the doctor left, Dan'l walked over to Matt. "Looks like you're gonna bed down here for the night. I'll bring you some blankets and pillows."

"Well, I'll jest tell ya somethin', Dan'l," Toothless said, watching Doc leave and shutting the side door behind him. "When Matt comes to, he'll be madder'n a wet hen, and I guarantee you he'll go after those varmints."

The rain continued through the night and into the next day. Matt slept through till evening. When he opened his eyes, he saw the ugliest face in the world smiling down on him.

"He's wakin' up, Dan'l," Toothless yelled out with a grin.

"You feelin' all right, mister?" Dan'l asked, kneeling down by Matt's head.

"Where am I?" Matt felt the pain in his shoulder, and elected not to rise.

"You're all right, now, Matt," Toothless said with his big grin. "Doc Parker fixed you up real pretty."

"What happened?"

"A gang leader shot cha," Toothless said. "All of 'em pulled their guns and you didn't have a chance.

Matt felt his arm for the moment, and cringed a little. "You get shot?"

"They shot my gun out of my hand, and I pretended to be dead. We both fell down in the mud, exceptin' you were shot. I weren't."

"No. Jest my luck, I suppose. You ran a slight fever, but Doc got you some laudanum in you and you slept like a baby all night and all day."

"He kiddin' me?" Matt asked Dan'l with a look of disbelief on his face. Much of the time, what Toothless said was a pack of lies, and the other half was all made up. Matt could not decipher which was which.

"He's speakin' the truth," Dan'l said. "The doc got the bullet out, patched you up and you sweated out the fever for near twenty-four hours."

Matt reached into his vest pocket for his money, and came up empty. Then he looked around for the saddlebags and found them nowhere in sight.

"The gang took everythin', Matt," Toothless said. "Dan'l here is puttin' us up with food and all 'cause we tipped him right good."

"Those sons-of-bitches." Matt's eyes rolled back into his head as he fell back to sleep.

"Let him sleep, Toothless," Dan'l suggested. "You can earn your keep by helpin' around here for the next few days. What he gave me paid the keep for the horses for a week. Not for you two, and not countin' what Doc wants."

Toothless looked a little disgusted at Dan'l, but knew he was right. He covered Matt up with a blanket, went to his own bundle of hay and slid into slumber.

A week went by, and Matt felt he was well enough to eat and walk on his own, so he and Toothless paid a visit to the sheriff.

"His name is Vern Steadman," Dan'l said, pointing the direction to the sheriff's office.

"Thanks. We'll be back."

Matt and Toothless walked down the sidewalk, and then crossed over to the sheriff's office in the middle of town.

"Mornin', Sheriff," Matt said, entering the office and removing his hat with his right hand, because his left one was still in a sling. "Nice day, isn't it? Your name Vern Steadman?" Matt asked.

"No secret. Yep. What's your's?"

"Matt Jorgensen, and this here's Toothless. Dan'l told us your name."

"You the man who got shot the other night, I take it?" Vern asked.

Matt could tell that Vern was slightly taller than he was, thinly built, in his early thirties, blond, with a thin moustache. He remained seated behind his desk with his legs stretched out across the desk.

"I'm glad you heard about me. This is my pardner, Toothless. We've come to file a complaint."

"Figured you might." Vern shoved a paper and pencil across this desk. "Write your complaint down on this here paper, and I'll follow up on it when I can."

Matt sat down and wrote.

"Did you get a good look at the men?" the sheriff asked while watching Matt write.

"I saw the leader's face."

"What did he look like?"

"He had a beard, and was soakin' wet."

"What else?"

"He was seen running in that saloon at the end of the street with his gang."

"Son," Vern said, standing up and walking over to the door, "you see him out here?"

"You don't figure on goin' after him, do you, Sheriff?" Toothless asked standing next to him in the doorway.

"Not with that description. It fits a hundred men walking up and down the street every day. Sorry."

Matt tore up the complaint, and walked over to Vern.

"Sorry," Vern said at their backs as Matt and Toothless stormed angrily out of his office. "If you see any of them again, come and tell me."

Matt and Toothless took their walk back to the stable.

The gang never returned to Mud Creek in the days that followed while Matt and Toothless were there, which pleased Vern no end. Closing his office, he mounted his horse and rode out of town, passing Matt and Toothless on the way.

"Where's he headed?" Matt asked Dan'l as he neared the stable.

"Home, reckon," Dan'l answered pumping his bellows. "He's a farmer."

"A farmer?" Toothless asked. "I thought he was the sheriff."

"Part-time sheriff, Toothless," Dan'l added. "Town can't afford a full-time sheriff."

"Oh," was all Matt could say as he watched the sheriff ride out of sight. "That would explain his attitude about not goin' after those varmints."

Two weeks later Matt was up and heating the smithy's fire with his good arm while his left arm remained in its sling. Doc had returned and changed the dressing a few times. Mrs. Berry's new eight-pound baby girl had no problems that needed his attention, and no gunshot wounds were reported in town.

When it came time for Matt and Toothless to leave, Doc was there to see them off, along with Dan'l.

"Are you satisfied with our trade of horses, Toothless?" Dan'l asked, combing the mane of Toothless' horse real careful like. "I'll guarantee ya, I'll take real good care of this horse from now on."

"Yeah," Toothless said, mounting a sixteen-year-old mare with an older saddle. "You sure this horse is healthy?"

"Kept him since he was born, Toothless. Now I wouldn't cheat you none."

Matt and Doc had their laughs as they shook hands.

"Can't tell you how much I appreciate your healin' me up, Doc," Matt said, mounting Skeeter. "You get a good price for that saddle, Dan'l, and split the money with Doc here."

"I know," Dan'l said. "Don't worry, I will."

"Oh, Matt," Doc said looking up at Matt. "You got any money to make out?"

"Don't worry, Doc," Matt said. "Dan'l paid Toothless the difference between the two horses and the saddles. We have enough to make out."

Matt took his reins, turned Skeeter south and spurred him gently along. Toothless smiled back at Doc and Dan'l, spurred his new mare, Lucy, and caught up with Matt.

# CHAPTER 3

## A Plow and a Mule

A day in the saddle made Matt and Toothless hungry, and Matt's arm was sore and needed a rest.

"How's your arm feelin?" Toothless asked, looking at a farmhouse up the road.

"Sore, but out of pain." Slipping it out of the sling, he straightened out his right arm to exercise it. "See. I can begin to use it."

"How much you figure we got for my saddle, pardner?"

"Your saddle brought in ten two-dollar gold pieces."

"Suppose there's another town up ahead some?" Toothless asked. "We've got the makings of one more meal on us, and that's it."

"I told you not to eat so much," Matt replied. "How a man without any teeth can eat so much, I guess I'll never know." Matt looked down the road and spotted a farmhouse, sat up in his saddle and rode towards it. "Wonder if we might find some hospitality there."

Staying in their saddles, they drew up a short distance from the house.

"Gotta be someone home," Matt said. "There's a fire burning in the yard."

A huge black vat sat on the fire with a wooden ladle sticking out of it as if someone was making lard.

"Who are ya?" a farmer yelled up at Matt and Toothless. He appeared to be in his early fifties, wearing bib overalls, a denim shirt, and a

39

straw hat. He had come up from behind a nearby tree on the other side of the road where he had been plowing. Leaving his mule and plow, he went to a nearby tree and fetched a bucket of water, and offered the men a drink.

"Matt Jorgensen from up in Wyomin'," Matt answered, dismounting and accepting a drink from the farmer's pail of water. "This here's Toothless."

"I'm Frank Hansen. What brings you to Kansas?"

"Headin to Texas," Matt replied.

"Me, too," Toothless added, dismounting and taking the ladle from Matt.

"What happened to your arm?"

"Busted it fallin' off my horse," Matt answered, looking over the farmer's shoulder and eyeing a feminine figure by the farmhouse.

"Was wonderin' if we could impose upon you for a good meal and a night's lodgin'. We'll pay you for it."

"Always willin' to help a stranger, mister," Frank said, taking the pail back when the two men were through drinking from it. "I'll have Martha fix you up something"

"Your wife?" Matt asked as he eyed a feminine beauty walking out to the vat. Her long red hair blew in the gentle breeze. She looked about his age.

"Yep. Martha. I've a daughter somewhere around here, too. Her name's Lori. I'll interduce you later when you get washed up over yonder when the dinner bell sounds." Frank pointed to a bench close to the well that was used for basins.

Even though Toothless was up in years, he still knew the joy of seeing a young, well-figured woman. Despite his age, just the sight of one was good enough for him.

Matt had not been with a woman for quite some time. Just the sight of a young good-looking female would appease him to no end.

"Need work?" Frank asked.

"We've got money," Matt replied. "I told ya we'd pay for it."

"Jest thought you might, with the busted arm and all. Could use some help, if you do."

"What kind ya got?" Matt replied.

"Got a horse for a strong back like yours," he said, handing the reins to him. "If'n you can handle it."

Matt slipped his arm out of its sling and stretched it out. "The ground looks pretty easy," he said, dismounting. "And your mule looks kinda easy. I think I can handle it. If I can't, I'll be the first to tell ya."

"Your arm up to it? I saw you stretchin' it."

"Feels real good. Maybe some good hard exercise is what it needs."

Frank looked at the tear in Matt's shirt. "You could use a new shirt, too. I'll loan you one of mine."

Matt took the reins from Hansen and threw them around his back.

Hansen looked at Toothless up and down. "What can you do?"

"I can cook," Toothless replied.

"Got a wife that does that," Frank said.

"Can shoe horses,' Toothless came back.

"Do that m'self."

"I can shovel horse shit," Toothless said with a grin. "Cut the weeds down by the tracks, chop kindlin', and castrate pigs, for starters," he continued. "I can go on."

"You're on," Hansen said. Then looking at Matt, he waited for his reply.

Frank was not too big of a man, but built through the chest and back from plowing. "I'll see that my wife, Martha has some vittles fixed up for ya right away," Frank said as he looked at Matt's horse. "Mind if I ride your horse to the barn? I'll stable him in the barn, and get your partner here started. Days' wages is all I can pay."

"Take good care of him. He'd like some hay and barley, and some oats if ya got any. My horse, that is," Matt added in jest.

"My daughter's good with horses," Frank said. "She'll take real good care of him."

Frank and Toothless rode over to the barn and put the horses in their stalls.

Matt started plowing, something he had experience with on the Double O. Of course, then he always pawned the chore off to his kid brother, Lukas.

*Daughter?* Matt thought, with a small grin on his lips. *This job might not be too bad.*

Being from Montana and now having gone through the flatlands of the Dakota Territory, Matt continued to see land without mountains for miles in either direction, and not have anything obstruct his view. Because of this the days seemed longer. He also began to feel the dry dusty taste in his mouth from the Kansas plains. It was a taste he didn't like, but was determined to become accustomed to it while he worked.

His intention at this time was to work a little here and there and travel on. His thought was that a good poker game once in a while with a few men with greedy appetites would expedite his journey. Greed, he determined, was the cause of many a man's downfall in a poker game. When it came time for one to go home with his winnings, the player would want to play one last hand to make a killing. By observing the greed in their eyes, Matt was good at winning the gentleman's last hand some of the time.

Toward dusk, Matt walked the mule to the barn.

Toothless came out of the house and took over, unhitching the mule and stabling him.

Matt walked over to the well and plopped alongside it. He pulled up the bucket from the well, and took a ladle-full of cold water to kill his thirst. As he drank, he looked around to see if Lori Hansen was nearby. He then followed Toothless inside the house and into the kitchen.

"What are you giggling about?" Matt asked Toothless who appeared to be hiding a grin.

"All washed up, I take it," the voice of a young woman broke into their conversation.

Matt looked up and saw a good-looking lady turn from the fireplace with a pan of cornbread. She appeared to be in her early twenties with lovely long red hair, and sparkling blue eyes. She busied herself while watching Matt and Toothless walk into the house.

Matt felt privileged to be in the presence of a beautiful lady who put a smile on his face.

"My name's Lori." The small girl walked in from the front room, stopped for a moment, curtsied, and looked at Matt. "I know his name is Toothless. What's yours?"

"I'm five-and-a-half years old, and I'll be going to school this fall," she said. She had long blond pigtails, cute blue eyes, and wore a clean blue cotton dress for supper.

Matt looked at Lori and realized that the little girl was the daughter. He had mistaken the young mother to be Lori, and was mesmerized by her beauty.

"This is Matt, Lori," Toothless interrupted, noticing that Matt was at a loss for words.

"And, this is my wife, Martha," Frank added, as he took the seat at the head of the table.

Matt stood for a while longer staring at the mother and daughter.

"Is there something wrong, Matt?" Toothless asked, still wearing the same silly grin. He sat next to Matt and admired the abundance of food.

"No," Matt answered. He took off his hat, placed it on a hook in the hallway, and sat down. Taking the plate of cornbread, he served himself.

"Ain't had home cooking since I don't know when, Ma'am," Toothless said, putting a calico napkin around his neck.

Tugging on his shirtsleeve, Lori whispered, "We have to say grace, Toothless." She folded her hands and closed her eyes, and then peeked up to see what Toothless was doing.

Matt put down the cornbread and bowed his head, along with Toothless and the Hansen family.

The prayer was short and to the point, as Frank asked the Lord for His blessing of the food and the company, and Lori put an "amen" at the end.

"We came here from Ohio," Frank said, serving a plate of biscuits to Toothless after he took one. "Me and Martha. Our daughter, Lori here was born on this farm five years ago."

"He's plowed through the Kansas dust and dirt, and made a decent living for us in spite of the dry weather, and sometimes, plain hard luck," Martha added.

"I knew I could make a living off this land, so I kept at it." He took hold of Martha's hand and squeezed it. "Glad I did. It's quite productive now."

After supper, Lori climbed upon a stool so she could be at the same level as the adults while she dried the dishes, which Martha washed. She then handed them to Toothless to put away.

Matt joined Frank in a game of checkers and a smoke from his makings. "Sure is a nice farm ya got," Matt said.

"We like it, Matt," Frank remarked, jumping Matt's piece. "We'll have corn, beans, tomatoes, and such by summer. Martha will jar them for the rest of the year. Why, we'll even have some pop corn."

"You plant pop corn?" Toothless asked from the kitchen.

"Yep," Frank answered, jumping one of Matt's men.

"Sounds like a great life, Frank. What do ya do for excitement?" Matt pondered his next move.

"Ever hunt, Matt?"

"All the time in Wyomin'," Matt answered, still pondering his next move.

"We do a lot of hunting in these here parts. Then we'll have a county fair in late spring, and see all our friends around here for miles. Swap yarns, buy and sell, and jest have a good time."

"And Martha?" Matt asked, looking toward the kitchen watching the back of her as she washed the dishes.

"I'm enjoying my life, Mr. Jorgensen," she answered over her shoulder. "Are you thinking of settling down yourself someday?"

"Lookin' forward to it, Ma'am."

Two checker games later, Martha, Lori, and Toothless joined the men in the front room.

Lori played a game against Matt. He graciously lost.

"Time for you to go to bed, little one," Martha beckoned Lori toward her bedroom, a little room off to the side with a sheet for a doorway. The bed was small, with two quilted blankets to keep out the cold. As the wicks in the lanterns were turned down in the kitchen, the glow from the stove and the crackling of wood died down making it an easy time for Lori to doze off. The voices in the front room were soft and didn't disturb her.

"Good night, Princess," Martha said. She bent down and kissed Lori's cheek, and received a warm smile from her beautiful little girl, ready to sleep.

"Good night, Ma," Lori returned with a slight grin, allowing her sleepy eyes to close gently.

# CHAPTER 4

## A LITTLE GIRL NAMED LORI

T he next couple of weeks were difficult but enjoyable for Matt He had feelings for Martha, knowing she belonged to Frank, she was so young and beautiful, closer to Matt's age than her husband's. He had youthful feelings bottled up inside him, not having a relaxing time since he left Montana. His enjoyable moments, lately, were when he watched Lori ride Toothless like a horse, or play hide-and-seek with Matt around the barn.

Toothless never had anything close to resembling a real family since he rode away from home at the tender age of fifteen. He was enjoying himself here with Frank, Martha, and little Lori. It seemed, there was never a moment that Lori was ever out from under his feet. She knew exactly where he was and hid around corners waiting to scare him. Toothless would act like he would about die of fright each time.

On one bright morning Toothless, fresh from milking chores, strode down the road toward the house. He concentrated on two full milk pails swinging from each hand, proud that he'd done his chore without spilling a precious drop.

"Boo!" A pile of hay at the porch corner erupted and Lori sprang up like a jack-in-the box. Toothless lurched back. "My stars!" Pails went up into the air, and the milk came down on top of him. With a dusty thud he landed on his backside in the dirt. Every precious drop he'd guarded now dripped from his hair and his nose. The shirt that

45

protruded over his belly was soaked into his pants, and he puddled around the depression where he'd landed.

When he blinked his eyes clear, he caught sight of Lori's blue dress disappearing through the screen door amid a peal of childish laughter until she ran right into her pa standing in the kitchen.

"What in heaven's name happened?" Frank pushed through the door and rushed down the steps.

Toothless felt warm wetness penetrate his clothes. His fingers disappeared under milky mud. Behind Frank, he could see Lori peeking around, fear turning her blue eyes to bright saucers. Suddenly the wild scene of a few seconds seemed enormously funny to him and he burst out laughing.

"Nobody's fault but my own," he said, tasting milk that still dripped from his hair. "I wasn't looking where I was headed." He scrambled to his feet, more interested in making sure Lori wasn't punished for her moment of fun. This was the closest thing to a family he'd ever had. He adored them all, Lori the most, and wouldn't do anything to hurt any of them.

On another warm evening, after dinner was eaten and the dishes were cleaned, Lori sat on Toothless' lap while he swung in the porch swing. Toothless felt that he had found his family at last. Knowing he was working for a family which he felt a part of, he sat there with a wide grin on his face. Lori looked up into his mouth. "Where's your teeth, Toothless?" she asked.

"Uh, teeth?" Toothless repeated, taken back a little with the embarrassing question. He thought fast, "Why, the tooth fairy came and took them all way."

"All of them?" she asked, scratching the side of her face.

"Well, yes Honey," he answered, "one at a time, 'til they were all gone."

"You ever gonna get them back? The tooth fairy took my tooth, but I'm getting one back. See," she said, opening her mouth and pointing to a new tooth coming in on the bottom. "And she even put a penny under my pillow for me. She give you a bunch of pennies, too?"

"Well, no, I don't suppose so," Toothless said with less of a smile, not knowing exactly which question to answer.

"Whatcha going to do from here on, Toothless?" she asked seriously. "You had a hard time chomping on that chicken leg last night.

You pulled it apart with your hands, and chomped it to death," she giggled.

"Well, if that don't beat all." He laughed with her. "Yep. You see, the good Lord is gonna give me some good choppers."

"What's that mean, Toothless?"

"Well, sweetheart. You see ..." he grew silent as he groped for words.

"He means, Lori, that the good Lord has some new teeth bein' made in town, and someday soon he's gonna get 'em," Matt came out onto the porch. "He'll have some dandies some day. I hope." He lit his cigar and looked out into the empty sky.

"Watcha lookin' at, Mr. Matt?" Lori asked politely.

"Oh, jest the night, little darlin'," Matt said. "The stars, the prairie out there."

"It's quiet here, Matt," Frank said, joining him on the porch.

"Yes it is, Frank," Matt replied, leaning against the column. "Reminds me of Wyomin', kinda."

"You said you're headin' for Texas," Frank reminded him, lighting his cigar.

"Soon."

"Why d'ya want to go to Texas, Mr. Matt?" Lori asked.

"Oh, I don't know, Lori," Matt answered. "Jest a place to be goin' to, I reckon. Far enough away from where I've been, I suppose."

"You don't like Wyoming any more?" Lori asked again.

"Love Wyomin'. Aim to go back some day." He leaned down to touch her hand. "Jest want to see what Texas is all about. Unnerstand it's big and it's wide and it's beautiful. I even hear it's got big steers with great big horns."

"The kind you blow through and make music?" she asked.

"Oh, they make enough noise without anyone blowing through them, Lori. And they got big rivers, and mesas, and ..."

"We've got some rivers," she said interrupting him. "I don't know what a mesa is."

"Well, little darlin'," Matt answered, "a mesa is a piece of land sticking out of the ground like a mountain, or a hill, but leveled flat like someone came along and chopped the top off with a sickle."

"What's a mountain, Mr. Matt?" she asked looking up at him with her face all puckered up.

"Well, you know what a hill is," Matt answered, assuming for the moment that she did.

"She's never seen a hill, let alone a mountain, Matt," Frank interrupted, lighting his pipe.

"Well, you take a lot of dirt and you build it up into a mound, like your hay over there by the barn. Pretend that's all dirt, stacked up real high. Higher than your house."

"Wow!" Lori said with her eyes wide open.

"Well, that's a hill, and take ten of those, and you've got yourself a mountain with a peak on top like your house here. Then, if you take off the roof of your house, there's no more peak. Unnerstand?" Matt asked, kneeling by Lori, and painting the picture with his hands.

"A house without a peak. I see. That's called a . . ."

"A mesa."

"Wow," Lori said, looking at Toothless. "Did you know that, Mr. Toothless?"

"Oh, yeah, little Lori," Toothless replied.

"Are you a farmer like my pa, Mr. Matt?"

Matt stood up and shrugged his shoulders. "No, I'm not a farmer like your pa. Your pa is a big man with a big farm. And he's raising a big family."

"Oh, pshaw, Mr. Matt. Our family is only me."

"For now, Sweetheart," Matt said. His attention turned towards the door.

Martha had stepped out of the house to join them. "What's this about our family?" she asked, looking down at Lori and drying her hands on her apron.

"I'm talking with Mr. Matt and Toothless, Ma," Lori said, and you ain't even told me to go to bed yet."

"Just came to get you," she said. "And you call him Mr. Toothless, little lady."

"Aw, Ma." Lori made a face, then reached up and kissed Toothless.

"I'll carry her in, Ma'am," Toothless said, standing up. "And if you don't mind, I'd kinda like tuckin' her in and tellin' her a story. And it's all right for her to call me Toothless, if it's all right with you, Mrs. Henson."

"Well, that's nice of you, Toothless," Martha said, giving Lori a goodnight kiss on her cheek. "Right to sleep after the story, young lady. Hear?"

"Yes, Ma'am," Lori replied as Toothless carried her atop his shoulders into the house.

Martha sat down on the stoop next to where Frank stood, and listened to the sounds in the night air. "Watching the fireflies flitter and listening to the crickets across the road gives me more wandering than I ever would want," she said.

Matt stepped off the porch and stood silently.

Martha watched him and studied his body. He was tall, strong, and good-looking, traits she had a difficult time finding in her husband. All she really knew about Matt was that he herded cattle in Wyoming, played checkers, and was heading for Texas.

Matt could sense her eyes on him. And he enjoyed the attention of the only woman for miles, and a good-looking woman at that. But every time he thought about her, all he had to do was look at Frank standing behind him to regain the right perspectives.

Matt turned to face the couple, and said, "Think I'll make one last visit and call it a day."

As he walked off, he saw Frank sit beside Martha and wrap his arm around her.

"Good night, Matt," Frank said.

Martha said nothing as she leaned back into Frank's arms and looked up into the star-lit sky.

# CHAPTER 5

## A TRIP TO TOWN

fter breakfast the next morning, Frank left the table and went outside. "Get the buckboard ready, Toothless," he said, watching Toothless clean himself up. "I've gotta go to town for supplies."

He turned back to Martha and said, "I'll be back before night-fall."

"Why don't you take Lori with you, Frank?" Martha asked.

"Not this time." Frank headed into the front room, reached up over the fireplace and took his long rifle down.

Martha watched him as he grabbed his jacket from the hook by the door. "Well, be sure to bring back some hard candy, then."

In a few moments, Toothless had the buckboard at the door.

"Want I should go with ya, Frank?" Toothless asked turning the reins over to Frank.

"No need," he answered, climbing into the buckboard. "When you get done with the animals you might want to fix the door on the barn. Rains are comin', and we'll need to keep some hay dry, as well as the horses. I'll be back tonight."

Lori climbed in next to Frank and received a kiss from her pa.

Frank then leaned from the buckboard, reached around and gave Martha a kiss. "I'll be back before Matt gets in. Lori, you make sure he gets his lunch. And no foolin' around with ol' Toothless over here."

"Oh, Pa," Lori said as Martha lifted her down from the buggy.

"I'll bring some hard candy home, and if you've been a good little girl, you can have some," Frank said with a wave.

Holding Lori in her arms, Martha waved goodbye to Frank as he whipped his horse into a trot down the road.

As he passed Matt in the fields, Frank waved to him. "I'll be back tonight, Matt."

Matt acknowledged him, waved back, and watched the buggy roll out and disappear around a bend in the road.

Lori was occupied helping Toothless feed the animals. Martha knew she loved the old man and followed him everywhere. One time, he fell in the sty trying to protect her from the sow that was protecting her suckling. Lori laughed until tears streamed from her eyes when a bantam rooster went after him after Toothless mistook it for a hen.

"Toothless," she said, putting her hands on her hips. "You don't know a banty rooster from a chicken."

He got back at her when they played a friendly game of horseshoes. He lobbed her horseshoes from a proper distance from the home stake, and did a good job at making ringers. Toothless was a good horseshoe player, and Lori got aggravated, walked up to the opposing stake, and simply tossed the horseshoe over the stake. She turned and smiled broadly at him with her little hands on her hips.

"There, Mister Smarty Pants," she said. "I threw it with all my might, and there it landed."

Toothless simply cussed and spit, turned and grinned his gums at her. She knew he was only teasing her.

Martha went out into the fields to give Matt his lunch. Martha was strong, solid in stature as well as having a fine figure. It was a warm day, and she wore her dress opened at the top. When she got to where Matt was working, she threw her bonnet back on her neck and let her hair hang down. She had primped herself up with her hair neatly combed and in place. Her face was clean and her teeth polished.

She watched Matt work the fields without his shirt.

He saw her coming towards him, and a warm feeling spread over his body. He was pleasantly surprised that she was bringing lunch to him.

"Hungry, Cowboy?" she asked, setting the basket of food, and the pail of cool water under the tree for him.

He plowed a row towards her, and said, "I'm surprised you came out here."

"Why would you be surprised?" She stood under the tree while the wind played with her loose-fitting dress. Like Lori, she wore no shoes.

"Gee, critter. Gee," he called out to his mule. "For one thing, Lori usually brings out my lunch."

"Well, I thought since Lori was helping Toothless, I'd bring it out to you myself."

Matt pulled up on the mule's reins and tied them to a low branch. He walked over to the pail of water and helped himself to a drink.

"That," he said, "is cold water."

"Fresh from the well. It should be."

Matt wiped his lips and replaced the ladle.

"Could I ask you a question, Matt? I mean without you getting angry?" Martha asked.

"Suppose so. What?"

"You weren't thrown from your horse like you told Frank, were you?" she asked looking straight into his eyes.

Matt said nothing, but took another drink of water.

"I found a bullet hole in that old shirt you threw away," she said, putting her fingers on his exposed and scarred wound.

"You want me to tell you how it got there?" Matt asked.

"You don't have to," Martha said politely. "It's none of my business. It looks pretty well healed."

"Pretty much so," Matt said, taking off his hat and wiping his brow with his bandanna. "Yes. I'd like to tell you. Toothless and I were robbed in town a few weeks back. We had more than enough money to make Texas. That's how come we're workin' for Frank."

"The man who robbed you, shot you?" She looked up into his blue eyes.

"At close range. I'll find him - someday, somehow, I'll find him."

"And you'll kill him, like he tried to kill you?" She turned back to her basket.

"I hope I won't have to, but if it comes to that, yeah, I suppose I will. Don't seem to be any law in this territory."

"We've got some law, Matt," Martha said. "But you're right. Our sheriff is not the man for the job. Too scared. Can't say I blame him any."

"There's no excuse for a man who's scared to be wearing a badge."

"Well, you see," Martha said, looking towards the farmhouse, "our land is being overrun with gangs. And it's not easy for a sheriff to go up against a whole gang. We all know that."

"What do the people do about the law then, Martha?"

"Hungry?" she asked trying to change the subject.

"Not now. But leave it here, and I'll eat it when I do get hungry."

Leaning up against the tree, he took out a cigar for himself.

"Oh, for most matters, we don't get involved. Sometimes, someone gets up a vigilante. Don't amount to much."

Reaching up, Martha took a match from his hatband, struck it on the bark of the tree, and put it to his cigar.

"You still think you want to catch these men?"

He took a hold of her hand and steadied it while the match lit his cigar. He held onto her hand for a while and looked in her eyes. Exhaling the smoke, he let go of her hand. "Thank you," he said. "I'll catch him some day."

He had not held a woman in his arms for some time, and it was becoming difficult to resist holding her. He knew he had to restrain himself, or else he would be sorry.

She leaned against the tree and watched him take another drink from the ladle.

The wind picked up a little and danced around them. They moved to the shadier side of the tree. As he dragged on his cigar, she watched him while he turned from her and looked away.

"You're a good looking man, Mr. Jorgensen," she said as she sat down on the grass. "I wonder why a man of your stature and wisdom puts his back into a plow."

Looking down the road, and away from her, he replied, "You're flattering, Martha. But, I'm just a man. No one special."

"I'm not patronizing you, Matt," she said, as she took an apple from her basket and began paring it with a knife. "Frank's a farmer. He'll never be anything else but a farmer. But, you're completely different. You wear a gun. And I can't see a man of your stature needing a gun."

"Or a plow?" Matt asked, turning to see her sitting on the grass. "You're very lovely, too."

"We're talking about you," she said, taking a slice of apple. "What's to become of you?"

"How do you mean?" His eyes drifted down her bare neck.

53

"I'm making you a little uncomfortable, aren't I? I'm sorry." She stood up and buttoned the top of her dress.

"You certainly are doing that," Matt replied with a grin.

"It's warm, and I'm not in the habit of having to watch how I dress on my own farm. Please forgive me."

Matt wondered how it would feel to ease Martha down on a green patch of grass and lay down beside her.

"What are you thinking?" She continued to slice her apple.

"I'm thinking I'm getting hungry." He knelt to retrieve a sandwich from the basket. When he rose, he found himself looking intently into her eyes. His face felt hot.

She smiled, turned her reddening face and looked down the road for a moment.

"I love this farm," she said, smiling as she kept looking away and feeling his eyes on her.

"You're married to a good man, Martha," he said, groping for words, hoping he wouldn't scare her away.

"Your ma raised a bright son," she teased, turning to face Matt with the paring knife. "Want a bite?"

"Thanks." He took a piece of the apple. "Want a bite of egg sandwich?" he asked, offering it to her.

"I'll have lunch with Lori when I get back to the house." She slid another piece of apple into her mouth.

"Real pretty girl, that Lori," he said. "Looks a lot like her mother."

"Thank you. I think so. She's my whole life. What about you? Any family?"

"Nope. Had a brother, but he got killed."

"Any girl friends? Wives?"

"Nope," he said, grinning a little. "Never met the right gal, I reckon."

"You've got another sandwich in there," she reminded him as she knelt down again to pick it out of the basket. "Here." She handed it to him. "I'll take the basket with me." She intentionally stayed down for a while, close to Matt's face.

The moment allowed her to see the sunbeams as they streaked through the branches and the wind played gently around them. The world outside seemed silent, with the exception of the occasional chirping of a bird.

"I'm sorry, but the sun is getting to me. Please forgive me," she said. "I can't stand a buttoned up dress." She unbuttoned the top button, took her dainty handkerchief from her apron pocket and wiped the light perspiration from her brow. "I best be getting back to Lori."

Matt reached down and gave her his hand to help her up. Her hand was soft and gentle to the touch, and as she neared him, he could smell the sweet fragrance of soap breathing in the perfume. If anything were to happen between them, he knew this was the time. He wanted to kiss her gently, and then passionately, but knew it would be just for a moment. She belonged to someone else. Still, it could be their moment, their one precious moment to share together.

She looked into his eyes as he held onto her hand.

"Will two sandwiches do?" she asked with a smile.

"I am going to savor the second sandwich later," Matt smiled back.

"Then," she said, "eat, and take a nap in the noonday shade. I'll be getting back to the house, for I can see my Lori running this way."

Matt watched Martha walk away, and continued eating his sandwich. He knew he had just let a beautiful dream pass by. He continued to watch as Lori ran in the plowed-up field to greet her mother.

Martha grabbed her daughter's hand in hers and they ran back to the house together.

*Where in the hell does she get her energy*, Matt kept eating and watching the pair run away. *Damn. Now what the hell have I got myself in for? Matt, you've gotta get away from here.* "Damn. Damn. Damn", he said over and over as he threw his sandwich down and kicked a sod of dirt into dust. *She is one helluva good lookin' lady. And, Matt, ol' boy, that's the problem. She's a lady, and a married one at that.* He stared at her back as she walked through the fields towards home.

# CHAPTER 6

## LEFT FOR DEAD

**M**ud Creek was the northern terminus town for the cattle drive from Texas. It would later become known as Abilene. Some cowhands at the end of their drive stayed and became ranchers or farmers.

The road to Mud Creek was uneventful for Frank. On this day, the town was quiet because the drives had to come through. Still trouble found Frank after he had loaded his buggy. A few men in town knew he was for a free state, and didn't own slaves. Frank always felt free to say what he pleased among those he thought were his friends. He was a simple religious man with a family and had no intentions of voting for slavery, nor was he an abolitionist. But speaking his mind was one of the only pleasures for a man his age.

"No man has a right to own another," Frank always said as he paid his bill at the hardware store. "We're a free state, and by the help of God, we're gonna stay free."

He got his hair and beard trimmed at the local barber. "Kansas is not like Missoura," he said. "We don't want slaves in our state."

A man from South Carolina who listened to him throughout the day was intent on doing something about it. Apparently well to do, he wore custom-fitted clothes, the type one would get from the east coast.

A gentleman in his late fifties, he appeared to be well educated from the way he held himself.

He contacted a young man by the name of Buck Tarbeck and paid him to make an example of Frank to the community.

Buck and three other men waited until Frank had his wagon loaded and was heading out of town before they approached him. They were called Pro-slavers. However, for the same amount of money, they would have easily fought for any side.

Around a bend in the road, and behind a group of trees, the four men hid from view and waited for Frank's approach. When the wagon appeared, they rode out in front and hailed it down.

"Hold up, farmer," the masked leader cried out as he held his arms up in defiance of the wagon's approach.

Frank halted as he was instructed, but showed no fear. This was the first time he had encountered any trouble.

"Get out of your wagon," the leader ordered Frank.

Frank complied with the leader's demands when the other three men dismounted, walked over to the wagon and looked through the goods.

"I know who you are, Buck," Frank yelled out. "No bandana's gonna disguise your voice." He knew the men well, he had seen them around town since they were teenagers.

Buck dragged his mask down. "Well, well. Now this does present a problem. We'll have to make you and your kind pay for the Pottawatomie Creek massacre," he said vehemently.

Two years earlier, John Brown and his sons had killed five Pro-slavery advocates at Pottawatomie Creek, which was a four-day ride south east of Mud Creek. It didn't slow down the growth of Pro-slavery. If anything, it increased the population of supporters. Since then, other Pro-slave men salted themselves throughout the eastern state of Kansas hoping to bring Pro-slavery there from across the borders of Missouri.

"We understand you got yourself some white men working for you," Buck said, watching his men tear through the goods. "You voting our way for slavery, or are you gonna keep your white workers? It's a lot cheaper buying a slave and feeding it. And you make more money in the long run, because you gets more work out of him."

"The men are out of work, and I hired them to help me," Frank said. "'Sides, what business is it of yours who I hire?" Looking at the men rifle through his goods, he moved towards them. "Leave those alone."

"What'cha gonna do about it, Frank?" Buck asked.

Frank attempted to climb aboard his buckboard, but was knocked off and to the ground by a fat man with a matted beard and mustache who stood on the packages in the buckboard. Frank got up, but Buck moved his horse into him, and knocked him back down.

"Stay out of it, Frank," Buck said again. "Tell us you'll vote for slavery, and we'll leave ya alone."

Rising to his feet, he reached behind the seat of his buckboard for his long rifle.

The fat man grabbed the rifle away from him. "You don't want this," he said, and flung it away from the wagon.

"If you want to go home tonight, you'd better be a good boy," Buck warned him.

"Who's paying you to do this, Buck?" Frank asked. "Taylor? Jones? McHenry? Which one?"

The three Frank named were rich men who had recently come into the area from South Carolina bringing with them poisonous ideas about how the States were going to become Pro-slavery.

"You'll pay for your sins, Buck Tarbeck," Frank said with his fist high in the air. "So will each and every one of you."

"Yeah? You farmers ain't got the guts," sandy-haired Tommy Benton said from atop the buckboard among the spilled goods. "Without slaves, you ain't nothin' but po folk ready to be swallowed up."

"And we're gonna do the swallowin'," Buck added, sitting high on his horse and laughing.

"You think what Brown did is gonna stop us?" one of the Johnson boys asked. He sat down on the buckboard seat. Their hyena-laughs and snorts only infuriated Frank more and he climbed the wagon to try to knock them out of it. Instead, Tommy's long skinny arm came around and met his head broadside, knocking him to the ground.

"Leave him be, boys," Buck said, looking down at Frank raising himself from the ground.

"You think Brown is the only one?" Frank asked through clinched teeth. "Right now Captain Montgomery is ridin' right along side him. We're gettin' rid of your kind."

Buck knew Frank was referring to Captain James Montgomery who'd become leader of a gang working out of Fort Scott. He had already shown his strength in a few violent assaults on the eastern edge of Kansas, and was prepared to ride the rail across the whole state. Yes, Buck had heard of Montgomery.

"Montgomery will champion the cause for the free-slave state of Kansas, and I'm fighting with him."

This only fueled the anger in Buck and his small band of men.

"I warned ya," Buck yelled out as they pounced upon him and mercilessly beat him until he was unconscious. Placing him in the back of the wagon, they whipped his horses to carry him home. Then they headed for Mud Creek.

The horses pulled the wagon into the road leading up to the farmhouse just before dusk. Matt was still in the fields when he saw them come in and, sensing something was wrong, left his mule and ran after the wagon, catching up to it only after the horses stopped at the barn.

Toothless and Martha with little Lori met the team ahead of Matt.

"Frank!" Martha cried out. "Frank! Oh, my gawd! Frank!" She ran crying towards Frank's splayed body in the back of the wagon.

Toothless picked up Lori and put her safely on the porch, then went after the horses.

"Unhitch 'em," Matt said, picking up Frank's body and carrying him into the house.

Martha bent down, picked Lori up in her arms, and cradled her. "Matt, what's happened to him?" Her eyes were filled with tears.

"Not sure yet." Matt put Frank on the bed.

Martha took a wet towel and wiped the blood and dirt away from his eyes.

"Where's the nearest doctor, Martha?" Matt asked.

"In Mud Creek," she replied staying with Frank. "Doc Parker."

"Yeah, I know Doc. Toothless will stay with you."

Matt rubbed Martha's shoulders for comfort then ran out the door towards the barn for Skeeter. With the help of Toothless, Matt brought Skeeter out of the barn all saddled.

"Stay here. I'll be back with Doc. Take care of them. Ya hear?"

"You don't have to tell me what to do," Toothless said. "I know my job."

Matt rode the trail towards town fast, but checking the sides of the road for any ambush. His eyes were trained in the dark from many times riding without moonlight. This night, the moon was full, which made him an easy target for any bushwhacker.

The trail led him back to Mud Creek, which had bedded itself down for the night. He rode slowly through town, searching for Doc Parker's office. When he found it, he hitched Skeeter to the post outside, ran up the stairs to the office, and pounded on the door.

A light flickered and the door opened. As luck would have it, Doc was in. He turned the lantern up to see who it was.

"Doc, you gotta come," Matt said, standing outside the door.

"What is it, young man?" Doc asked.

"Frank Hansen, farmer up the road, was bushwhacked and beaten. He's almost dead."

"I know Frank," Doc said, going back for his clothes. "He was just in town today getting supplies. What would anyone want to bushwhack him for?"

Doc dressed quickly, then grabbed his bag and opened it. "If he's in pain, he'll need some laudanum," he said, putting a bottle in his bag. Doc followed Matt as he ran back down the stairs.

"My buggy is over at the livery," Doc said, walking up the street. "Ride over there and wake them up. It'll speed things a little. I'll catch up."

The ride back to the farmhouse was easy in the moonlight, and Matt was feeling a little more comfortable with the terrain, still concerned that someone could still spring out of the shadows and bushwhack them like they did Frank.

Matt escorted Doc into the house where Frank lay.

When he finished patching up Frank's cuts and bruises, Doc closed the medicine case. "He should regain consciousness by morning. He'll have some scars, but all in all he'll be fine."

"You sure, Doc?" Martha asked to feel at ease with herself.

"He'll be all right, Martha," Doc assured her as he packed up his bag. "He's got a bad head bruise, but his eyes show no signs of hemorrhaging. No internal bleedings that I can tell. He'll be quite sore for a while. Keep some cold rags on his face to keep the swelling down. I'll check back with him in a day or two."

"Thanks, Doc," Martha said. She and Matt saw him to his buggy.

In the late morning, Frank was slightly awake, and still in bed. His swollen eyes searched the room where he laid, and rested on Matt's rugged face that looked down at him.

"Where's Martha?" he asked with a slight groan.

"I'm here, Honey," she replied, entering the room from the kitchen with a small pan of cold water.

She sat down next to him in a chair and applied more cold compresses to his face.

"Feeling better?" she asked with a smile.

"What happened, Frank?" Matt interrupted.

"I feel like a bull hit me," he answered. "Matt, this is a free state," he remarked, feeling the top of his head. "Why would anyone want to bring in slaves?"

"Don't rightly know what you mean, " Matt replied.

"Missoura has slaves for working on the farms," Martha answered. "They buy them, work them hard, and for nothing but meals and scanty housing. They take away their freedom, keep their kids from any learning, and treat them like cattle."

"Why?" Matt asked.

"To make more money," Martha answered. "We're small potatoes. Down state there are bigger farms. They grow grain. With slaves doing all the work, their owners simply live a life of leisure. We're not that way. We're dirt farmers, pure and simple."

"Then why did they beat up on this little girl's pa?" Toothless asked, entering the room with Lori in his arms.

"Frank likes to argue in town," Martha added. "It's his only vice and it thrills him to want to protect his land, even if we are small. It gives him a voice. Well, with all his rhetoric in and about Mud Creek, people listen to him and would vote his way. He'd like to be mayor some day, and this way, he feels he might achieve that goal."

"And now, your big mouth has gotten you into trouble," Matt said, folding his arms and looking down at Frank.

"If we let them take Mud Creek, they'll take Topeka, and Wichita, and Kansas will become a slave state," Frank winced as he talked, feeling pain throughout his whole body.

"We've no law as it is, Matt," Martha added. "With slavery will come more violence along with greed and murder."

"They'll take my farm," Frank said, keeping his eyes closed because of feeling great pain. "I can't let 'em."

"They'll jest come in and take it?" Matt asked.

"If we let them bring in slaves, they will," Martha answered. She rose and left the room. "I've got to get some colder water."

"I'll get it, Ma'am," Toothless said, taking the pan of water from her.

"Thank you," Martha said, looking into Matt's eyes as she stood by Frank. She wanted so much to say something to Matt.

"Do you know the men who did this to you?" Matt asked still looking into Martha's gray eyes.

"Tommy Benton, Buck Tarbeck, and the two Johnson boys. Martha knows them," Frank uttered as he passed out.

"It's their word against Frank's," Martha said. We have a part-time sheriff in Mud Creek. You know he's no match for these four vermin. They were born mean."

"I've met your part-time sheriff. You tell us how to go about finding these men, and Toothless and I'll do the rest." Matt strapped his Colt to his side. "Toothless, let's saddle up."

Toothless put little Lori down. Matt grabbed his gun belt from the wall, strapped it to his side, and sauntered out the kitchen door for the barn.

"We can't ask you to do this, Matt," Martha pleaded as she walked him to the kitchen door.

"I didn't hear any one asking anything, Martha." Matt picked up his hat and gun belt from the hooks off the kitchen wall. "How do we find these men?"

"It'll be four against two, you'll get yourselves killed."

"If my memory don't fail me, you mentioned something about a part-time sheriff, and that would make three agin' four. Jest about the right odds, I'd say."

"Vern Steadman," Martha yelled out to Matt as he walked towards the barn. "He knows where they are."

Matt and Toothless rode past the house, while Martha stood there gripping tightly onto her apron. *God keep you safe, you big idiot,* she whispered to herself.

Doc's carriage rounded the roadway as they stopped to greet him. "How's our patient today, Matt?" he asked.

"He's awake," Matt answered. "Then he passed out. I know he's in pain, but that's about all I can say."

"I'll change the dressings."

"Is he gonna make it, Doc?" Matt asked.

"He's a strong man," Doc replied. "His will to fight is what's keeping him alive now. I'd say he's got a fifty-fifty chance, with that bump on his head."

Matt waved him through, and with Toothless, they rode towards Mud Creek.

The two men rode over to the livery, when they arrived in town, and found Dan'l outside bellowing up the embers.

"Hello, Matt. Toothless. What can I do for you?" He stopped his work and looked up at the two men sitting in their saddles.

"Looking for a Vern Steadman, Dan'l," Matt said brushing his hat back on his head.

"The sheriff? In back, last time I saw him, groomin' his mare."

"Thanks," Matt replied.

The two men dismounted and hitched up their horses, then went to the back of the livery stable where they found the sheriff.

"Strangers in town," Vern said, as he continued to comb his horse's mane. "How can I help you?"

"Remember us, Sheriff?" Matt asked.

"Can't say."

"Some men relieved me of all my money one rainy night, and you said it'd be no use lookin' for them."

"Oh, yeah. You couldn't recognize them, as I recollect."

"We're farmhands now, workin' for Frank Hansen. We're looking for some men."

"I know Frank. I have a farm on the other side of Mud Creek, small one like Frank's. Who are these men, and what're you wantin' 'em for?"

"They beat the hell out of Frank. He might be dead as we're talkin'," Toothless answered.

"Buck Tarbeck was one name," Matt added. "Johnson boys, a couple of others. Who was the other one, Toothless?"

"Tommy Benton?" Vern asked. "He'd likely be the fourth. They hang out together."

"Do you go after them, or what, Sheriff?" Toothless asked.

"They're tough. I'll go talk with them and see what I can do," Vern said, reaching up and taking his hat off a hook on a post nearby.

Noticing that he wasn't packing a gun, Matt asked, "What are you going to use for persuasion, Sheriff?"

"Gun? I'm a farmer," he reminded Matt. "If they did beat up Frank, I'll try to bring them in, but I'm not going to risk my life for it."

Vern untied his mare and walked her outside. Matt and Toothless sidled Vern to their horses. Unhitching them, they followed as he walked out of the stable towards the only saloon in town.

Inside, the man who had hired the boys was sitting at a table playing cards with two other rich and portly gentlemen.

"Who you looking for, Sheriff?" the man asked as he looked up at Vern with Matt and Toothless standing by his side.

"Buck Tarbeck," Vern replied. "Know where I can find him?"

"Try his house, Sheriff," the man answered. "Did he do anything wrong?"

"Thanks," Vern said, and turned and walked out.

Matt sized up the men at the table, noticing particularly the way they were dressed. He and Toothless turned and followed Vern.

They climbed into their saddles and rode out of town towards the Tarbeck farm. It was one of the largest farms Matt had seen so far, and they saw several slaves working the land as they rode up.

"Notice something peculiar, Matt?" Toothless said, eyeing the slaves.

"I see them," Matt answered. "Keep a lookout for those four men."

As they rode up to the house, a plump well-dressed man and his wife greeted them. "Care for some lemonade, Vern?" the man asked. "You and your companions are welcome. Why don't you light down and set a spell?"

"No thanks, Paul," Vern said, staying on his horse. "I'm looking for Buck."

"He's in town," Paul Tarbeck replied.

"I didn't see him."

"He's there. They left this morning for town. You might talk to a man by the name of Phil Taylor. He's been working for him lately. What you need my boy for, Vern?"

"Frank Hansen claims Buck and his friends bushwhacked him," Vern replied holding tight on his reins.

"When?"

"Last night."

"Couldn't have been him, Vern," Paul said, taking out his pipe to fill it. "Buck and his buddies just returned from a hunt this morning. They were east of here."

"Yeah?" Vern replied, pulling the brim of his hat down over his eyes. "I wonder what or who they were hunting."

"Don't go half-cocked," Paul warned as he watched them start to ride off.

"They're good boys, Sheriff," Mrs. Steadman added.

"Who's this Phil Taylor, Vern?" Matt asked as they rode back onto the highway.

"Remember that rich fella at the saloon?" Vern asked.

"Him, eh?" Matt responded.

"Yep. You don't want to tangle with him or his two buddies. They're rich, and they've got more money backing them."

"Are they crooks?" Matt asked.

"Worse," Vern answered.

"Worse?" Toothless came back. "What could be worse than crooks?"

"They pay others to do their work for them. They're agitators. They come into town, do their job, and leave."

"What's their job?" Matt asked.

"They're Pro-slave men who want Kansas to become a slave state," Vern replied, kicking his horse into a canter back towards Mud Creek.

Paul Tarbeck was right. When the men reined up at the saloon, Buck and his three accomplices were standing outside its doors laughing and talking loudly.

Vern, Matt and Toothless alit from their horses and tied them up to the hitching rail.

"Gotta talk to you," Vern said walking up on the boardwalk. "You and your friends."

"What about?" Buck put his thumb on the hammer of his gun. "Or is it Sheriff Vern today?"

"I'm always the sheriff, Buck, and I'm totin' no iron," Vern said. "Jest need to talk. That's all."

Matt and Toothless backed out into the street and stood their grounds, waiting to see what was going to happen.

"That go for your friends out there, too, Sheriff?" Buck asked. "I see they're totin' iron."

"They claim you bushwhacked Frank Hansen last night, and left him for dead" Vern said.

"Frank hurt?" Buck asked, smiling at his buddies. "First I heard anything about it, Sheriff. Why, Frank's a good friend of ours."

"He was never a friend of yours, Buck. I want you four down at the jail, right now."

Buck stepped off the boardwalk and walked past Vern.

"You arrestin' me?" Buck asked, rubbing his gun grip with his thumb.

"You'll have to stand trial. Might go light with you if Frank lives," Vern said, watching the men crowd him.

"And if he dies?" Buck asked sarcastically.

"If you did it, you'll hang."

"Nobody's gonna hang me," Buck said, turning back around to face the three men. "Nobody, 'cause ol' Buck never did anythin' wrong."

Looking at Matt and Toothless with their gun belts, Buck said, "Now we don't trade words here in Kansas, mister."

"Sound familiar, Matt?" Toothless asked.

"Yeah," Matt answered, walking away from the group towards the street. "Let's move out, Toothless."

The other three men stepped off and walked around the tied-up horses, crowding the men for a fight.

Matt remembered to keep six bullets in the chamber this time. His thoughts traveled to all those hours when he pulled his gun fast out of its holster on the prairie and fired it at tree limbs, and tin cans. Now it had to pay off.

He watched Buck's hand as it started to clamp down around the butt of his pistol.

"You touch that hog leg, and Matt Jorgensen will fill you so full of lead, you'll be dead before you fall," Toothless warned Buck. "He's the fastest gun in the territory, killed three outlaws in one draw without any help. Now he's got me and the sheriff."

This is the first Vern had heard about Matt, and he did a double take at what he'd just heard.

"You the one from Wyomin'?" Buck asked.

"That's me," Matt replied taking a couple steps backwards with his hand above his Colt. "And I'm calling you a thief and a coward, and I've got something to give you that I borrowed from you."

Buck stepped out in the street alone, his three cohorts dropped their gun belts and backed away on the boardwalk.

"We heard about you," Buck said. "Some men told us about a fast gun from Wyoming. Until now we didn't know who that man was. You ain't got nothin' for me."

"I have six of them."

"I see you didn't learn your lesson the other night," Buck said, confirming Matt's suspicions.

Seeing his pals on the sidewalk, and knowing about Matt, Buck became a little nervous. "You guys chickening out?" he asked, as he stepped out to meet Matt. He tried to hide his fear, but his hand shook as he held it close to his gun.

"Like I said before, we don't trade words, mister," Buck said as he drew his .36 and cocked it.

Matt's Colt was out of its holster first, and from his hip he fanned it, hitting Buck right between the eyes. Buck stood, wobbled, and fell to the ground, dead. His gun discharged as he went down, sending the bullet into the ground.

Matt turned quickly on the other three men who were standing scared and frozen.

"We don't trade words in Wyomin', either," Matt said with his gun still smoking. "Anyone else?"

"You did it!" Toothless exclaimed loud and clear. He took his gun out and pointed it at the other three men.

Matt was surprised at how his reputation had traveled this far south. Of course, Toothless blabbing it everywhere might have helped.

Now, with another fast-draw killing under Matt's belt, ol' Toothless began to dance a jig right in the middle of the street.

"I knew it. I knew it," Toothless kept saying with a broad grin on his leathered face. "Fastest gun in these here United States. Matt Jorgensen, people," he yelled as the townsfolk gathered around. "Fastest man there is. Shot him right between the eyes."

The three agitators left their table and came out to see Buck stretched out, bleeding in the street, face down. They knew they had lost their key player. When they looked at the other men being escorted down the street by the sheriff, they went back inside for their belongings and left town that day.

It was a big day in Mud Creek for Matt and Toothless. Toothless had finally seen his first real gunfight with bullets flying, and it was between his pal Matt and a would-be killer.

While the mortician cleaned up the street, and Matt spent some time at the jail with the town's part-time sheriff, Toothless spent the rest of the day in the saloon, being offered drinks, which he gladly accepted. He could not stop telling the many and various and untrue stories about Matt Jorgensen from Wyoming, one of the first of the fast draws.

Back at the jail, a couple men entered and brought a saddlebag to Vern.

"We took the horses over to the livery, but figured you'd want his saddle bag," one of them said, handing it to Vern. "Feels like it's got some money in it."

"Thanks, gentlemen," Vern replied, and watched the men leave.

"That's my saddlebag, Vern," Matt said.

"Was Buck the man who shot you?" Vern asked.

"Must have been," Matt replied looking inside the saddlebag. "Looks like he spent a lot. Only thirty, thirty-five, forty double eagles left, but it'll do."

"How many were there?"

"Less Ma's, we had around seventy. I won't complain. We got this much back."

"What about it, gentlemen?" Vern asked the three men he locked up.

"It was all Buck's doin', Sheriff," Tommy blurted out. "We had nothin' to do with it."

"This his saddlebag?" Vern asked.

"It's his," a Johnson boy replied. "Buck spent the rest on his women. He didn't give us none. Not a damn cent."

"You'll have to sign for it, Matt," Vern said, writing out a form.

"S'all right with me. But, Vern, could I ask you one more favor?"

"What?"

Matt whispered in Vern's ear so that the three men could not hear. Vern went over to the jail, unlocked it and let Matt enter it.

As the three men cowered away from Matt, he asked, "you didn't have anything to do with my getting' shot?"

Without any warning, Matt pasted his fist into Tommy's face hard enough to knock him unconscious.

"And you didn't have anything to do with beating up a harmless farmer?"

He brought the back of his hand against one of the Johnson boys, sending him against the wall. Coming back with a full swing of his body, his fist met the other boys' jaw, breaking it, sending him to the ground.

"Doc Parker will be over when he's not delivering a baby and patch you boys up," Matt said with a smile as he rubbed his knuckles and walked out of the cell.

Vern locked the cell and followed Matt out of the jail with a slight grin on his face. "They'll probably get off someway or other, but I'll guarantee you they will never forget you, Matt Jorgensen from Wyomin'."

Matt shook hands with Vern and stepped up on his horse.

"Thought you were a sissy, Vern, when you didn't help me the first time," Matt said. "Now, I see you're all right."

"Jest like any other man," Vern said. "One of these days, Mud Creek will have a real marshal, and hopefully a new name."

"New name?"

"Yeah. Who'd want to have their kids grow up in Mud Creek?"

The two looked out at the muddy road and laughed. Matt tipped his hat and rode over to the saloon where he caught up with Toothless.

Outside of town, Matt said, "I got my saddlebags back, Toothless."

Toothless laughed and grinned all the way back to the farm.

It was at least three weeks before Frank could get up and around. Matt and Toothless had plowed the forty acres and planted seed. Now, it was time for Matt to move on. He felt he had earned his keep many times over, and staying on would only increase his desire to invite trouble into his bunkhouse.

Martha continued to help take the water and food out to him while he was farming, but for insurance, she made a point of taking Lori along with her when she went. Each time she came with a little more bounce, and Matt knew some day there would be one bounce too many. Just being around her made Matt skittish.

Toothless on the other hand had different ideas. He fell in love with a pretty little girl for one of the few times in his seventy years, and decided to stay put. Little Lori had won his heart, and he felt it was his duty to teach her all about farming, or the other way around. Frank and Martha were grateful for his decision to stay on as their hired man.

The day arrived for Matt to push on towards Texas. After a full breakfast, the last one Martha had fixed for him, he saddled up ol' Skeeter.

Toothless and Lori helped Matt saddle Skeeter, while Martha and Frank stood on the porch waiting for the last goodbyes. On the main road, they saw two men in a horse-drawn carriage heading their way. A horse was trailing them tied to the carriage.

"Wonder who it could be," Martha said with her hand shading the sun from her eyes.

"It's Vern Steadman," Frank said. "Don't know the other one."

"What in the world is he bringing someone way out here for?" Martha said, staying on the porch with Frank.

Matt walked over to the carriage and greeted the gentlemen.

"Good morning, Vern. I was jest leavin'."

"Good morning, folks." Vern pulled his team to a halt. "This is Marshal Whittaker from Topeka."

"Good morning," Whittaker greeted them as he stepped out of the carriage.

"What in thunder brings you men out our way?" Frank asked. "Martha, get them some lemonade. They must be thirsty."

"We surely are that," the marshal answered. "Thank you."

"Matt, the marshal needs to talk with you," Vern said. "Can we go inside?"

"Sure. Toothless, take Skeeter for me."

"I'll take the saddle off, too. Looks like you'll be here for a while," Toothless said, walking Skeeter back to the barn.

Lori stood there watching everything going on, like any five-year old would do.

"Comin'?" Toothless asked Lori.

"Yep," Lori said, and turned and followed him.

Inside the house, the men settled in the front room with their drinks. Martha and Matt stood as Frank sat down with the other two men. Toothless and Lori returned and stood in the hallway just outside the room behind Martha. Matt stood by the front window.

"Matt, I'm the U. S. Deputy Marshal and I rode all the way from Topeka," Whittaker said, taking off his hat and showing his dark wavy hair. He sported a long thin black moustache, and a goatee to match, and appeared to be somewhere in his forties. His suit was black, and he sported a silk vest, which held a marshal's badge and a watch with a chain and fob. His shirt was gray, and he wore a shoestring bow tie. He had a muscular-looking face with a cleft in his jaw, making him look rather handsome in some people's eyes, Matt supposed.

"I'm here to solicit your help," he continued.

"How the hell can I be of help to you?" Matt asked, taking out his makings. "You're a marshal."

"We have a big problem here in Kansas, one that has gotten out of hand. I don't know if you're aware of it."

"This slavery thing?" Matt pointed to Frank. "He got beat up because of it."

"And you killed the man who did it," Vern interrupted.

"Anything wrong?" Matt asked, lighting his cigar.

"The capital received my report, Matt," Vern said, "and it came to the marshal's attention. He wired that he would like to meet you."

"No one until now would go up against any of these men?" Whittaker continued.

"What men?" Matt asked.

"The three we arrested, and the one you shot," Vern said. "They were paid to ambush Frank."

"Remember those three men who left town all of a sudden?" Vern asked.

"The rich dudes?"

"The three men in Mud Creek, including the one who hired Buck, were ambassadors for Captain Charles A. Hamilton, the guerrilla leader for the Pro-slavers. Joining forces with these three men meant in essence joining up with Hamilton. They paid Buck and his men to beat up Mr. Hansen. They were evidently sponsored by the Southern Emigrant Aid Society and were also members of the Dark Lantern Societies," Whittaker added. "We know that much. Their main objective is to terrorize the Free-State settlers into voting for Kansas to become a slave state."

"How does any of this concern me, Marshal?" Matt asked.

"They've brought in people from outside Kansas, Matt," Whittaker said, taking out cigars from his vest and offering them to the men.

"Do you know who they are?" Frank asked.

"We know the leaders by name," Whittaker answered. "We don't know them by face."

"Why don't you arrest them?" Frank asked.

"They've got protection, at least two hundred armed men. We don't have enough men, Mr. Hansen. My deputies have their hands full in Lawrence."

"And?" Matt said.

"And, our hot spot is a place called Fort Scott," Whittaker continued. "It's on the border between Missouri and Kansas. You talk about the leaders. Hamilton runs slaves across the border, and a man named Montgomery who chases them back."

"Any soldiers?"

"The governor has allocated us some men at times, and only when they're not needed elsewhere," Whittaker returned dragging on his cigar. "Yes, we've got a few soldiers down there trying to keep the peace."

"It seems to me," Frank interrupted, "Governor Geary would concentrate our soldiers on that very spot if that is where it's needed."

"He's talking about our governor, John Geary, who became our new territorial governor after the last one resigned," Whittaker added. "He's helping restore order and making Kansas a free state. But, when we go in to arrest anyone, they become like ghosts. We can't find them."

"Ghosts?" Toothless asked. "How do you mean, Marshal?"

"They run home and turn into pumpkins. They go from terrorizing and become dirt farmers once again. If we knew who they were, we could go in and arrest them. That's why we need you inside, to find who they are, and help us stop them. If we let Hamilton and Montgomery have their way in Fort Scott, I'm afraid Kansas just might have its own civil war. I need you to put a stop to this bloodshed in Fort Scott."

"Why me? Why not Vern? He's a sheriff. I'm headed for Texas."

"You're a fast gun, Matt," Whittaker said, enjoying his cigar. "We need a fast gun at Fort Scott. The government is willing to pay you for it."

"The government has soldiers, Marshal, remember?" Matt returned.

"That's the problem, Matt. Our hands are tied. We have to be unbiased, neither for nor against slavery. We need someone who's not afraid to bring this gang warfare to a halt, and who is against slavery."

"And, jest how do you propose one man like me is going to do this?" Matt asked.

"This is the day of the fast gun. By joining up with Montgomery, and becoming his hired fast gun," Whittaker said, standing up. "Gain his trust."

"That sounds like spy work," Matt said looking into Whittaker's dark eyes.

"You hit the nail on the head," Whittaker said chomping down on his cigar.

"Now, I know I'm stupid about some things, but don't it make sense that if he's against having slaves, he should be working with you?"

"He's a jayhawker, Matt," Frank said.

"What in the hell is a jayhawker?" Matt asked.

"He's using the cause to further his own ends. He pretends to fight for a free state, but then he raids farms, threatens farmers with ruin, and steals from them," Whittaker said.

"We never know who they are, and that's a fact," Vern added. "Hell, had it not been for Frank, we never would have suspected Buck and Tommy to be part of Hamilton's gang. Especially Tommy. They were good kids."

"Both gangs do the same thing?" Matt asked.

"Both men are scrupulous. They came here with good intentions, I suppose, but both men are thieving bastards," Frank added.

"I join up with Montgomery, and I help him get rid of Hamilton. What if they get rid of me?"

"That's the chance you have to take, Matt," Vern said rising.

"I don't mind tellin' you, I don't like the odds."

"A hundred dollars a month salary goes with the job, with the first month in advance," Whittaker said.

Matt looked at Frank, and then turning his back on the men, looked into Martha's eyes. She closed her eyes and turned her face away. He knew her feelings were for him to leave. On the other hand, she knew he was no coward, and for this she would be proud of him, he was sure of that.

"You've done enough, Matt," Frank said stepping into the center of the room. "They can't ask you to do this."

Matt looked over at Toothless who was holding Lori in his arms, a grin of pride lighting his face.

"Can't tell you what to do, Matt," Toothless said. "If you're a goin', I'll ride with ya."

"What if I don't accept?" Matt asked, turning back to Whittaker.

Nobody answered. Matt stood up in the middle of the room and looked into their faces.

"And if I accept, and disperse these gangs, with your help, what then?"

"Then your job is done," Whittaker said. "You can ride to Texas knowing you've done your part for your country, or you can join with me and be a Deputy Marshal, settle down and start a good life."

Matt rubbed the gun grip as a habit, and walked to the door.

"Heaven help you that you do make it out alive," Whittaker said. "They can be mean, and vicious, Matt. Both men want power, and they both came from separate states and settled here in Kansas thinking it will be handed to them on a silver platter. Hamilton is the more ruthless one, but don't think Montgomery won't carve you up for dinner, cause he will."

"Then what happens to Kansas if I fail?"

"Like I said, Kansas will have its own civil war, and hundreds if not thousands of people will be killed. Farms like Frank's here will be ravaged. It'll take years to rebuild what a civil war will destroy. That's why I'm here to try to persuade you, Matt."

Matt scanned the land in front of him at the work he, Toothless, and Frank had done these past few weeks. He envisioned how it was going to look. He then turned and looked at Martha and Frank, and little Lori in Toothless' arms.

"You saw four men, Matt," Vern said, "who were paid by Pro-slavery men to hurt Frank. The same men were willing to kill you."

"Where are those men, the agitators who paid Buck?" Matt asked.

"Probably back in Fort Scott by now," Whittaker said. "That's their headquarters. You find them, you'll probably find Hamilton."

"I have a sister down there," Frank said. "Her name is Sandi. Appreciate it if you'd look in on her if you run across her. She's a little thing, twenty years old."

"Sure," Matt answered, not really paying attention. His mind was still struggling with the decision of whether or not he was going.

Matt returned to the middle of the room where Whittaker was holding out a cigar.

"It looks to me as if my country is calling me," Matt said, taking the cigar.

"Then you'll do it?" Whittaker asked.

"Got no choice," Matt said, lighting his cigar. "How does the government figure on protectin' me?"

"You're on your own," Whittaker said. "Only one man there who will know your identity, Deputy Marshal Sam Walker. If the sheriff or the government troops capture you with the gang, you'll have to take your chances."

Matt puffed on his cigar, cheated a peek at Martha, and envied Frank for his settled-down life with her. He felt a sense of apprehension about what he was to do, but knew that the deal was made, and there was no backing out. He was going to become a spy for the government.

"Toothless," Matt said, looking intently at him.

Toothless's eyes widened as he waited Matt's decision to take him along. "I'm acomin', too. Ain't I?"

"No, you're not. One man can get in and out a lot easier without havin' to worry about another one."

"You won't have to worry 'bout me. I can take care of m'self."

"Sure you can, in a one-on-one situation. This here is different."

"He's right," Whittaker agreed. "Matt's worrying about your safety could get you both killed. He'll have enough on his hands."

"You can join up with me once I get through this mess." He looked into Toothless' face and thought, *If I ever do, Toothless. If I ever do.*

Toothless' felt hurt but senses the men were right. He picked Lori up and held her close to his chest.

Later, Vern took his horse, untied it from the carriage, and headed back to Mud Creek. Matt followed Whittaker's carriage back to the main road.

Martha stood with Frank on the porch and waved as Matt rode off. Toothless and Lori both waved goodbye to him, and Lori threw him a kiss.

Matt caught up to the carriage as it headed north in the fork.

"His name is Marshal Walker," said Whittaker.

"So, if I get into Montgomery's gang, I tell your Marshal Walker who I am. How do I find him?"

"He'll find you," Whittaker answered. "Safer that way. He's tall, muscular, in his thirties, wears a moustache. All I can tell you about him."

"Sounds like every dude I've met so far," Matt said, and spurred Skeeter east to Fort Scott.

# CHAPTER 7

## A QUEST FOR HONOR

April, 1858

It was mid-April. Heading south, Matt tried his best to avoid talk of slavery issues along the way. When he stopped at a general store, he would hear the checker players and merchants talk, sometimes loudly and heatedly, while at other times quietly so as not to bring attention to themselves. The topic of conversation was always the same, slavery.

When asked his opinion, of course he would simply say he was from Wyoming, and was just riding through. Whichever way he rode, the problem was there ahead of him. He wished he had never left Montana, and then again he wished he were already in Texas where he was headed.

He became aware that the more prominent people were for slavery, while the farmers were against it. He heard every opinion, every side to the issue, and everything about two men in particular, Captain Hamilton and Captain Montgomery.

Running slaves across the border from Missouri to Kansas among the farmers was risky and dangerous, but was rewarding for Captain Charles A. Hamilton, the guerilla leader for Pro-slavery. Member of a wealthy Georgian family, Hamilton knew about the Kansas disturbance. He moved into the state and established residency in order to propagate his Pro-slavery beliefs.

Matt knew that Captain James Montgomery was no better, but he used his shield as fighting for Kansas to remain a free state. What Whittaker told Matt appeared to be true; both Montgomery and Hamilton were fighting for the glory and for wealth rather than for the cause. Each leader would confiscate honest, hardworking farmer's goods and distribute them as he felt fit among their men, and keep the best for himself.

Matt knew that the government wouldn't take either side, although they seemed to be more against slavery than for it. Their duty was simply to enforce the law of the land. There was a fine line among all three parties, which Matt found out when he met up with Hamilton's foe, Captain James Montgomery.

Matt calculated that a four-day ride south of Kansas City would bring him to Fort Scott, putting him right in the middle of one of the hottest fights in Kansas. There was no way around it. As he entered Linn County, he heard shooting in the distance. He rode to a crest where he could see a group of men chasing another band of men across the land.

Sitting his horse high on the mound and in a grove of trees, Matt took the moment to light a cigar as he watched, not wanting to get involved at this juncture in time. It would have been a mistake to choose the wrong side to sidle in with.

"Hold your hands high!" a voice commanded from behind him.

When Matt turned, he saw a long rifle pointed at him. The man appeared to be in his mid-twenties, tall and lean with dirty-sandy hair and dark brown eyes. He wore chaps with large Conchos decorating them.

"Are you for a free state?" the man asked, cocking his rifle.

"With that rifle pointing at my gut, it doesn't look like I have a choice, now does it?" Matt asked with a smile.

"No, it doesn't. Smells like I have a filthy Pro-slaver, boys. What d'ya want me do with him, Capt'n?"

Matt sat still studying what was going on around him. A group of seven men had surrounded him, and the one with the rifle appeared ready to blow a hole in his belly. Matt kept his hands high and away from his holster.

"I'm ridin' through to Texas," Matt said, "if that helps matters any here."

"What do we have here?" another voice pierced the air from the other side of Matt.

Matt turned in the direction of the commanding voice. He could have been a businessman or a lawyer with his stately look, fine clothes, black long hair and a well-trimmed beard and mustache. Judging from the reaction of deference from the other men, he was the leader of a gang of Free-State fighters.

Reaching out his hand, he said, "My name's Captain James Montgomery. Who are you, might I ask?"

Matt accepted the firm grip. He assessed the man to be in his middle forties, even though the deep lines in his forehead and around his eyes made him appear much older. At least head and shoulders shorter than Matt, Montgomery appeared lean and wiry in his tailored coat.

"Matt Jorgensen," Matt replied. "I'm from Wyomin', if that will help ya," Matt answered. "I jest left Mud Creek a few days ago."

"Do you buy that, Capt'n?" the man with the rifle asked.

"Yes. He's not from around here," Montgomery answered.

"Mud Creek?" Montgomery asked. "Hmmm," he continued as he rode his horse around Matt's horse while stroking his beard. "Matt Jorgensen." He dismounted and handed the reins over to the nearest man. He took a cigar out of his vest pocket and lit it.

Matt followed Montgomery and alit from his horse.

"Mud Creek," Montgomery repeated, lighting his cigar. This is Ben Rice," Montgomery gestured toward the man with the rifle. Ben was a wiry man with heavy dark eyebrows, which gave him a sinister look. "He's my right hand man, fast with a gun, too. But, from what I hear, you could be faster. I understand you killed some of Hamilton's hired guns, and chased the rest the hell out of Mud Creek single-handedly. Now that takes a lot of guts. What you did in Mud Creek is exactly what we need here in Fort Scott."

Matt was dumfounded that someone this far south had heard of him already. "I heard about you, too, but I didn't expect to meet up with you so soon. Glad I did."

"Men," he shouted, holding his Sharps rifle up high, "this man here is about the fastest with a gun in Kansas."

"We don't need him, Capt'n," Ben said, putting his rifle back into its boot.

"What's Fort Scott?" Matt looked around the group of men.

"I said we don't need you," Ben came back angrily.

"You got a problem, mister?" Matt turned his back on Ben to talk with Montgomery.

"I'm afraid I don't exactly know what you're talking about, sir," Matt took a long draw on his cigar. "Never heard of Fort Scott."

"Then why are you riding this way if you ain't heard of it?" Ben asked.

"Isn't Texas this way?" Matt asked.

"Whatcha mean?"

"I'm headin' south, and I'm told that Texas is south."

"Fort Scott's an old army post up ahead," Montgomery replied. "I'll tell you all about it in due time. Got business in Texas?"

"Jest set my sight on it," Matt answered, wary of the question.

"Is anybody there expecting you any time soon?" Montgomery asked.

"No one."

"Good," Montgomery said, hands clasped behind his back, and chewing on his cigar. "Kansas will enjoy your stay. See those men down there?" Montgomery pointed to the band of men chasing the other group eastward. "Those are my men. They're running those damn Pro-slave men into Missoura where they belong. Ben here doesn't like Pro-slave men. None of us do, but he's got a real dislike for them."

"And if I choose to leave?" Matt asked, taking a long drag on his cigar and holding on tight to his pistol grip.

"Take off right now. Nobody will harm you. Just don't stop at Fort Scott."

Matt knew that, working as a government spy, if he was going to get in with Montgomery's gang to help get at Hamilton, this was the time. He might never get another opportunity. Of course, at this time, it didn't appear to Matt that Montgomery needed any help, the way his men were chasing Pro-slavers back to Missouri. Yet, he had sworn to Marshal Whitaker that he would act in the position of a deputy marshal to help make Kansas a free state. He knew what he had to do, and without any hesitation that might mess up his plan, he charged right in with eyes wide open.

"Like you said, I have time. Fort Scott intrigues me."

"Good. Ride with Ben and me."

"What about those men down there?"

"They'll finish their work and go on home. In the meantime, I want you to see my home."

The men rode to a close-by location, a large unfinished farm-house that sat a good quarter of a mile off the main road. Because it was late and the sun had just dipped below the horizon, Matt had little time to see much of the farm as he was ushered into a bunkhouse adjacent to the barn, where a few of the riders slept so they could be close to their horses if they needed them. A couple of them took Matt to a bunkhouse in back. Dick Coulter appeared to be the younger of the two. Sandy-haired and barely twenty, he was half a head shorter than Matt. Matt felt his eyes staring at his gun.

Some of the other men went home to their own farms, while a few tented in the woods close by. In a group of a few dozen men in the bunkhouse, there was found discipline and order where the men shared commonalities.

"You can have the upper bunk," Dick said. He pointed to a double cot. "Only one left." He laughed and sat down on the bottom bunk. "I sleep here."

"Do any reading, Matt," the other man said, picking up a small book from his cot next to Dick's. From its worn pages, it appeared that it had been the only one read many times over. "M'name's Chaps. Nothin' much to do around here when we ain't out there ridin' or workin' our farms." Chaps had dark straight hair, and a smile that was cockeyed, as if he enjoyed making fun of others.

"Thanks," Matt replied, taking off his gun belt and laying it on his cot. "Not a book man."

"Is it true you're the fastest draw in Kansas?" Dick asked, watching Matt remove his pistol from its holster.

"Workin' on it," Matt responded, spinning the chamber. He emptied the bullets and laid them on the bed next to his gun belt. He took a rag lying nearby and began cleaning his pistol. "It's a Colt .36. Little heavy, but once you get the feel of it, it slides out of the holster real nice and easy like. Fires fast, too." He cocked it and released the hammer back into position. After reloading it, he twirled it, and placed it back into its holster.

Dick still couldn't take his eyes off Matt and the pistol.

"Capt'n wants to see ya, Jorgensen." An older man stomped into the bunkhouse.

He waited for Matt to strap his gun belt back on, then he led him to the room where Montgomery sat at the table drinking a cup of coffee. Ben stood next to him. On the table was a map strewn open.

"Come on in, Matt," Montgomery said, waving for him to sit down. "Coffee?"

"Sounds real good to me." Matt grabbed the pot from the stove and a fine china cup. "I was wonderin' when we were gonna eat," he said, examining the cup.

Montgomery's table had a clean white tablecloth, exquisite china, crystal glasses, and a vase of flowers in the center. Cloth napkins in silver holders lay along side the china and fine silverware. There was a setting for four put in place by a gentleman in an apron.

"Got Vince fixing dinner right now," Montgomery said. "Sit down. I want all of us to get better acquainted."

Matt noticed that Ben rubbed his pistol grip as a nervous habit. "I wouldn't do that too often." Matt held his cup in his left hand. His right hand hovered above his pistol grip.

"You nervous?" Ben asked.

"Not me," Matt answered, "but some fast gun might think you want to draw down on him, and might jest cut you to ribbons."

"Do what he says, Ben," Montgomery ordered. "I don't want you two getting into a fight with one another. No sense in it. Ben's my right hand man, Matt. He's been with me since we started, he's loyal and dependable." •

"I respect that in a man," Matt said, sitting down at the table.

"You can sit down, too, Ben." Montgomery kicked out a chair.

A young lady approached them, and Ben pulled out a chair for her, the fourth plate setting. Sandi nodded without looking at Matt and sat down. Her cut blond hair pushed up inside her hat gave her a boyish appearance. Her eyes were gray, she appeared to be in her early twenties, and she wore a loose dress that hid her thin shape.

"This is Sandi," Ben said. "She's my woman," he declared with a look that told Matt he was a dead man if he even touched her. "This here's Matt Jorgensen."

Upon hearing her name, it registered with Matt that she could be the sister Frank Hansen told him about. Her coloring and features were similar, but the age difference threw him. If she were Frank's sister, she would have to be a half-sister because of the age difference. Frank was over thirty years older. Still, Matt kept looking at her, until he felt uncomfortable by Ben's stare.

"She's my woman, mister," Ben reminded him. "All mine, and nobody else's."

"I was just admiring her beauty, Ben. You make a fine looking couple."

"That they do," Montgomery agreed, and then turned to his aproned cook. "Vince, bring us a bottle right away."

"Ben and Sandi live with me in my house. They share separate bedrooms in the back. One of these days, they intend on getting married. Right Ben?"

Ben nodded but said nothing.

Matt watched a Negro man, slightly bent by age, bald and wearing a chef's apron, head for the kitchen.

"I'm from Ohio, Matt," Montgomery told him. "Came out here when I saw the first opportunity for a good way of living."

"How's that?" Matt asked.

"Helping Kansas farmers keep out slavery," Montgomery said. "We don't have it in the north, and Kansas should be free of it, too."

"I'm not political, Capt'n," Matt said. "I jest have my sights set on goin' to Texas."

"Texas?" Montgomery said. "When you see what we're doing in Kansas, you won't want to go to Texas."

"Maybe not, sir," Matt answered, watching Vince bring a decanter to their table.

"Vince, this is Matt Jorgensen from Wyoming. He will be joinin' us at this table from now on."

"Yes suh," Vince responded, bowing to Montgomery. "And Mister Jorgensen, how do you like your liquor, sah?"

"Straight," Matt answered.

"Pour it in a crystal glass," Montgomery corrected him.

Vince poured it into clean crystals for the three men.

"Kentucky bourbon," Montgomery stated, picking up his glass. "I do hope you like bourbon."

Matt picked up his glass, looked into it like a kid, and smiled. "Yes sir. I'm a bourbon man," he lied.

"Good. May I propose a toast? Gentlemen. I give you a free Kansas."

Montgomery noticed that Matt did not readily pick up his glass, but stared at Vince walking back into the kitchen.

"You're not joining us, Matt?" Montgomery asked. He saw a question of concern in Matt's eyes. "Oh, I see. Vince. You're thinking he's a slave. No. No. He's a free man here in Kansas. We pay him for his services. He's the best, and he knows my tastes almost as well as I. He comes from Kentucky. Lost his wife a few years back, and came to work for me."

Matt turned and looked at Montgomery and smiled, and then joined the two gentlemen and said, "To a free Kansas."

This was his first bourbon, and fine bourbon at that. He was more accustomed to poorly made Red Eye out of a bottle.

"Tomorrow, Matt," Montgomery said, lifting his glass of bourbon, "we'll show you Fort Scott."

That night a relationship grew between Matt and Montgomery. Matt was so carried away with Montgomery's praise for his heroics in Mud Creek that he had little time to sift through the two theories related to the slavery issue. When he did, his beliefs became strong that Kansas should be a free state, as he was against slavery. He never had it in Montana, and felt Kansas should be the same.

Suddenly he realized he was becoming caught up in Montgomery's passion for a free Kansas and knew he was in for a long spell with the captain. And it all began as a fight for the cause which he felt Frank and Martha would have approved. Perhaps one day he would ride back to Mud Creek, and Frank would be its mayor.

He remembered Toothless with Lori in hand, standing on the roadway watching him as he rode out. It would be forever etched in his mind. To him, it was typical America.

# CHAPTER 8

## BAREFOOT SANDI

Evening came and Ben had not shown up at the house for supper. Sandi sat on the porch where Montgomery found her waiting. He took a cigar from his vest and, lighting it asked, "Mind if I sit with you?"

She sat looking out into the night as if counting the fireflies or just listening to the crickets and said nothing. Sandi had no dislike for Montgomery, but her man was Ben. It was her belief that the men felt that she was some whore Ben found in town and brought home, and that he would eventually discard her. And now that he was gone, she worried that he might never come back for her.

"We're not a bad bunch, Sandi," Montgomery said carefully, trying to become friends with her.

This friendliness was a first for him, because he had been disappointed in Ben when he brought her home after a drunk. And now he was off again on one of his drunks, and Montgomery wondered what or who would turn up next.

"You know, he'll come back," he said sitting in the swing. "How old are you, Sandi? Twenty? Twenty-one? You've got yourself a pretty good man."

"He'll come back this time," she said, her knees tucked up under her chin as she sat on the porch stoop.

"What's your real name, Sandi?" he asked.

"It's Sandi. Really."

"How about a last name? I've never asked you."

"You never cared," she said, still looking outward. Then she added, "It's Hansen."

"Sandi Hansen. Sounds pretty. Where're you from?"

"Up around Mud Crick," she replied still looking out at an empty road leading up to the house.

"He found you there?"

"Yep," she answered, looking over to Montgomery. "I was brought there by some other men. They were unkindly men, I didn't like 'em. When Ben saw me, he liked me, and brought me here."

"Do you want to stay here, Sandi?" he asked, looking into her hurt eyes.

Apparently no one ever paid too much attention to her before. The men certainly would not bother her. They knew she belonged to Ben Price. Montgomery had regarded her as extra baggage, and he didn't want to soil his hands. But now he felt he had a problem that had to be solved, a hurt little girl who felt no one cared for her. In the midst of strife and war, he was beginning to take a liking to her.

Just when he felt he was finally communicating with her, she stood up, smiled, and ran down the road. She saw a rider coming in and knew it had to be Ben. The rider rode slowly and carefully. Sure enough, it was Ben.

She ran alongside him as he trotted his horse to the barn to bed it down. When they emerged, she held onto her man, gripping his muscular arm..

"Evening Ben," Montgomery said as they came up to the porch.

"I'm a little drunk, Capt'n," he slurred, "but I'll be all right in the morning."

"Better be. We're riding into Fort Scott at daybreak."

"What we goin' there for?"

"I'm fixin' to hire us a fast gun."

"That Jorgensen guy?"

"We need him, Ben. If he's as fast with the gun that I'm led to believe he is, he'll help us beat Hamilton's gang and move me right into the capitol."

"Like I said before, we don't need him," Ben said, sitting on the stoop and bringing Sandi to sit on his lap. "I've got a fast gun, right Sandi?"

"Right, honey," she said, giggling and nibbling at his neck.

"Not fast enough to scare Hamilton, I'm afraid. Hell, they know you. And they know Matt. They told me all I need to know about his reputation. Damn good thing he didn't wind up on their side."

"Am I still going to be your right hand man?" Ben asked.

"Right into the governor's seat, Ben. Right into the governor's seat. Now I have another question for you."

"What's that?"

"Are you going to be able to lead a raid yourself in a few nights?" Montgomery rose from the swing. He was getting set to let Ben become the leader he wanted him to be. At the same time, he wanted Matt to see what his organization was doing.

"Damn right I will," Ben answered, putting Sandi aside and walking up on the porch. "I'll pick out my men in the morning."

"I know you won't like the idea, but I want you to take Matt along with you."

Ben stopped and said nothing. He bit his lower lip. His loyalty for Montgomery was unquestioned for two years now. But the addition of Jorgensen didn't sit well with him, and resentment boiled inside him.

"He's got to become part of us, as I sure as hell am going to hire him," Montgomery continued, grinning a little to ease Ben's concern.

"Think he'll ride under me?" Ben asked.

"Like I said, we've got to make him ride with you. Take a couple of farms. Show him what we do."

Ben grabbed Sandi by the waist and took her inside. "See you in the mornin', Capt'n."

Montgomery stayed on the porch to finish his cigar and sat back down in the swing. He knew his plans for becoming governor were closer than ever before as soon as Matt would make up his mind to ride with them.

# CHAPTER 9

## FORT SCOTT

T he next morning, Montgomery walked briskly out of the house, wearing a clean suit of clothes, vest and hat, a long frock coat and dress gloves. He looked more like a banker than the leader of a guerrilla group.

Ben walked out with him to two geldings, which were saddled, by a couple of the wranglers who were holding the reins.

Matt had already eaten with Montgomery and Ben earlier and now sat on Skeeter ready to ride.

"Saddle up, men," Ben said as he mounted his horse.

Montgomery led his men down the trail to the main road, and cut south through Linn County. The sun was up high when they reached Fort Scott.

"Fort Scott is a growing community, split by both sides of the slavery issue," Montgomery told Matt as they rode in. "The issue is very clear; we do not want slavery in Kansas like they have in Missoura. Charles Hamilton's living somewhere here in Kansas, we don't know where. He wants to own slaves, and he's fighting so Kansas can become a slave state. I say, let him go to Missoura. Nobody's stopping him. Most of us want a free state."

Montgomery's strategy was to nip slavery in the bud by keeping adversaries out of Kansas. However, the Pro-slavers were the more predominant of the two factions, while the Free-Staters lay in the surrounding territory.  Because of the slavery factions, Fort Scott quickly grew in size.  Its location on the border of Kansas and Missouri was another contributing factor.

The gang rode through the parade grounds past one building, and came to a second building.  Behind it were stables where they bedded down their horses.

Matt followed Montgomery and Ben inside the second building where they went into a large room on the first floor.  The room housed a large bed, a table and four chairs, which were for Montgomery's private use.

Montgomery rolled out a map on the table.

"I want to acquaint you with our illustrious Fort Scott, Matt." He then took his Bowie knife from his belt and pointed out the various locations on the map.

"As you can see, it was an army post at one time, and now it's abandoned.  Notice there are two buildings, here and across the parade grounds.  We've taken up headquarters in this building here on the far side of this parade ground.  We're located on the border of Kansas and Missouri, which affords us a great meeting place for leaders of Free-Staters when they come to town."

"I saw another building as we rode in," Matt said, sipping hot coffee.  Pointing on the map, he added, "That's this one here, I see."

"That's for our adversaries," Montgomery informed him. "Those who want a slave state use that building as their headquarters. The leader is one Captain Charles A. Hamilton from Georgia.  He came here with the same aspirations I have, except with different ideals and different tactics of course."

"Wow!" Matt replied setting his coffee down.

"Coffee hot?" Montgomery asked.

"No, No.  Well, yeah, but . . ." Matt searched for words.  "You mean to tell me, those men you were chasing are holed up in that there hotel?"

"Not exactly," Montgomery answered.  "Those men we were chasing were just a few who came across the border to test our response. That's why we come out in strength, enough to send them flying back. We flanked them on two sides, while our third group went up the middle. They saw our numbers.  Had they made their way farther into Kansas, others would have followed.  We have access to many more men at all times out in the countryside who will ride with us." He walked over to the window, pulled back the shade and looked towards the Western Hotel.

Matt saw the value of that strategy.

"Now, the people in the Western Hotel over there are leaders of the Pro-slavers who pretend they rent rooms from time to time here, when all the time we know it's their main headquarters," Montgomery continued.

Vince rapped on the door, entered and announced that supper was ready.

From his room, Montgomery led Matt to a dining hall where the men began to gather on long benches and tables. The food was passed down the center of the table as the men dug in.

"We sit here, Matt," Montgomery said, as he sat at an isolated table decorated with a fine tablecloth and all the accoutrements that went into making it a fine setting. "Please join Ben and me."

The rest of Montgomery's men served themselves towards the back of the room. They also knew to keep the noise level down in their talking so that Montgomery could enjoy his meal in peace.

"Thank you, Vince," Montgomery said as Vince brought out the decanter and filled the glasses with fine bourbon.

Taking two glasses, Montgomery offered one to Matt. He took the second, and Ben took the third.

"To Matt," he proposed as a toast. "May he prosper in the wealth and fame of the good state of Kansas."

The glasses clinked together, and Matt's mind started to wonder. *What in the living hell have I got myself into this time?*

During dinner, Montgomery continued feeding basic information about his organization to Matt. Matt was certain he was not divulging top secrets by any means, but he was allowing for some confidentiality. How much, Matt was not sure. At this point, he didn't feel too sure about anything, especially his safety.

Throughout the evening's meal, he kept watching out of the corner of his eye at Ben's constant stare at him.

After a while, Ben got up enough courage to talk to Matt. "You don't look so fast," he remarked dropping his eyes to Matt's pistol.

"You know somethin', Ben?" Matt chewed slowly on a piece of beef, swallowed. "That's jest what the last man said."

"One of my men?"

"No. One jest before I met up with you."

"Where's he at?"

"Dead," Matt said, and spit out a piece of gristle.

Montgomery laughed and watched Ben's face grimace. "You asked for it, Ben. You want to try Matt out some time, be my guest. You're a big man."

"One of these days, I jest might," Ben replied. Rising, he walked over and joined the other men.

Matt and Montgomery finished their dinner, and then walked out onto the veranda together. "I think Ben's nervous about havin' me around," Matt said,

"Wouldn't you be?" Montgomery took out two cigars from his vest pocket, sticking one in his mouth, and offered Matt the other one. "You're a threat to him. He sees that, and I think that's good, keeps him on his toes, right where I want him. Don't get me wrong. He's my right hand man, and always will be. This is Kansas. It's a state that needs leadership, and I'm here to offer her my services. And I aim to give myself to her. In return, I'll become her governor one day."

Vince was on the porch with a pair or crystal glasses and another decanter of bourbon.

"Do you like good Kentucky bourbon?" Vince asked as he poured it for Matt.

"I'm beginning to get spoiled with it, Vince, ol' fella," Matt said with a smile.

He sat down on the banister of the veranda and sipped his drink slowly. He took the cigar and lit it, savoring the peace of the evening.

"How do you figure on gettin' Kansas to make you her governor, Capt'n, if you don't mind my askin'?"

"What are you drinking, Matt?" Montgomery asked, more of a statement than a question.

"Good ol' Kentucky bourbon," Matt replied. "That's what Vince keeps tellin' me."

"And what are you drinking from? I'll tell you. Pure crystal. And the food is made to suit a king. And my clothes, they're custom tailored. Good living, Matt. How do you think we got it?"

"Never occurred to me," Matt answered. "But I'm sure you're about to tell me right now."

"We raid farms," Montgomery said without wavering or any hesitation. He waited for Matt to respond.

Matt took a drag on his cigar, and let out the smoke. Then he looked at the crystal, swished the bourbon in it and took a slow sip.

"Are you all right with that?"

"I don't know," Matt said, taking another sip. "What you're sayin' don't seem to make for good votes. Jest what kinda raids are we talkin' about?"

"Oh, not the kind you're thinking, Matt," he answered with a laugh. "No, no, no. What we do is for the cause. We are Free-Staters. We'll raid a farm that is using slaves, and to teach them a lesson we'll take some of their excesses. Oftentimes it's money. We know which farmers are doing this, and we simply take from them. Makes me sort of a Robin Hood."

"Take from the rich and give to the poor, thing." Matt concurred.

"Eventually, we will make Kansas a free state. Any questions?"

"Does anyone get hurt?"

"I'm a Christian, Matt," Montgomery answered. "I don't go for killing. Not me, nor any of my men."

"How are you on maiming and beating?"

"We have never had to resort to that kind of force. We merely use scare tactics. We scare the hell out of them by threatening to rape their women and burn their barns. It's all a game we play."

"And what if the people are unwilling to part with some of their, so-called, 'excess goods'?" Matt asked, flipping his cigar ashes out into the field.

"Like I said, we've never encountered such. Once we ride in with twenty or thirty men, all in masks, they are so afraid, they give us what we need right away. In fact, you are to ride along tomorrow night with Ben." Vince, who had followed the two men onto the veranda, saw Montgomery's glass was empty and quickly refilled it. "You are not to do anything, unless you are absolutely sure you want to. If at any time you want to ride away, you may."

"You have that much confidence in me that I won't tell the authorities about you?"

"Now, you're putting me at a disadvantage. I said you may ride out. I'm taking you at your word that you won't go to any authorities."

Matt stood there looking back at Montgomery, attempting to make himself a little more comfortable with his drink and cigar.

Matt dragged on his cigar, and Vince surprised him by filling up his glass again.

"I'm waiting, Matt. If you like the idea, fine. If you don't, I hope you ride the hell out of here right now, with my blessings."

"You have your army, Montgomery, " Matt said rolling his cigar in his hand. "Hell, you got more'n two hundred men, I hear. One more won't make that much difference, as I can see."

"One more, Matt?" Montgomery asked speaking up close to Matt's face pointing with his fist. "One person won't make the difference? Why the hell do you think I'm spending so much time with you?"

Matt smiled to break the tension. "'Cause ya like me?"

"Only one person is stopping me. One person!" he said biting his lip.

"Can't be me," Matt said smiling nervously.

"It's that son-of-a-bitch Hamilton. With him out of the way, I've got Kansas."

"What's in it for me, Capt'n if I do join up?" Matt asked.

"I was waiting for you to ask that," Montgomery said. "My men are all farmers. They come when I call them. Not one of them is a gunfighter. I aim to use you and your reputation as much as I can. And I'm willing to pay your price."

"My price?" Matt asked.

*What the hell is my price?* Matt thought. He had never figured on selling himself out as a hired gun.

"I'm willing to pay you one-thousand dollars Matt to ride with me and help me win Kansas."

Matt's mouth opened and the cigar fell out when he heard this. Catching it as the ashes fell off, he turned and looked away from Montgomery to compose himself. After he placed the cigar back in his mouth and faced Montgomery, he met a lit match from Montgomery's hand.

"You all right?" Montgomery asked.

"Oh, yeah, I'm all right," Matt said, dragging on the cigar and staring at Montgomery.

"I'll go fifteen hundred." Montgomery threw the match to the wind and watched it die out. "I want Kansas."

Matt walked over to the banister of the veranda and sat down on the rail. Looking over Fort Scott and the empty black sky, he enjoyed his cigar while pondering Montgomery's offer. He was quickly learning that farming was going to be a thing of the past, and he would never ever have to look at another cow again except to eat it.

Of course, he thought, the government is paying me one hundred dollars a month, and I've got my first month's pay burnin' a hole in my pocket right now. A man can't collect from two sources, or can he? Matt felt uncomfortable being in the wrong place at the wrong time, but he knew he had to stay and play out the hand that was dealt him.

He turned toward Montgomery. "And what you say about just using force, no killing, goes?" Matt asked holding out his cigar.

"Merely by force, Matt. Sheer force. I don't believe in violence. But I do believe in force. There's a difference. But, we need that one element in our group to make this work. And that element is your fast gun." Montgomery paused then walked over to him.

"Is it a deal then?"

"I can still leave any time I want, as you said?"

Montgomery nodded.

Matt found himself without any say in the matter. He was a prisoner of the Free-State men by virtue of his reputation as a gunfighter and he had to ride along with Montgomery because of his relationship with Marshal Whittaker. He just didn't want Montgomery to think it was going to be easy to get him to join in with him, otherwise he figured he would lose his credibility. His next thought was, when to meet up with Hamilton.

"I assume you've made up your mind to work for me?" Montgomery prodded. "You come in with me, it'll be strictly for your gun hand." Swishing the glass of bourbon around in the crystal, he held it out for Matt's decision. "Well?"

"Good bourbon," Matt said as he watched Montgomery's hand. He knew that accepting the toast, he would be sealing the bargain. His main concern now was whether or not he would be sealing his fate.

He stood up, reached out with his drink in his right hand, and accepted the toast. "Mister, you've got yourself a hired gun."

Ben returned with a cigar in one hand, and a glass of bourbon in his other, and sat down next to Matt.

"Shake hands with our new man, Ben," Montgomery said. "He's joined up with us."

Without looking at Matt, Ben lit his cigar. "I know."

Ben never joined in the toast, but rose and walked back to the table and joined in with his friends in a poker game.

"Good! Now, Ben has a couple of farms to raid, he wants you to ride along with him and the gang. Nothing big. Just to get you acquainted with our operations. Up for it?"

"Might as well," Matt replied.

"He'll fill you in tomorrow or the next day. Relax and have a good time while you're here. You're in good company." Montgomery settled back in his chair.

"Think I'll join the rest of the men," Matt suggested. "Mind?"

"Not at all. Get to know them. It'll do you and them some good. I'll stay here and enjoy my bourbon and cigar, and then head for bed. See you in the morning, Matt."

Matt went over to join in the conversation with some of the other men.

On the opposite side of the room, half a dozen men sat at a table with Ben playing cards. Ben laid his cards down, stood up and watched as Matt sauntered over. He kept his eye on Matt's gun hand riding on his gun grip loose and easy. He kept watching Matt's seemingly long and calculated walk to his side of the room. It was almost deliberate in a way, he figured, challenging him to draw.

"Gentlemen, I see you're having a friendly game of cards. Mind if I join you?"

"You got the money, sit down," said the man with the cards in his hands. "Ben. You in?"

"Sure. Hell. Why not." Ben sat back down.

"Name's, Matt." Matt took a chair, and sat down with four men playing poker, while two other men stood watching. The games lasted into the night, and when they were over, Matt had a little more money than when he started, enough to let the men know he knew something about cards.

Later, when everyone settled down for the night and Ben had gone to his room, Matt had a lingering uneasy feeling over the day's events. He decided to take a walk around the grounds.

The night was cool, and he enjoyed the gentle breeze that swept in that time of evening. A figure stepped out of the shadows and spoke to him, nearly making Matt jump out of his skin.

"Whittaker," he whispered hoarsely, and disappeared back into the shadows for a moment.

Matt stood silent. This might be a contact, or a set up. Whittaker was the name of the U S Marshal who had hired him.

"Matt Jorgensen," he responded, looking back inside as the men deserted the room he just left.

"Good," the voice whispered. "Step over here without turning around. You were described to me, so I knew what you'd look like. Thank God you made it this far."

"How'd you know where to find me?" Matt backed cautiously.

"Not too many strangers ride out this way. I have contacts. Trust me. Don't turn around. Are you in with the gang?"

"Yeah. But I'm kinda wishin' I weren't, if you get my drift."

"I don't envy you none. Anything coming up?"

"Marshal Walker?"

"Shh. Yes."

"What's your first name?"

"Sam."

"Good enough for me. I heard of a couple of raids on some farms. Don't know anything else."

"When?"

"Two days, maybe three"

"Good." Sam let out an uneasy breath.

Matt watched the figure disappear in the thick of the night. He walked some more, and thought about Walker meeting him like he did. Then he returned to the hotel with more questions dangling inside his head. He found Montgomery sitting back on the porch with Ben, which made Matt more uneasy.

"Enjoy your visit with us, Matt. It isn't often we come in the company of a gunfighter such as yourself," Montgomery said.

Matt looked up and gave Montgomery a dumbfounded look. "I thought you were goin' to bed."

"I guess like you, I wasn't sleepy."

"Listen, you have other men around you, Capt'n. And Ben. I'm not the only gunfighter in your employ, am I?"

"No, but you're the best," Montgomery answered.

"We made a bargain tonight," Montgomery said, sipping the last of his drink for the night. "And I'm keeping you to it." He rose and went to his room. "Let's go to bed, Vince."

Vince checked the lanterns, turned them down but not completely off, and followed Montgomery.

In the silence of black, it might appear as if the whole world were empty and void. Yet, here it was an abandoned fort turned into a village full of people and homes. The windows were darkened and the people's voices waned through the emptiness of the night. The sound of the crickets and the choir of frog voices broke through the night like distant thunder, with an occasional owl joining in with its deep bass voice.

Matt sat and listened to all that was happening around him, and to the thoughts dancing around in his head. Home felt to be a million miles beyond the blackness.

# CHAPTER 10

## PAINT CREEK

T he Montgomery gang left Fort Scott and returned to the Montgomery Farm early the next morning. Two days later, Ben had his gang mounted up and told Matt to hit the saddle and ride with them.

"We're gonna show Matt here some fun, men," Ben said as he swung up into his saddle. "Let's ride."

To make sure no soldiers would interfere, they set men up at posts at different intervals. Their job would be to fire warning shots to let the rest know if any soldiers were in the area.

When they reached the first farm, the sun was still high enough for them to catch slaves in the field.

"Stay here, greenhorn," Ben said, motioning for Matt to stay behind. "We'll ride in and give you a show."

The farm reminded Matt of Frank and Martha's farm, and the thought of raiding it put a knot in his stomach. He remained silent and watched the "show" as Ben called it. It was a larger farm than Frank's and they had four Negro slaves working it.

Up to this point, there existed an air of mystery surrounding the anti-slavers. But when Ben and his men, bandannas covering their faces, shouted out and shot their guns, Matt knew what type of predicament he was involved in. It went against his grain and his sense of right and wrong. In the chaos, the slaves scattered in different directions. Matt sat still and took in the scene.

The farmer came out with his shotgun, but at the sight of Ben's gang of thirty men, he dropped it and raised his hands.

"You're showing good sense, farmer," Ben said, as he galloped in full speed, and reined up in a cloud of dust at the porch. "You're a slave owner, and we don't cotton to slave owners in Kansas. I'm gonna tell ya jest once. Get rid of 'em. I'm not gonna waste my time chasin' 'em, and I'm not gonna bust my knuckles on you. We'll jest help ourselves to some of your excess goods." Then, with a wave of his hand to the men, he said, "Go on in, men. Take what we need."

Ben sat his horse all the while, watching the farmer stand there shaking.

"Hand me the shotgun," Ben said as Dick alit from his horse.

Dick handed it up to Ben.

As the farmer reached out to retrieve it, Ben moved his mount forward and knocked him down. The farmer's wife came out with a baby in her arms and screamed.

"If it's all the same to you, ma'am, don't scream," Ben said softly. "It makes my horse nervous. See what he did to your man."

Dick took a gentle hold of the wife and baby, and looked into Ben's terrible face. "They're new parents, Ben. Leave 'em be."

"Boy, don't you ever talk to me like that!" Ben yelled down. "You get in there and make those men get a move on."

Dick ran into the house but looked back at Ben with an angry stare.

"You take what you want," the wife said, cradling her infant. She was about the same age as Sandi, but much cleaner in appearance. "Jest leave us be."

By the appearance of his weathered-beaten face, her husband appeared to look at least twenty years her senior. He rose from the floor of the porch and went to his wife's side.

Ben waited until Dick came out with the men, all carrying food, and trinkets. Then he shouted a command. "Chase those niggers 'til they can't run no more!"

The men from the house put their booty into cloth bags and threw them across their saddlebags. The other men rode after the Negro slaves, tromping the planted fields as they rode.

Matt watched all this as they finally regrouped and rode towards him to get away.

"Come on, Matt, let's ride," Ben said as they rode past him.

Turning Skeeter around, Matt put him into a gallop and quickly caught up to them.

Across the hill, they rode to the second farmhouse just as the sun was about to go down. This one house was larger, with more acres, and more than a dozen Negro slaves. Matt conjectured this stop might have been a mistake on Ben's part because a couple of the slaves knew how to ride and had horses. Two of them spotted the gang coming, and they rode out for help.

"Get those damn niggers," Ben yelled at his men.

Dick was a rider, and caught up with one of the slaves. He grabbed the bridle and pulled the plow horse to a halt. The slave threw up his hands, jumped from the horse and walked back. Dick hit the horse's rump and sent it on its way.

Three of the other men were still riding for the other Negro slave when Ben fired a shot to bring them back. The slave kept riding.

The farmer and his wife stood outside the house helplessly and watched the gang pilfer their land and rummage through their house. The wife kept her tears inside her as the farmer held her in his arms. His soul cried out for revenge, but he stood helpless.

"If you were a little younger, Ma'am," Ben said, "I'd make a pass atcha. Hell, you're one handsome woman." He dismounted.

The farmer took a swing at Ben and missed. Ben came back with his fist to the farmer's stomach. When the farmer doubled over in pain, Ben kneed him in the chest and knocked him off the porch.

The woman stared at him in fright. Ben reached out and grabbed her.

At the same moment, Dick's arm came around his neck and brought him away from the woman.

Ben turned his full body around, and he caught Dick with the back of his hand drawing blood. Dick fell to the floor. Ben pulled him up and was ready to smash his face when five quick shots rang out from a nearby hillside.

"Soldiers!" Ben shouted out angrily and pushed Dick to the ground.

The men quickly filled their bags, mounted their horses and rode like the devil. Ben stopped and looked at the woman glaring up at him.

"Hell," he said, "it might have been fun." He spurred his horse and rode out.

Matt spurred Skeeter into a gallop, and caught up to them.

Sure enough, the Negro slave had found the soldiers nearby as · they were waiting for the gang. Matt's information to Marshal Walker three days prior about an impending raid had alerted him and his deputies, and they were roaming the hillsides.

It was not the first time Montgomery's gang had been chased, but this time Ben was in command and riding in front. When he saw the soldiers, he yelled for them to burn leather. The soldiers opened fire at them as they continued to flee. The chase ran along well-traveled roads, and finally across open meadows where the gang had no place to hide.

"What're we gonna do, Ben?" Matt asked trailing him by a few feet.

"Ride your ass off," Ben returned. "If those soldiers catch us, we've had it. Montgomery, too."

"A few miles more is a place called Paint Crick," Ben shouted at the men. "Once across that crick, we should have shelter on the other side. Keep ridin'," he ordered and spurred his horse on.

The early spring had melted the snows, and the creek was higher than usual. The high waters slowed their crossing considerably, and the soldiers almost caught up with them.

Once on the other side, Ben's gang returned the volley of gun-fire.

Matt, caught up in the excitement and danger of it all, and to show the others that he was a real part of the gang, swung his mount in the creek, and returned fire along with the rest of the men. His intent was not to hit anyone, but to fire over their heads and cause the soldiers to run.

Then, as the men were all together on the other side of the creek, Ben could see that the soldiers were not about to stop, so he ordered his men to ride through the thicket.

Matt lagged behind and caught Ben out of the corner of his eye aiming his Sharps carefully at a soldier's back, bringing him down with one bullet. Then he turned Skeeter in time to see the soldier fall as Ben passed him and headed for the thickets.

No other soldier was wounded, and only one was killed. None of Ben's men was hit. The soldiers rode away, carrying their dead soldier with them, as Ben and his men rode to safety.

Ben didn't claim the kill, and because he didn't, Matt became the big hero of the hour among the men. They all thought he had made the hit.

Montgomery was not pleased. He called Matt to his room that night, and again laid down some hard and fast rules.

"We know how good you are, Matt," Montgomery said, pacing the floor while Matt sat in a straight back chair rubbing the handle on his gun. "You're too good. That might be the trouble."

"If you're talkin' about that soldier getting' killed today, Capt'n," Matt returned, "you're runnin' up the wrong road, 'cause I didn't kill him."

Montgomery took a decanter of bourbon and started to pour Matt a drink. Matt refused, and Montgomery poured one for himself. He looked at Matt suspiciously. He obviously believed what Ben had reported earlier to him after they returned from the raiding party.

"What I'm saying is I'm against killing. You know that. I didn't come all this way to kill." He dropped in his large chair and took a sip of his bourbon. "I told you at the start. Why couldn't you see it my way?"

Matt could see that he was upset about the killing, but wasn't sure that telling Montgomery about Ben's murderous moment would be safe.

"Begging your pardon, sir, but what was the shootin' all about, if someone wasn't goin' to get killed?"

"Matt, I'm a politician. Oh, I know it seems me like I'm a guerilla, a Soldier of Fortune. But, I have to do this to get to where I'm goin'."

"Which is, sir," Matt said sitting in a chair next to him and feeling more confident talking with his commander on an even level. "To become governor of Kansas right?"

"Yes, of a free state," Montgomery added. "I didn't stand as good a chance in Ohio, because we're not at war with anyone there. Here, I can claim victory through votes. Votes, Matt, not killing. If we ever get into a war, God help us, I'll have lost my chance for governorship. And your killing that soldier just might have killed my chances, too. If so, I'll chase you to Texas if I have to, and tie your heels to a running steer," Montgomery threatened.

Matt knew Montgomery was serious, and he refrained from even smirking at what he said.

Matt was up early the next morning, and waved at Ben and the men having their breakfast at the tables as he sauntered over to the kitchen. Montgomery was just pouring his coffee, and Matt headed for the pot.

"Mornin', Capt'n."

"Good Morning, Matt. Make sense out of what we talked about last night?"

"Yes and no."

"Spit it out, then."

"I'm confused. When we do our next raid, just what do we do, Capt'n, when any soldiers confront us again? Run?" Matt took a sip of coffee. "Not use our guns?"

Montgomery ignored the question. "I'll get Ben and organize a meeting." He grabbed his hat and went outside.

There had been much talk about the killing, and how Matt turned his roan in the middle of the stream, and fired point blank at the soldier, bringing him down. At the meeting, the men were in a rare mood.

"That takes a man with fortitude, gentlemen," one of them said, toasting with his cup of coffee. "To stop in mid-stream, turn and fire at on-coming soldiers."

Montgomery and Matt confronted the group, and the men raised their coffee cups in unison and said, "To Matt!"

"Hold it," Montgomery said as he brought them to attention. "This is not a time for adulations. My rules are simple, no killing. Not by you, any of you, and not by me. Plain and simple. Matt should not be praised for what he did. Because this was his first raid, I'll chalk it up as an accident. But I don't want any of you to ever forget this happened."

Montgomery stood for a long while and looked at them. Being confident that he had made his point, he walked back into the house.

Matt felt compelled to stay and talk with them. He noticed Ben getting fidgety and sensed that he could not restrain himself much longer from revealing that he was the one who shot the soldier after listening to them praising Matt for what he supposedly had done.

Ben heard Montgomery go easy on Matt for violating his rule. Montgomery would never let him or any of the others out of that without fit punishment. Why he'd all but condoned what Jorgensen did! He clenched his fists. Betrayed by his own captain. Well, he'd show Montgomery. He'd show them all. And he'd take care of this Matt Jorgensen once and for all. His fingers felt wet with sweat, and he worried whether he could draw without the gun slipping out of his control. He had to make Matt back down.

"That soldier got shot in the back!" Ben accused, waited for reaction from any of them. No one said anything, just stared at him. Sweat beaded on his forehead. He spit into the dirt. "Hell, we never killed anybody, no matter how many times we went out. First time it happens, and he's at the other end of the gun." He pointed directly at Matt.

Matt waited for Montgomery to come back from the kitchen at the sound of the outburst, but he didn't.

"That's right." The voice came from someone in the gathered men.

"In the back, did you say?" Another stepped forward.

"Jorgensen did it?" another asked.

"I saw him do it." Ben leveled a glare in Matt's direction.

Matt saw the sweat spread over Ben's face. "You're a liar," he gritted. The glare he returned made Ben step back.

"Prove it." Ben's hand shook near the gun handle that rode low on his hip.

Matt knew he was in a tight spot now. This hothead was in a tight spot as well. Ben had to show something to these men, to Montgomery, to himself probably just to prove he truly was the Captain's number two man. Ben had to test Matt's reputation as a fast gun. In a way, they were facing the same thing. Matt wasn't so sure he was as fast as everyone thought. He'd had an edge on Jerry in Mud Creek with the scare Toothless put into him just before he drew on him. But now Toothless wasn't here to back him up.

He was alone, and he knew he would have to prove his worth.

"Make your play, Ben."

The nerves in Matt's hand twitched. Ever so slowly he raised it near the gun at this thigh. He concentrated hard on Ben's eyes to catch a slight twinge, a flicker in them. His mouth went dry and his lips began to beg for moisture, but he kept his tongue from licking them, fearing any sign would give Ben that much edge to draw his gun faster. He felt alone, and so damned far from any place he could call home.

*Here goes,* Matt thought. Sweat spread in his armpits. *Take your time. Can't back down now.*

Ben stood while Matt began to circle him, and at the same time keeping his eyes on the rest of the group.

"I have no quarrel with you, Ben," Matt said. "Keep your gun holstered, and I'll ride away."

"Big talk," Ben said, attempting to still his hand, which was nervously shaking by his holster. "Hear that, men," he taunted, "he wants me to let him go."

"Else I'll have to kill ya."

Slowly Ben lifted his hand away from his holster, and put both out in plain sight and rested them on his hips.

Montgomery was not oblivious to what was happening, but hoped he would not have to step in to stop it. He waited to see how the two men would resolve it, hoping it would not be in gunplay. He waited patiently to make his move.

"I don't think you're as fast as you make out to be, mister," Ben said. "Don't push your luck."

"Luck don't have anything to do with it," Matt replied. "Anytime you want to try me, go ahead. I jest got through cleanin' my gun, but I'll dirty it up agin, jest to please you. Which will it be, Ben?"

Matt felt he had a bullet somewhere with his name on it. Whether it was this night, or some other time, he figured he might just as well get it over with. He also knew that his call had to be sure and certain, and that he could not back down. He realized deep inside that he had gone past the point of no return, and he kept his concentration centered on Ben's eyes and his gun hand.

Sweat began to roll down Ben's face, flowed down his nose and dropped to the ground. His eyes twitched as he turned his head to see Montgomery leaving him to face Matt alone.

Matt calmly bent down, picked a weed with his left hand, and stuck it in his mouth. His eyes stayed intently on Ben.

Ben turned and walked towards the house. "He shoots a man in the back and stands here and denies it."

Matt tightened his hands into fists. "Stop right where you are, Ben," Matt ordered as his hand touched his gun grip.

"What?" Ben asked, without turning around. "You gonna shoot me in the back? See men? He's a back shooter. Well, go ahead, Jorgensen, shoot me."

Matt drew and fired a shot at Ben's heel, knocking it off the boot. Ben fell, and then picked himself up, again without turning around.

"In the leg, if I have to, you mangy polecat, and I'll work my way up. Tell them who shot the soldier in the back."

Ben shook more.

Montgomery threw open the door and ran down the steps toward the dueling men. "What's going on?" he shouted.

"I called your right-hand man a liar, Capt'n," Matt said, keeping his eyes on Ben.

"I told you there would be no killing, here or anywhere. What's it going to take for me to make my point?"

"He drew and shot my boot while my back was turned," Ben said, pointing his finger at Matt.

"I heard you from inside Ben," Montgomery said with deadly calm. "And I didn't like any of it. You got a just fight, Matt?" Montgomery asked.

"No, he ain't!" Ben retorted.

"I'm asking Matt."

"He's got something to tell you, Capt'n," Matt returned, "about that soldier gettin' killed."

"What is it?"

Ben stood there silent, sweating it out, but did not answer Montgomery.

"You got a fight, take your gun belts off and use your fists like men," Montgomery said. He turned around and motioned with his cigar to the rest of the men to spread out, allowing Matt and Ben to finish their brawl. "This is their fight, men. We'll stay out of it. You two settle it between yourselves."

"You gonna leave me here with him, Capt'n?" Ben yelled, shivering, but trying to control himself.

"Yep," Montgomery said chomping on his cigar. "I'm damn curious as to who's telling the truth. This should prove it."

Ben looked at the men's faces as they moved out into a circle. He realized no one was coming to his aid. Finally, his left hand went to his gun belt and he dropped it, keeping his right hand up in the air. "One of these days," he said, kicking his gun belt away.

"You talk too much," Matt returned and readied his fists.

Once again Matt knew he had won another gunfight without much danger. But he also knew he was in a territory where, if he turned his back now, he would be hunted down and probably killed. Taking his gun belt off, he also dropped it.

Ben had a few pounds on Matt, and sensed that he had the advantage to whip him. He turned quickly and rushed Matt, causing him to lose his balance, and the two rolled down the slight embankment, stopping at the foot of a tree. Ben was the first up, and grabbing a stronghold in Matt's shirt, pulled him to his feet and filled his face full of fist.

Matt felt like his jaw was broken on the first punch. He realized then that he might have made a mistake in throwing his gun away.

He rolled farther down the embankment and landed near a boulder. The blur of Ben charging at him spurred him to move fast.

Ben swung and missed, hitting hard against the rock. The impact dizzied him.

Matt seized the opportunity and yanked him by his hair. He swung the back of his hand across Ben's face with such force that blood flew out of his nose in a wide spray.

Ben fell back and Matt jumped him. The two rolled farther down the embankment. Matt landed on Ben's back and shoved his face into the hard soil. He regained footing and dragged Ben to his feet. He spun Ben's limp body around and plowed a lightning-fast fist hard into his already bloodied face.

Ben turned as if to go down, then spun back with surprising strength. He grabbed Matt's arm and threw him to the ground. He stood over the stunned and surprised Matt, than kneed him in the groin.

Matt got back up and felt Ben's boot connect under his chin sending him flying backwards.

Matt's eyes rolled back in their sockets and he saw the beautiful white clouds gathering in the sky above him. He felt like the angels were coming to get him. He got a grip on himself and saw Ben's boot again coming down upon him. He dodged and grabbed a firm hold of Ben's leg, yanking upward. He flipped Ben over, causing him to land on the back of his head, almost breaking his neck.

Matt knew he had him. Matt snatched his strength, leaned on his legs, breathing hard and panting. He looked at Ben stretched out on the ground with his face down. When he caught his breath, he took Ben's arm and rolled him over. Ben lay there with his eyes closed.

Matt was confident that the fight was over, and started up the hill.

Ben waited for his moment, playing possum, to catch Matt off guard. He picked up a rock and was about to pounce on Matt from behind when Matt heard the crack of a twig under Ben's foot. Matt turned, and with lightning speed, bent down out of range of the rock. He came back up and planted his fist squarely into Ben's midsection, making Ben fold. Ben tumbled down the embankment and rested at the bottom.

Matt knew this time that Ben would not be getting up, left him there and climbed up to where he left his gun belt.

A rifle shot rang out and clipped the dirt ahead of his gun belt. Quicker than a jackrabbit, Matt grabbed his gun from its holster.

"Hold it, mister," a woman's voice shouted. She held her rifle over her head. "I'm Sandi."

"Woman," Matt yelled back, "you damn near got yourself shot."

Holstering his Colt, he walked over to Sandi, grabbed the long rifle away from her and threw it out into the field. "Get her out of my sight before I use the rifle on her."

A couple of the men rushed on the porch, parked her back in the house, kicking and scratching.

"All right!" Montgomery interceded, "that's enough. I think I've made it quite clear. From here on in, no killing."

"That go for that damn woman, too, Capt'n?" Matt asked, gasping for fresh air.

"She's Ben's woman, Matt," Montgomery replied, laughing. "She almost killed you."

"Yeah," Matt responded. "Damn near. And I almost killed her."

After the dust settled, Ben was helped to the watering trough where a couple of the men cleaned his wounds. They assisted him as he hobbled towards the house. That's where Matt stopped them.

"Hold it right there, men," Matt ordered, walking over to them. Picking up Ben's head by his hair, he asked him, "You have something the men want to hear!"

"What?" Ben said incoherently, trying to focus.

"Who shot the soldier?"

"You did" Ben said weakly.

"Tell 'em," Matt said, holding his head up by his hair.

Finally, in a scared voice, Ben got out two words. "I did."

"In the back?"

"Yeah. Yeah, in the back," he confessed.

Matt dropped him into the men's arms, letting them carry him into the farmhouse.

"How do you feel, Matt?" Montgomery asked.

"I'll mend," he said, spitting out blood.

"Now, Capt'n," shouted the blacksmith, Eli Snyder. "I'm not condoning Ben's dirty work, but this shooting was in self-defense. They came after us, and you always told us to cover our ass."

Another agreed. "They could have killed any of us, Capt'n."

"I know," Montgomery said, "but I feel certain that you could have gotten away once you were on the other side of the creek. We know this territory a lot better than those soldiers do."

"So, what do we do next time?" Eli asked.

"If you ride with me, we don't kill unless I tell you otherwise," Montgomery said. "We just don't kill, damn it."

"You gonna tell that to Ben, Capt'n?" Matt asked, picking up his hat and dusting it off.

"Same goes for him," Montgomery answered. "Don't worry, I'll take care of him."

Captain Charles A. Hamilton, the guerrilla leader for Pro-slavery, who had been informed about the soldier being killed, attempted to use the incident to get rid of his adversary, Montgomery.

Hamilton, a large man, sporting a dark moustache and a salt-and-pepper beard, came from a wealthy Georgian family. Chased out of Georgia by legal authorities for his unscrupulous financial misdealing and violent bigotry, he moved to Kansas, a state in political turmoil, to more effectively perpetuate his Pro-slavery beliefs. He did it for the glory and wealth that his fight for Pro-slavery would bring him. His gang consisted of men from Missouri who diligently saw to it that slaves were brought across the border into Kansas.

Hamilton tried to pin enough evidence on Montgomery to convict him of murdering this soldier. The killing of a soldier was a state concern, and he hoped that the authorities would believe him about Montgomery's gang killing the soldier, and bring in the government troops to hunt them down. By getting rid of Montgomery, Hamilton would have free reign towards making Kansas a Pro-slavery state and he would accomplish his ultimate goal. However, what he looked for to pin against Montgomery was what he himself had unsuccessfully planted in the minds of the citizens, and the authorities refused to bring in the troops. He felt he was losing the battle without anyone's help, and sought to destroy Montgomery himself on a personal level.

Montgomery sensed that someday his command would crash the longer he engaged in his brand of warfare. He had hoped that his command of a couple hundred men could instill enough fear in the farmers by the sheer numbers that they would not have to resort to killing. Time was running out, and he knew he had to act quickly.

He saw Ben and Sandi walking fast to the barn but gave it no second thoughts. The couple came out riding their horses and, without a word, rode away.

That evening, Montgomery found himself alone on the porch alone with a glass of bourbon in one hand, and a cigar in the other. He decided to get roaring drunk.

Vince kept a steady eye on Montgomery's drinking this night, as he had on other occasions. When he saw the glass empty, he came out with a decanter and poured Montgomery another drink.

"Leave it, Vince," Montgomery ordered, set upon drinking the night away.

Matt came out of the bunkhouse and walked up onto the porch, sensing Montgomery wanted someone to talk with.

"How's he going to be?" Matt asked, taking out a cigar and lighting it.

"He'll be all right," Montgomery said.

"What kinda woman is his gal?" Matt let a ring of smoke flow out of his swollen lips.

"Sandi? Quiet, unassuming, I suppose. Where he goes, she goes," Montgomery answered with a smile. "She stood by with her rifle to see to it that you didn't kill him. She didn't interrupt your fight, though. She just wanted to make certain you didn't lay a hand on her man again. Pretty sensible woman, once you get to know her."

"Is there anything on your mind, Capt'n?"

"Just that gawdam killing".

"I thought you got over that."

"Hell, I won't get over that 'til hell freezes over. My upbringing, I guess. Just don't believe in unnecessary killing."

"Good to hear," Matt responded. "You all right with it, I mean, with it being Ben who killed that soldier?"

"Aren't you?" Montgomery asked, pouring more bourbon into his glass. "Want a drink?"

"Now, that I can go for," Matt said, and gratefully accepted the glass.

Montgomery drank more than his usual round of bourbon and Vince found him passed out in his room.

The next morning, when the sun had split the sky from the horizon, Matt went to Montgomery's room. Vince had already couched Montgomery up on his bed. Montgomery's aide since he began his campaign, Vince showed loyalty to the man by keeping Matt from entering and sending him away.

Matt went alone for breakfast, keeping the captain's condition to himself.

He listened to the chatter that came from the men at other tables around him. He served himself his own breakfast and sat down at the table. After he heard enough, Matt stood up. "All right! I thought we cleared the air last night, but I see some of you are still harboring a grudge agin' Ben. Forget it. I have."

"You're a real man, Matt," Dick said.

"You seem to have a head about you, Matt," an older man returned.

"I'm all for getting' on with Matt," another man stood up and said, attempting to clear the air. "If ever we come agin' any soldiers another time, I want him ridin' next to me."

"Will ye be a stayin' with us, Matt?" Eli asked.

"Yeah," Matt said, "I'm stayin' because the capt'n needs me, and wants me. I'll use my gun to help where and when I can. And you won't ever see me shootin' anyone in the back, either."

"And he's from Wyoming, gentlemen." Montgomery's voice boomed from behind him as the men sat up straight in their chairs.

Montgomery entered the outside arena. Vince's coffee had worked wonders to help sober him up.

"Cheyenne, Wyoming to be precise, right Mr. Jorgensen?" he continued. "Why I hear it's purported to be the wealthiest city per capita on earth. They've got more money per person there than anywhere."

Carefully he sat at the table and surveyed the men.

"He has no reason to fight our fight," Montgomery continued. "I vote that he can leave any time he wants, and we won't do a damn thing to stop him."

Matt caught some grumbling from a few.

"They're my men, Matt, and they'll do what I say," Montgomery said with a slight smile. "I'm grateful to you staying. Enough said."

Vince brought a decanter over to him.

"Now here's my breakfast. Thank you, Vince."

Matt joined him at his table as usual and the two men continued talking. Some of their talk was pure show for the men. And some was careful clarification for themselves.

"Would you have let me take my leave now, Capt'n?" Matt took a swig of coffee.

"Hell no," Montgomery came back. "I'd a still chased ya into Texas and tied you to a steer." Montgomery smiled and took a swig of bourbon.

Ben and Sandi rode back to the ranch a week after they'd left. They stopped at the front porch where Montgomery was standing, watching them ride up.

Montgomery was accustomed to Ben's tantrums, but this one had lasted longer.

"Hungry?" Montgomery asked.

"A might, Capt'n," Ben answered dismounting.

"Vince already saw you riding up. He'll have something for you in the kitchen. Now go get cleaned up."

Sandi dismounted, and Ben took the two horses to the barn to bed them down for the night. She walked up to the porch, and for the first time threw her arms around Montgomery.

"Whoa, little lady," he said with a surprised look on his face. "What's this all about?"

"I jest had time to think about what we were talkin' the other night." She stood on tiptoes and peered into his eyes.

"How's Ben?"

"Better," she said, planting a kiss on his cheek. "You're like a father to us."

"He gives us all that feelin'," Matt said coming through the door. "Hello, Sandi. Glad to see you're back."

Ben jumped upon the porch and glared at Matt without saying anything to him. "The boys took the horses," he said, slipping an arm around Sandi. "We decided to get married, Capt'n."

"Well, if that don't beat all," Montgomery said, a little shocked. "This calls for a celebration." He whipped out a cigar and gave it to Ben.

"You know I can't stand cigars, Capt'n," Ben said, but took it any way. "But, I'll give it to Matt, if he'll take it."

Matt was taken aback at Ben's attitude, but accepted the gift. "Thanks, Ben," Matt said, "and congratulations."

"It took Sandi to make me see things the way I should have seen them before. She told me how you could have shot her and didn't."

"Sometimes things like that happen in the heat of a fight," Matt said. "Too many people shoot before they look."

"Meanin' me, I suppose," Ben said.

"Capt'n," Sandi interrupted, "it weren't the way everybody thought it was. Ben told me how really it happened."

"I know. Let's go inside, and you can hit the feed bag," Montgomery said.

Sandi didn't wait for Ben to start eating. She started in the moment Vince had laid it down on the table.

"So why did you accuse Matt?" Montgomery asked.

"I don't know, Capt'n," Ben said. "He was taking all your attention, so I figured to go one step further and put the total blame on him. You would have found out about the shootin' in the back one way or t'other. I figured I had to tell you."

He looked at Matt and held out his hand. "No hard feelings, Matt?"

"Hell no," Matt said. "Like Eli said, we were runnin' scared, and seems like to me, now that I hear your side of the story, you were just coverin' our ass. Like you said, he could have got either one of us."

"Vince," Montgomery yelled out, "round up our best fixin's. We're gonna have a party."

Vince came back in with a big smile, and asked, "What kind of party?"

"A wedding party, Vince, a wedding party."

"Oh, yeah," Vince said, and turned to go. He stopped and turned around. "Who's getting' married?"

"Ben and Sandi. They're already married."

"Oh, hooray!" Vince went to Ben and Sandi and shook hands with them. "This on the level?"

"Afraid so," Ben said, showing Sandi's finger with the ring on it. "Ain't much, but at least it's something."

"Matt," Montgomery said, "get the men to gather as many people as they can, and get them here by Saturday night. Tell them there's gonna be the best wedding ever right here at the Captain's place.

It gave Matt and the rest five days to get the word out. By Saturday night, the people came, and with them came two of Matt's friends.

# CHAPTER 11

## THE WEDDING DANCE

O ver three hundred people attended the party that night at the Montgomery Farm. Farmers from Linn and Bourbon Counties arrived, and some came from even farther away.

Ben and his bride were two of the happiest people on earth that night.

The band of three fiddlers and two banjo players played the *Virginia Reel* most of the night, with other tunes intermingled to keep the party light and lively.

Montgomery was never without a dancing partner. He loved to dance. He was honored by any woman who would accept his hand. As it turned out, he was quite the ladies' man, though never serious with anyone.

The punch bowl had more whiskey in it than anyone had suspected, but Montgomery had his own special drink, which Vince would supply him with from time to time.

A buggy with a team of horses drove up and parked under an elm tree in front of the house. Matt thought he was seeing things when he recognized the couple as they got out, Frank and Martha. They walked over to the far side of the lawn where the dancing was going on and Matt rushed up to greet them.

"Frank! Martha!" He just about shook Frank's hand off. "How the hell did you know about this wedding?"

"Oh, my stars," Martha said, overjoyed. "Matt."

"Me in the flesh." He gave her a crushing bear hug.

Frank looked over at the dancing on the lawn. "Sandi?"

"Sandi? You know her?" Matt asked.

"She's my baby sister," Frank answered.

"Why, yes, of course. I remember you mentioned her. Just never really connected it. She's only twenty."

"Half-sister, Matt. My pa remarried a young woman after Ma died."

"That explains it," Matt replied. "Real fine looking woman."

"She wired us about the wedding, and naturally we came. Of course, we were hoping we'd run into you, working for Whittaker."

"Shh! You didn't mention about my being a deputy marshal, I hope?" Matt asked in a low voice looking around to make sure no one was listening.

"Of course not," Frank answered. "We came because of Sandi getting married. How is she, Matt?"

Matt, Frank, and Martha sauntered over to the punch bowl. They wanted to keep the evening a joyous occasion, but they realized that the uneasiness of their conversation could have dire results if they were heard.

"As far as I know, Frank, Sandi is clean as a whistle. Oh, she's a little feisty, but women her age tend to be at times, right, Martha?"

The feelings Matt felt for Martha were still there, maybe more intense. Out of respect for Frank, though he kept them hidden. But every once in a while, his eyes met hers and set off sparks.

"I suspect so, Mr. Jorgensen," she answered, and avoided his eyes by watching the people dancing.

"I'm glad to hear that. She's a great little girl, once you get to know her. Well, I see Martha's got that dancing fever, Matt," Frank said, taking Martha by the hand, and leading her out on the lawn to dance."

She danced with her husband, but caught Matt's watchful eye from time to time.

Late in the evening, Frank finished a dance and took Martha back to the table. "I've got to dance with my sister," he told Martha, and moseyed over towards Sandi.

"We haven't had much of an opportunity to talk, Sandi."

Matt was close at hand, and he pushed Martha and him together. "Would you mind dancing with Martha?"

Martha fell into Matt's arm, and he led her onto the grassy dance floor. She felt so natural in his arms.

"I haven't danced a reel in a coon's age," Matt said nervously. "I'm probably gonna trip all over."

"No you won't," Martha encouraged him. "You happen to be a marvelous dancer."

With that said, how could a man like Matt not be the best dancer on the floor? He spun her around, put his arm around her waist, and danced her to the rhythm of the music as if he wrote the dance himself.

Lanterns lighted the night, but looking up, Martha saw the myriad of stars dancing right along with her and Matt. Her flowing dress, the one she had made for Sunday occasions, billowed outward and flowed with her every movement.

The two were unaware of any other dancers on the floor as they drifted together across the silky grass floor in each other's arms, reeling back again and again and again. For the first time in years, she felt like a girl.

Her mind filled with wonderful thoughts of how only she and Matt were dancing together on a snowy white cloud, keeping in tune with each other's heartbeats. She could feel his hand caressing her side, and enjoyed the moments when occasionally his cheek met hers.

Matt could feel energy emotion in his body heighten as she pressed against his chest. Then, as carefully as he could, he swung her to his side and danced apart to show the rest that they were only dancing. Their attraction went unnoticed by most because their eyes were set on Montgomery and his partner.

The Captain had found his dancing partner for the evening, a tall brunette, young and beautiful, barely out of her teens. Suzan Martin attended the party with her parents, Charles and Linda Martin. They enjoyed watching their daughter having fun.

Montgomery was not the smooth dancer that Matt proved he was. He danced with a straight back, and his right arm was high in the air as if it were stiff. But he enjoyed the style of dancing he learned in Ohio, and was having the time of his life moving across the slippery grass and staying upright.

Not everyone danced that evening. Many simply milled around the punch bowl, men enjoyed smoking their cigars, while women chatted about the latest news. Because of the distance from which they all came, most didn't get the chance to see each other except on special occasions like this one, or at church and church socials. Religion was a strong bond in Kansas. It was a breath of fresh air to talk anew with some they would rarely see.

Then as the reel called for it, Matt spun Martha around and away from him, and for a brief second, her face brushed Frank's and Matt reeled her in again. From a moment of emotional fantasy, back to reality, the couple fell into each other's arms, and out again. The dance ended, Martha curtsied, and Matt gave a gentle bow. For a brief moment, their eyes met and held.

Frank walked Sandi over to Ben, and returned her arm to him. The reel began again, as if the tempo had only paused for a moment. Frank walked back to Martha and the two waltzed back onto the lawn together.

"She's a wonderful dancer, Matt." Frank danced off with Martha.

Matt saw that Ben was not dancing. "Mind if I waltz with your bride?"

Ben shrugged his shoulders and gave her to him. He sauntered back to the punch bowl for a refill.

"Montgomery paid you a compliment, Sandi." Matt slid his arm around her waist. She was much smaller than Martha, even with the shoes she was wearing. "You danced quite well together."

"You and Martha were wonderful on the floor, too."

Matt danced her away to the music and nervously wondered how many other people had been watching him and Martha. "You really think we were that good?"

"Dance with me like that, and Ben will shoot both of us," Sandi said with a slight laugh.

"Really?" Matt added. "Let's see, shall we?"

"Matt, I'm wearing shoes. I can't dance fast like you."

"Good," he replied. Finding her waist a little thinner than Martha's, he relied on her following his every command as if he were demonstrating the art of dancing, his style. Sandi had never before found dancing to be quite so enjoyable. She wore bloomers under her thin dress, and at first became embarrassed when she revealed them at their first twirl around the floor. Matt's arm rested on her back, and she fell naturally into his gripping power, relying totally on his movements.

Matt saw the eyes of the ladies as well as the gentlemen on them as he twirled her around and back again as he did with Martha. He enjoyed dancing, a practice he picked up in Montana watching the ladies at the saloon when he was a kid.

His dancing became a requirement with a few other ladies that evening. They told their husbands that they would be delighted if they could dance like that. Rather than attempt it themselves, some husbands relinquished a dance with their wives and allowed Matt to enjoy their company on the dance floor.

Matt's next-to-the-last dance was with Martha. Their eyes looked deep into each other's, and their tender young hearts intertwined. They knew that this might be their last moment together before the music would fade away and the evening would end. Frank had saved the same dance for his sister Sandi.

The music faded, then started up again. The caller announced, "Go back to your original partners, and dance the last waltz. This one's for the bride and groom, Mr. and Mrs. Ben Rice."

Ben and Sandi joined together for the last dance and waltzed across the trodden dance floor of grass as two lovers. Ben had more to drink than he had realized, and almost fell. Catching himself, he smiled at the guests, and continued.

Frank and Martha joined Ben and Sandi, and soon other couples joined them in the final dance of the evening. The lawn was packed with sleepy-eyed dancers.

Matt stood on the sidelines and watched.

Montgomery gave Suzan back to her parents as the lanterns dimmed low, and the people boarded their carriages for home. He knew he would see her again, and from the light in her eyes, he knew she looked forward to seeing him again.

Many of the carriages with their passengers, and the horses with their riders drifted out into the evening with the full moon lighting a pathway home. Montgomery asked Vince to show Frank and Martha to their bedroom.

"Have a good time?" Matt asked Montgomery. He waved to Frank and Martha as they walked to the house and tried to ignore the tug in his chest at seeing them go off together.

"What do you think? She's a beautiful girl." A slight grin played under his moustache.

"Yeah," Matt said. He watched Martha and Frank disappear into the house and the door close behind them. "Very beautiful woman."

Both Montgomery and Matt smiled.

The next day, Matt was up bright and early, but Vince had beaten him by a few minutes, and already had the coffee on the stove.

"Great coffee, Vince." Matt sipped his coffee and warmed his hands around the cup. He found the breakfast was even better, as Frank, Martha, and Montgomery joined him around the table.

"Where are Ben and Sandi?" Martha asked, opening a hot biscuit.

"They're still in bed," Montgomery answered, swigging down his first cup of coffee for the day. "How was your sleep?"

"I was too tired not to sleep," Frank said. "How you guys manage is beyond me. You people know how to have a good time."

"Don't include me," Montgomery said. "I'm stiff as a board when it comes to dancing. Those two are the ones."

"Someone should have told me to take off my spurs," Matt laughed to avert suspicion of his romantic intentions. "I kept tripping on them."

"You didn't," Martha put in. "You were an excellent dancer. And you told me you forgot how to dance. Speaking of forgetting, I meant to tell you. Lori celebrated her sixth birthday last week."

"Six years old," Matt said. "Where is she? Why didn't you bring her?"

"Oh, pshaw, as Lori would say. Toothless is taking good care of her. They both said to say 'hello', and to tell you that they miss you."

"I take it that Lori is your daughter?" Montgomery asked.

"Our one and only," Martha answered.

"Wait here," Montgomery added, and went back to the house.

Frank took this moment to talk with Matt. "If anything happens here," Frank whispered, as he watched other men busying themselves around the farm, but none close enough to hear what he was saying, "get my sister out safely. Promise me that."

"You can depend on it, Frank."

"Ben looks like a pretty nice man," Martha added. "What's your opinion of him?"

Matt bit his lip, and then lightened up a bit, knowing he didn't want to say anything that could hurt two people he'd come to appreciate. "He's Montgomery's right-hand man, Martha. How Montgomery thinks, he thinks. I hope everything will turn out okay."

In a short moment, Montgomery returned with a bag, which Matt recognized as one they had got from their raid on one of the farms.

"Okay?" Montgomery asked, hearing the last few words Matt said. "What's okay?

"Oh, uh, I was talking about their leaving so soon. I told them we just got to know each other, but that their leaving was okay."

Montgomery ignored Matt's words and addressed Frank and Martha. "You can stay here as long as you want, you know that. But, I know, you've got a farm and a little girl to get back to. I know if I had a little girl, I'd be riding out, too. Here, give these to her, and tell her they're from her two uncles, Matt and Montgomery."

"Oh, you don't have to do that," Martha said, taking the bag and looking inside. "Oh, my word. Her eyes are going to go saucer up. Look at this, Frank. It's an assortment of hard candy, the kind she always looks forward to getting when you go to town."

Frank looked at the bag full of candy and remarked, "It's a whole year's supply, that's what it is."

"Not quite, but you can give some of this to that toothless fella you mentioned," Montgomery said, curling his moustache with his fingers. "He doesn't have to chew any."

"Thank you, Uncle James," Martha said, folding the top of the bag so nothing could fall out on their trip home. Then she leaned into him and gave him a kiss on the cheek. "That's for Lori."

When it came time to leave, Matt and Montgomery walked Frank and Martha to their carriage.

"I had the men freshen up and feed your horses, Frank," Montgomery said, as he untied the reins from a lone hitching post and handed them to Frank.

Matt escorted Martha to the passenger side of the carriage and offered his hand to help her up. When she took it, a moment of ecstasy danced between them. She had to let go, because he didn't have the willpower to do so himself.

Frank smiled at Matt and shook his hand. "Visit us when you can, Matt. Goodbye, James, and thank you for your hospitality and for watching out for my sister." He swung up into the carriage and took the whip in hand. "Tell Sandi goodbye for me, too."

"I'll do that, Frank," Montgomery said.

"Good bye, Uncle James," Martha said, allowing him to take and kiss her hand like a gentleman. "How sweet. Thank you."

"Good bye, Frank," Montgomery said, adding, "good bye, Martha. You are a lovely lady, and Frank is a very lucky man."

"I remind myself every day," Frank said.

Matt stood there, almost speechless. "Good bye, Frank. Tell Toothless to stay out of trouble. Give a kiss to Lori." Then he looked at

Martha for almost the longest time, and choked quietly on the words, "Good bye, Martha."

"Good bye, Matt. "

Montgomery scratched his goatee, looked at Matt, smiled, and said nothing.

The carriage got smaller and smaller as it remained on the road heading for Frank and Martha's farm. It disappeared into the horizon.

Matt's mind told him it was time to ride on, too. He had come to like Montgomery, and was not interested in working as a deputy marshal to bring him to justice.

He had come to like Ben a little, now that he was hitched to a run-away little girl named Sandi. He liked the red-bearded Eli, the second in command. He'd come to like all the men, and felt that betraying them now was not in keeping with his principles.

Montgomery picked up his coffee cup and walked back toward the house.

Matt lit a cigar, kicked a hunk of dirt, and said, "Capt'n!"

Montgomery stopped and turned around.

"I'm leavin', Capt'n."

"What brought this on all of a sudden?"

"Jest got itchin' feet, I suppose. All's I know is, I gotta get down to Texas and start a life of my own."

"I thought this was your life," Montgomery said, looking into Matt's eyes. He could tell Matt was hiding something, but couldn't figure out just what it was. "I'm paying you good money. All you have to do is ride with me. Forget it. You're staying."

"Sorry, Capt'n," Matt said taking a drag on his cigar. "I'm jest not the right man for your company. I don't like usin' my gun to further your cause, a cause, I really don't have the slightest concern about."

"Damn! What would you do in Texas?" Montgomery asked, throwing his arm to the wind. "Hell, Texas ain't got nothing Kansas can't give you. You'll be a big man with me, Matt. Watch and see. You don't have to use your gun all your life. When this is all over and I'm governor, you'll have a position with me, fine clothes and a good house. You'll get yourself a good-looking woman and live out your life raising kids in a country that you helped tame. Think of it, Matt."

"Sounds real good, but I'm jest not interested in settin' down my roots in Kansas soil. That's all there is to it."

Montgomery's mind went to Martha, and the spark he saw between the two as she rode away. "You have a thing for that pretty woman, Martha?"

"Hell no," Matt resounded, throwing his cigar to the wind.

"That's it, isn't it, Matt?"

"Capt'n, you can accuse me of anything you want, but the real reason is jest I aim to go to Texas. There's no woman involved, never was, never will be."

Matt put his hands on his hips and looked at Montgomery, with a smile on his lips. "Of course, I saw how you got along with Suzan. Now you two could make a couple. You get married, like Ben and Sandi, and who knows what will happen next?"

"She was pretty, wasn't she," Montgomery came back with an upturned moustache. "I want to see more of her. But damn it," Montgomery added, punching Matt in the shoulder, "I'm not the one talking about leaving. What if we get you a gal?"

"You can get me a harem, I'm still goin."

The two walked back to the house together and Montgomery continued to try and get Matt to change his mind about leaving.

Ben and Sandi were still in their bedroom.

The evening crept upon the Montgomery Farm quieter and faster than a chicken laying eggs come sun-up. Matt and Montgomery sat on the front room floor with two empty bottles of bourbon between them.

"I'm leavin' when the sun comes up," Matt told him.

Montgomery had passed out, and Matt soon joined him.

Vince came into the room wearing his nightgown, and helped Montgomery to his bedroom. Once Montgomery was neatly tucked in his bed, Vince returned and picked up the empty bottles, and straightened out the front room. He left Matt to sleep away the night.

Ben and Sandi never came out of their room.

# CHAPTER 12

## THE MASSACRE

May 19th, 1858,

**M**att never did leave. Montgomery talked him into staying and learning the ways of Kansas. As mundane as it appeared to be, Matt decided to stay until he felt there was a better time to leave. He was a man driven by destiny, and he knew he would have to follow it. He knew this was merely a stopover on his journey to Texas.

Montgomery kept his men out of action for the next several weeks, sending most of them home to work their farms. A remnant stayed behind and worked his farm.

Matt filled his hours practicing his fast draw and shooting at moving targets. He amused himself watching Montgomery ride out every day to meet with his newfound love, Miss Suzan Martin.

It was almost as if Montgomery had given up his looting the farmers of Kansas, and Matt was feeling more comfortable about it; still, he was not comfortable with his spy work for Marshal Whittaker.

Matt reasoned with himself that Montgomery had all he needed right here on his farm, and that he might eventually become enticed by Suzan to quit his reign of terror and settle down to politics. After all, Matt imagined, Kansas was becoming a quiet place to live.

When Captain Hamilton failed to get authorities to arrest Montgomery for murder, he went after one redheaded, red-bearded man, Captain Eli Snyder. Eli was a leader in Montgomery's gang. To get him, Hamilton figured he could easily destroy the rest, for Eli was a man the gang would follow.

Eli was a blacksmith by trade, a family man, and a commissioned captain in Montgomery's gang.

Hamilton begged the government again and again to intervene on his behalf in the capture of Eli. The government refused to go after him, like they refused him when he tried to get them to arrest Montgomery. Hamilton angrily mounted up with his gang and rode out to Eli's home in Linn County. He told his men as they rode out, "We'll bring him in, and then we'll get the rest. But he's the one we need now. Once we have Eli, the rest will come easy."

Fort Scott stood on Eli's property, and for this reason, he had become a very wealthy and solid citizen.

Hamilton was a committed man with little morals. Unlike Montgomery, he would stop at nothing to get his way. Eli's home was not difficult to find. Upon reaching it, Hamilton dismounted and with his shotgun, pounded on the door for Eli to come out. The rest of the men sat their horses, guns drawn.

Eli spotted their approaching and had run out the back door and hid behind a stack of firewood on the backside of his house.

"I'll set fire to your house, you damn idiot if you don't come out!" Hamilton shouted, mounting his horse.

"He's back here!" one of his men yelled as they rode their horses around the house.

Once they had him out in the open, they surrounded and crowded him with their horses.

"You come with us or I'll blow you through," Hamilton threatened as he leveled his shotgun at Eli.

"If you don't get off my land, I'll tumble you from your horse," Eli came back. The red-bearded man wearing his tam lashed at them with a poker, striking one of the horses a smart blow. The horse reared and Hamilton's men fired their pistols, mostly in confusion. Eli felt a bullet pierce his shoulder, but he managed to reach the back door of his cabin.

The men followed him, and when they reached his cabin, his young son rushed out and fired a shotgun.

"Burn the devils," Eli shouted, as the boy opened fire. "Cut away at them with the other barrel."

After seeing the futility of getting Eli out of the house without injuring his son, Hamilton and his men left.

Defeated by one blacksmith and a lad, Hamilton and his men rode back to Fort Scott. In the meeting room of their hotel, they made a list of farmers that belonged to Montgomery's gang. He ordered his men to follow him and scour the countryside to kidnap farmers and bring them to swift justice.

The next morning a downpour of rain soaked the area and caused some flooding. Hamilton's men equipped in rain gear mounted up for their ride.

"No damn rain is going to keep me from getting my revenge," Hamilton said with clenched teeth as they rode down the muddy road towards Linn County. "They won't suspect us coming in this weather."

His fight against Montgomery had become personal since the authorities would not go after them for killing the soldier. Hamilton felt justified in taking the law into his own hands and went after farmers he suspected of being members in Montgomery's gang.

It was worse than Montgomery's raids on the farmers. The Hamilton gang was ready to take people from their homes. Thirty men visited eleven farms, dragging the husbands and fathers away from their families. "We'll teach you, you filthy murderers," Hamilton said as the rain soaked his black beard.

They refused to let their captives ride. Instead, they marched them off with their hands tied behind them to a nearby ravine. None of the captives ever rode with Montgomery, but their denial didn't satisfy Hamilton.

Once at the ravine, Hamilton stopped his men, and then rode slowly around the kidnapped farmers, gloating over his capture. "You killed, and you shall be killed, as the Good Book says."

Hamilton ordered his men to use their bandanas to blindfold them. "Line them up in a file."

His men felt this was some sort of a joke for Hamilton to pull. Certainly he was not going to execute harmless farmers in execution style. This had to be his way of scaring them, perhaps leaving them tied up in the rain to escape on their own.

"You men are to dismount, take your Sharps and stand in file opposite these murderers. "Turner, you will give the command, when ready, for them to fire."

"You're actually going to kill them, Charles?" Turner, his right-hand man, and a few years older than Hamilton, had ridden with him since '55. Medium build, he sported a small dark moustache, and wore glasses streaked with raindrops. He was a man of culture and education, yet his views on slavery as he had been brought up to believe were right and proper reasons enough to ride with Hamilton. Now he was being forced to be responsible for the deaths of innocent farmers.

"You can't kill these men, Charles. It would be cold-blooded murder."

"What do you think they did to that soldier?" Hamilton retorted. "They shot him in the back. A man barely eighteen, shot in the back."

Sitting tall in his saddle, he glared at Turner. "Your duty, Turner, is to order them to fire when you are ready. Do you hear me?"

"We were supposed to teach them a lesson, not to kill them," Turner said defiantly.

"And teach them, by gawd, we will," Hamilton shot back. "Get your men lined up and give the order."

His men watched as the two argued, and Hamilton could feel their resentment towards him.

Turner looked at Hamilton and spit on the ground. "You go to hell, Charles." He spurred his horse away from the scene.

"Damn you, Turner," Hamilton yelled at the top of his voice.

The men watched as Turner rode away, and then looked to Hamilton for their next orders.

"Peterson," Hamilton called out.

Homer Peterson third in charge was more a docile man than Turner.

"Get your fat ass up here," Hamilton ordered.

"Yes, sir," Peterson answered and spurred his horse to the top of the ravine where he met Hamilton.

"Line up the men to fire when ready, Peterson."

"Beggin' your pardon," Peterson addressed Hamilton in a low tone of voice.

"Damn you, Peterson. Get those men lined up, and fire when you're ready. That's an order," Hamilton screamed at the top of his voice.

"No," Peterson said.

Hamilton had made previous plans with Turner that this raid would strictly be to scare the farmers into believing Hamilton's influence was strong, yet controlled. Yet, he had not planned to kill any of them that day. However, the more the men fell apart after receiving his orders to kill, the more enraged he became.

Hamilton moved his gelding next to Peterson, bent over and backhanded him.

"Get down there with your men," Hamilton ordered. "I'll give the gawdam orders myself."

Peterson turned and rode back to join the rest. The men looked at him perplexed, and showed their fear.

Turner reined up on the crest, and through the rain watched Hamilton's maniacal moves. He could not believe what he was witnessing, as they had discussed there would be no killing. They only wanted to drive fear into them.

The hostages stood there in great fear believing no one would save them from their fate.

Turner spurred his stallion to breakneck speed towards the direction where he saw smoke rising in the near distance. It was Montgomery's camp. The storm was reaching its peak when Turner rode in. Suddenly, he realized he was headed for the main tent. Alighting from his horse, he found Matt and others outside the Captain's quarters.

"It's Turner," Ben called, taking him by the arm. "Hamilton's man."

"Turner! Why is he here in our camp?" Montgomery stepped outside.

"Sir, Hamilton is returning bullet for bullet."

"What the hell do you mean?" Montgomery glared.

"Hamilton is shooting some farmers believed to be the killers of a soldier," Turner said. "Retaliation. If I'd known what he was going to do, I wouldn't have ridden with him."

"You're deserting him?"

"Yes, sir."

"Where?" Montgomery shouted. "Where?"

"I'll lead you to them." Turner headed for his horse.

"It could be an ambush," Ben suggested, untying his horse.

"With God as my witness," Turner said, "it's the truth. Ride with me, and pray it's not too late."

Montgomery turned and ordered his men to mount. "Ben, you and Matt lead them out, and for God's sake, stop Hamilton's murderers! I'll catch up."

Matt mounted up, and Ben followed. They rode with Turner east towards the border.

Hamilton had lined up the farmers and made them kneel in file. He ordered his men, "Take out your rifles and prepare to fire."

"I don't want to do this," said one of the men, whose sentiments were repeated through the file. Nobody wanted to do it.

"Ready," Hamilton ordered as he sat his stallion.

"Aim," he continued the count looking at both the farmers and his men.

A humming noise came from within the farmers.

"What? What's going on?" Hamilton asked loudly looking at the farmers.

"They're humming, sir," one of the men said as he put his rifle down.

"Pick it up, boy," Hamilton ordered. "You're going to fire when I give the order. Stop that gawdam singing!" he yelled.

They were humming to the tune of *The Battle Hymn of the Republic*.

A young boy stood there, defiant of Hamilton's orders. The farmers sang louder.

Hamilton spurred his horse and rode to the front of his men. He dismounted and strode over to the young man that had let his rifle fall, and smacked him with the back of his hand.

"Pick that rifle up."

The boy had no choice. He picked up his Sharps, stood there, and watched this madman.

The singing grew louder when all the farmers turned from humming and were now singing.

Hamilton took his pistol out of its holster. "Aim your gawdam rifles, men. Shoot, or so help me, I'll shoot you."

The men knew he was dead serious about his threat. No one had the courage to back him down.

Montgomery's riders, with Turner leading them, rode hard and fast, but the downpour impeded their progress. The road was swollen with streams, and the mud made traveling slippery.

Hamilton brought his .36 into sight of the first man and held his arm straight and stiff. "Why are you singing so loud, my sick friend?" he asked. "You're going to be shot."

"I am the father of a baby boy, you son of a bitch," the man answered with a proud grin. "Kill me and he'll avenge my murder. Kill me and he'll search out your blood."

Anger had intensified Hamilton's grip on his pistol. His finger pulled the trigger. He fell into the rhythm of pulling the trigger and seeing men fall, he pulled it again and again, aiming at the next man standing. A volley of firing followed from some of the other men who for the most part fired over the heads of their captives.

Two riders, not from Montgomery's gang, rode up to a crest overlooking the site of the ravine. With their rifles, they fired single loads. The bullets pelted the dirt around Hamilton's men. One man was hit in the shoulder, and another in the leg. The riders' accuracy caused the men to scramble and head for safety.

Gunshots resounding like thunder through the valley. Montgomery and his men rode hell bent for leather towards the sounds and discovered a group of men riding north.

Turner led the men in the direction of the gunfire. It was not long before they came upon the grizzly sight in the ravine. They witnessed the departure of Hamilton's gang, and the arrival of the two riders, one waving a white flag of truce.

The two riders reached the ravine ahead of Montgomery's men, and sat their horses waiting for them.

"Dismount and take cover," Matt ordered as his horse almost slid into the ravine.

Montgomery's men cautiously ran to help when they saw the bodies of several men who had been shot.

Catching up to his men, Montgomery dismounted and joined Matt who was already at the site moving bodies to see if any of the men were alive.

"Who are you?" he asked pointing his cocked Colt at the two riders.

"Just happened to be riding by when we saw those men shooting at these tied-up men," the younger man said, untying the white flag from his rifle.

"Pretty fancy shooting from where I saw," Matt said. He turned over a body to see if there was any life in him.

"We've got one over here, Capt'n," Eli said, untying the man's hands and lifting him to his feet. "He's not hurt at all."

"Bring him here," Montgomery said, walking over to meet them.

The man had been trying to help his friends with his hands tied behind his back. He had tears, but was not crying, and not cowering. "They yanked me away from my wife and kids. Then they brought us here with our hands tied behind our backs. We knowed they were gonna kill us. But we stood firm." The man grew weak but continued. "Jeb told 'em, 'Gentlemen, if you are going to shoot, take good aim.' There was no flinching from any of us. No sir. We simply looked into their eyes and spit in their faces."

"Give this man some whiskey," Montgomery ordered as he helped lay the man down by the nearest tree.

"Had it not been for these two men," the man continued, "you would not have found any of us alive. Hamilton meant to kill all of us."

"I've never seen anything like it before," Matt said, untying the hands of one of the dead men.

Two more men were found, still alive. Groaning from the ravine signaled the presence of yet another man, and then another. Six men survived the massacre.

The two riders dismounted and helped in the search.

"Three more, sir," another man said as the count came in. "But these will never see their wives or sweethearts again."

Four men lay dead.

"What happened here, mister?" Montgomery asked. He walked among the bodies and stopped at one man whose wounds seemed to be slight. He was a young man with curly brown hair, whose face was muddied up from the stream where he had lain face down.

"I don't know, sir," he said almost incoherently. "I was knocked out, and came to in this ditch with my hands tied. Am I gonna live?"

The younger of the two riders spoke up, "A rugged man, tall, looked to be their leader, stood where that man is layin' and shot at these men point blank until he saw us firin' at them.

"When we started firing, he holstered it, mounted up and started riding," the older rider said, bringing his horse over to Montgomery. "We wounded two or three of 'em."

"More like five or six, my count," the younger one said, bringing his horse next to the other rider's mare. "I got three myself, and I know you got more than me."

"They came at us before daybreak like vigilantes, hooded," the unharmed man said from his seat by a tree. "Right in front of my family. Threw my wife down, hit my sons. The filthy, murderin' bastards."

"Easy, mister," Montgomery said, giving him a swig of whiskey from a canteen. "Rest a bit."

"They've been comin' regularly for several weeks," the man continued, giving back the canteen after a deep swallow. "They called us murderers, and said they were going to kill some of us to teach us a lesson. Then, today they came and got me."

"Why, mister?" Matt asked, giving some water to a wounded man not too far away.

"You," the wounded man said, pointing to Montgomery. "You caused it."

"You're out of your mind," Montgomery countered, walking over to him.

"They told us that you killed some soldiers for no reason," the man continued.

"The soldier!" Montgomery said in a low but angry voice. "Now you know what I meant about no killing. See what it's caused." He glared at Ben, slapped his leg, turned and stomped away.

Matt and a few of the other men used their bandannas to clean and cover the wounds of the wounded.

"Hamilton's gang did this to you?" Matt asked.

"Hamilton?" the younger man asked. "Captain Charles Hamilton?"

"I don't know," the man said. "I don't know." He was an elderly gentleman who had been shot in the shoulder. His raging against Montgomery did not help him any. He made the fifth fatality that day.

The man by the tree spoke up. "They wore masks. The leader was a big man. He tried to get others to fire, but they didn't. I saw him take his pistol out. That's all I can recall."

"I told you that," the young rider reminded them.

"They were Hamilton's men," another wounded man said. Aided by a rider, he limped towards Montgomery.. "I'd knowed them by their yell, and their horses."

"Damn!" Montgomery exclaimed, taking in the bloody sight of innocent men shot with their hands tied behind their backs. "Gawdam you Hamilton, you son of a bitch! Well, Matt, it kind of looks like I'm up to my ass in war. You still figurin' to ride away to Texas?"

Matt looked around at the gory sight and shook his head. He now knew why U. S. Marshal Whittaker had sworn him in as a deputy to help clean up Fort Scott. Whether he liked it or not, he knew he was totally caught up in it and would do his job.

Montgomery placed his hands on his hips and faced the two strangers. "Who the devil are you men?"

"Name's Rod Best," the young rider introduced himself. "This is my brother, Phil. We're from Lawrence."

"Lawrence?" Montgomery repeated. "See any fighting up there?"

"Yes, sir," Phil said. "Somebody shot five men dead center, and chased five more out of Lawrence."

"Pro-slave men, I hope," Montgomery said, rubbing his chin.

"I believe they were," Rod added. He was about Matt's age, an inch shorter in height, and standing six-foot-three in custom-made boots. His eyes were a gentle gray, his long blond curls dangled nicely from under his large black brim hat, and he sported a drooping moustache. He wore a black Prince Albert frock coat that showed off his broad shoulders, and a loose bandanna, which left his throat free. He carried two Colt .36 pistols at his waist with their handles turned forward for the underhand or "twist" draw. He appeared to be absolutely cool and composed considering what had just happened.

"I take it then, that you're glad these men were killed," Rod said, stroking his moustache.

"I always say a good Pro-slaver is a dead one," Montgomery gestured. "How did they come to get themselves killed? A fight with some soldiers?"

"No sir," Phil replied. "Jest two men."

"Two men? Only two men? I've never heard of two men killing five men and chasing out five more. They must be mighty fast with the gun."

"Oh, yes sir, they are," Rod added, pointing to themselves. "We're the two men."

"You?" Montgomery asked. "We seem to be obliged to you gentlemen," Montgomery said.

"Might obliged," Matt added.

It was the first time Matt and Rod met, and from then they would become the best of friends.

Ben walked up, after helping bandage a wounded farmer, and stood behind Montgomery. He looked at the two revolvers in Rod's gun belt and how their handles faced outward. He eyed Phil's pistol hanging low on his gun belt, and saw how both men carried their Sharps as if they never left their side.

"Where are you men heading, now?" Montgomery asked.

"Looking for a man who calls himself, Captain James Montgomery," Rod said with a smile. "Reckon that might be you?"

"It is," Montgomery answered with a surprised look on his face. "Now that you found me, what is it you want?"

"To join up with you," Rod said, pushing his hat back on his head. "We heard about your run in with the soldiers down here, and figured you might need our help. For a price, that is."

Montgomery was excited that these two men wanted to join up with him. He thought of how Matt's guns and the addition of two more fast guns would help in wiping out Hamilton and his gang.

"We'll talk later," Montgomery said, as he turned and walked away with Matt and Ben.

Matt looked back at Rod and felt comfortable about him. There was something about his stature and the way he held himself that caused Matt to appreciate him.

Rod and Phil continued helping the wounded and had little time to watch Montgomery.

"One dead soldier caused all this," Matt said. "Hamilton had no cause to go this far. Hell, he couldn't get the soldiers to arrest us, so now he's trying to kill us off himself.

"He wants to bring me out against him, Matt," Montgomery said. "It's a personal fight between us, now. He's using the killing of the soldier as an excuse to get at me."

"Beg your pardon, Capt'n, but I think he did this to get the soldiers to hunt you down. He wants you dead, any way he can cause it. Hell, he doesn't have to fight you personally, once word gets out that it was you who killed these men."

Montgomery knew Matt might be right, that Hamilton would blame this massacre on him and his gang. He had to prepare himself for that. He also knew that he had to face Hamilton if for no other reason than a quest of honor.

"Find out which one is Jeb, Matt." Montgomery turned and walked back to the ravine. "I want to see this brave man who gave his life so the others could live."

"Yes, sir," Matt answered and ran on ahead.

Montgomery reached the spot where Matt brought the man to meet him. "Where's Jeb?"

"He's the first one in the middle, Capt'n," the man said slowly, still shaking from what had happened.

Jeb lay face upward in the mud as the rain continued to pour down. He was dead.

"He took my bullet. Hell, it seemed they concentrated more on shooting him than the rest of us. I fell down with the rest, thinking I had been hit, too. I lay there a while until I heard them ride away. I wish I had been shot. You came ... and I was tryin' to help the others." He collapsed in Matt's arms.

"Ben," Montgomery called out. "Have the men bring up a wagon. We'll take them back to their families. I want the dead properly buried, and this man, Jeb with dignity."

"Yes, sir," Ben answered. "All right, you heard him. Some of you ride back and bring a wagon."

Ben walked over to where Jeb lay, and once he saw his body, Ben yelled, "Oh my gawd!"

"What's the matter, Ben?" Montgomery turned to see Ben's face filled with remorse.

"We raided his farm. He jest became a father."

The killing, execution style, became known throughout the state as the Marais des Cygnes Massacre. And soon the whole area from Mud Creek to Wichita and to Fort Scott heard about it.

Most of what Montgomery thought was true, Hamilton was using everything he could to fuel the fire of hatred between them, hoping Montgomery would come out in the open to fight him.

# CHAPTER 13

## ONE GUNFIGHTER TO ANOTHER

May, 1858

**M**att and Montgomery were right. Hamilton made sure that word spread like wild fire around Fort Scott that Montgomery's gang had caused the massacre. The story of the massacre filled the land with terror. Posters were already spread around, and soldiers were on scouting missions for any sighting of the gang.

Rod and his brother, Phil, had been made members of Montgomery's gang by virtue of the fact that they stopped a full massacre from taking place.

Several nights afterwards, in the front room, Montgomery met with his leaders. The rain had brought a slight chill to the land, and a fire was built in the fireplace to take away the dampness.

Montgomery had invited his new recruits, the Best brothers, and one Hank Turner to the meeting. Each man was well equipped with a fresh cigar and a glass of bourbon, which Montgomery supplied from his cache. They became a tradition for his meetings.

Suzan and Sandi added their presence to the décor of the room, as they sat on the divan and listened.

"Gentlemen," Montgomery started out as he stood by the fireplace with his lit cigar in hand, "we are blessed to have in this room men who are going to change the history of Kansas. I've already discussed with each of you individually how you fit into my plans. I know you will live up to your part of the bargain, as well as I will live up to mine. We are at a juncture in time where we have been forced to play out our hands.

"Hamilton has got to be stopped! He has to be punished for his cold-blooded murders. I lie awake nights and the sight of those men keeps going over and over in my head. Many nights have gone by, and tension is still so high in Fort Scott, it's difficult for ladies to walk the streets. Turner has informed me that the massacre was conspired in the Western Hotel across the way. And he tells me no man can make him come out of hiding into fighting. He hits and runs. That's why he's never been caught."

"The same way we fight," Ben added.

"Well, it might sound ironic, but you are exactly right. So, how do we get him out in the open to fight?" Montgomery asked.

"You're right." Rod walked to the other side of the room, brushed back the window curtain and stared out into the night. "You and this Hamilton will have to duel it out."

"Ben and Matt know my theories on killing."

"He don't believe in killing," Ben replied. "That's why he hired us."

"I realize killing is necessary in war," Montgomery continued. "I don't want to kill."

"And Hamilton knows this," Matt added. "That's why he's goading you into a fight on his terms. It's time for me to use my gun." Matt slammed his fist down on the table. "Those men were murdered with their hands tied behind their backs, Capt'n."

"I was there, Matt," Montgomery said looking strong into Matt's steely blue eyes.

"Then we're your hired killers, so to speak?" Rod asked.

"You're my hired guns. If you can get Hamilton without killing anyone, all the better."

"You saw those men in the ravine, Capt'n," Eli said. "Don't that tell you nothin'? I'm for killin' 'em. An eye for an eye."

"It tells me also that those farmers would still be alive had we not killed that soldier," Montgomery said, stepping into the middle of the room.

"No, sir," Eli said, standing up for all to see his arm in a sling from being shot by Hamilton. "It happened because they thought we were weak. They'll continue to kill 'cause they think nothin' will be done about it. I'm fed up to here. I could have been one of 'em, but I fought. When they came to kill me, I fought, and they left took off a runnin'."

"What do you propose to do, Capt'n?" Ben asked, sitting close to Sandi.

Phil stood up. "I suggest we storm Fort Scott and burn the gaw-dam Western Hotel to the ground, Capt'n."

"What about innocent people?" Matt asked.

"There's no innocent people in that hotel," Eli said, pounding his fist on the table. "Quit mealy-mouthing, and let's get this damn thing over with."

"My brother's got a good idea," Rod added, "if we examine it further. We need to teach them a lesson. Why not burn the hotel? We'll shoot those who run out, and chase the rest out of the country." He looked up from under his hat and grinned.

"I have to admit, I think he's right, Capt'n," Matt added. "If there are no innocent people in that hotel, but only leaders, we need to get rid of 'em. Now we have strength on our side, and the element of surprise. We should be able to flush Hamilton out."

"What do you mean, surprise?" Montgomery asked.

"Those two men right there," Matt pointed to ROD and Phil. "Hamilton doesn't realize that we have two more fast guns, and one hot-blooded Scotsman ready to do battle. We ride in force."

"Scare tactics, Mr. Jorgensen?" Montgomery asked. "Now you're learning.

"Yes, but this time we back them up with guns to kill if we have to."

"Heaven help us if we have to. Then, gentlemen," Montgomery proclaimed waving his glass of bourbon in the air, "here's our plan of attack. We'll use Phil's idea. Ben, take your men and pour coal oil around the perimeter of the hotel. Light it, then ride like hell and shoot up the town."

"What's your point, Capt'n?" Ben asked.

"To get them the hell out of Fort Scott, so scared that they won't stop until they reach the border.

"One man will stop," he added with dead seriousness on his face, "because I'm going to stop him. I'll be waiting in the street outside the hotel."

"You?" Matt asked.

"It's my fight, Matt. I'll be there to meet him face to face."

"With us," Rod added.

"No, alone."

The room grew quiet. Suzan and Sandi both stood up.

"You're not going to commit suicide, Mr. Montgomery," Suzan said walking up to him. "Matt, tell him."

"He's fast, Captain," Turner said.

"I heard in Lawrence that he's one of the fastest men in Kansas," Rod said, watching Suzan's reaction.

"Don't be a fool." Matt threw his cigar into the fire. "You've got us. It's time we earned our money."

"If I don't make it, Matt, you can have him."

"After you're dead," Suzan came back. "No thank you. Matt, Rod, knock some sense into his head. We're going to be married."

"Hey!" Matt said with excitement. "Congratulations, Capt'n. Who's the best man?"

"After this is done, whichever one of you is still alive."

After dinner that evening, Matt began checking and cleaning his Colt. Noticing Rod pistols, Matt asked curiously, "Why do you wear two guns, when most of us wear only one?"

"Why do you wear one gun, when I wear two?" Rod answered.

"You got me," Matt returned.

"How long does it take you to reload, Matt? If I had more than five people coming at me, the sixth one could kill me."

"I keep six chambers full," Matt said, taking a bandanna from his back pocket and wiping his Colt with it.

"I only keep five. Reason being, when I'm riding, or fighting, I don't want it to go off."

"Good point," Matt agreed. "I'll think on that."

"Of course, when I know I'm going into a fight, I fill up the sixth chamber."

"I see," Matt agreed again. "How many do you have filled now?"

Rod slipped his pistols out of their holsters, and putting one under his armpit, he spun the chamber of the other one to check. Then he flipped it back into its holster with a backward flip of the handle.

"Say, I've never seen that done before. Do it again," Montgomery requested.

Rod stood up, spun the cylinder of the second gun, checked it out, and flipped it back into its holster. Faster than Montgomery could keep his eyes on Rod's hands, he drew, spun them, cocked them, uncocked them. Without warning, he did the roadhouse spin and offered them, butts in, to Montgomery. When Montgomery went to retrieve them, Rod spun them back into his palms with both hammers cocked again.

He released the hammers, spun the pistols again and flipped them back into their holsters with the handles turned outward. Turning his back on Montgomery, he spun around and did a fast cross draw, bringing the Colts out at lightning speed, again with the hammers cocked.

"Wow, I've never seen anyone faster," Montgomery said, taking his bandanna out of his coat pocket and wiping his forehead with it.

Matt drew his pistol with equal speed, spun it, cocked it, and then released the hammer, spun it again, and holstered it with equal amazement.

"You still got it set in your mind to go up agin' Hamilton, Capt'n?" Matt asked.

"Only thing I can do, Matt." Montgomery took out a cigar and lit it.

"In the morning, Capt'n," Rod said walking over to him, "Matt and I are gonna teach you some new tricks that could save your life."

The next morning was the first of June, and before breakfast, Matt and Rod were on the other side of the barn practicing with their pistols.

"You are fast, Matt," Rod said, watching him draw and shoot.

"Thanks" Matt returned. "Coming from you, that's the damnest compliment a man can receive."

"You wanna be faster?"

"From a compliment to an insult."

"Nope. Just stating a fact," Rod continued. "Phil, throw a tin can up in the air for us."

Phil fetched a tin can from the barrel around the corner of the barn, walked back to the men standing by the fence, and waited for his brother's order.

"When I say draw, try to out draw me and hit the tin can, Matt."

Matt slipped his Colt out of its holster and back down again, like he usually did when he was ready to draw to make sure of its slickness. He kept his holster well oiled, but made sure his gun was clean of all excess oil that would cause the gun to slip out of his hand.

Rod watched Matt's eyes, and when the time was right, he gave the command to his brother. "Draw!"

One shot from Rod's pistol sent the tin can flying. Another shot from his second pistol sent it to the ground. Matt's Colt dangled in his hands, cocked but not fired.

Matt thought, a*nd you're getting' paid to be fast. Hell, mister, you better think twice about this line of business before you get your head blown off.*

"Notice anything different about us?" Rod said, holstering his pistols.

"Yeah," Matt said as he still held onto his .36. "I'm standing here with egg on my face, and your guns are smokin'."

Rod and Phil laughed. "Even Phil could take you, Matt. Barely, but I'd bet even money."

"Hell, I thought I was fast."

Rod motioned to Phil to check for anyone watching. Phil returned with an all-clear signal, and another tin can in his hand.

"Give it a try," Rod said with a smile that lifted his drooping moustache and made Matt feel a little more comfortable, but not quite like the man he was five minutes earlier.

Matt looked at Phil, drew his holster out and slipped it back into its holster.

"You nervous, Matt?" Rod asked.

"Damn right!"

"Never ever slide your pistol out of your holster before you're ready to use it. It takes another second away from your draw. If you're not ready by the time you're up against your target, you never will be. That one second of confidence is all you need."

"Hell, I never gave it another thought. I jest wanted to make sure I could get the damn thing out okay." He started to grip the handle again but stopped. "It's a damn habit."

"Now, jest draw when you're ready. Don't shoot. Jest draw."

Matt stood and relaxed his body. When he felt the moment, he drew his Colt fast and easy. He could have shot his opponent dead center if he had to.

"How was that?" Matt asked with a nervous twitch to his voice, waiting for Rod to criticize it.

"Good. Damn good."

"All right," Matt said with a grin.

"But, not good enough. Do you want to be fast, or do you want to be dead?"

"What did I do wrong that time?"

"Not a thing. Your draw was natural, but look at Phil. He drew behind you. You outdrew him, but barely, 'cause he's fast, too. And you could have shot and killed him. Phil has too many bad habits. He has more good habits, because I taught him, but, he refuses to give up his bad ones."

"Mind tellin' me what my bad habits are?"

"Not at all. Get ready to shoot a can out in that direction." Rod pointed out into an empty field. "Draw again when I tell you. This time, when I say 'draw'. Go ahead Phil. Throw it."

When the can was high enough, Rod gave the order, "Draw!"

Matt drew his revolver, fired, and hit the can three times, sending it out into oblivion.

"That is really good shootin', Matt," Rod said with a whistle.

Phil's jaw dropped and he threw up his hands. "He don't need no lessons, Rod."

"See what I mean, Matt, your stance for one thing. You aim with your shoulders and your feet in the direction you're goin' to fire."

"Knowing that could be used agin' me, too?"

"Not really. It's good. I wouldn't worry about it. Another good thing is that you look at your target and you don't blink. Now for tip number one. Watch the man's fingers, not his hand. A good magician uses his fingers. So does a good gunfighter. If a man's finger is curled, he has to uncurl it to fit it through the trigger housing, losing another second, or part thereof. You have that down pat, so there's little to tell you about any of that. You've developed some good habits. Damn good."

"Then, pray tell, what am I doin' wrong that could get me killed?" Matt said, slapping the side of his leg in anger.

"Look at Phil's holster, Matt, and mine."

Matt looked and said, "Yours aren't tied down. Mine is, so I should be faster."

"Not necessarily. Notice ours are at a slant. That shaves at least another second on our draw. You're drawing with a tied down holster, and your pistol is pointed down."

Rod unbuckled his gun belt and pointed to the leather ties in the back.

"Your holster slides on your belt. That's okay for you, but, I found, by latching my holster at an angle, the gun come out faster. My handle is pointed upward because my gun grip is twisted. Yours should be pointed more downward."

Matt handed his gun belt over to Rod and watched him carefully.

"Work on tying it here, and you'll improve your draw, maybe one half to one second, but it could make all the difference between who hits the dirt first.

"Here, Matt," Rod said, handing his gun belt to Matt, "try my gear. See how it fits you."

Matt exchanged gun belts, and strapped Rod's to his hips. "Damn," he thought as he eyed the slickness of the pistol, and felt the curvature of the gun as it fit perfectly inside his palms. It was evenly balanced, and the pearl handle not only looked good to Matt, but felt perfect. He knew he would have to own at least one Colt with a pearl handle.

At first, it felt awkward to him to draw with the holster slanted, but after several tries, it became natural for him.

"Now, draw and shoot."

Matt attempted, but found he was still a little awkward. He tried again and again, until it finally became easier.

"I want you to practice with my gun belt until you become as fast as me," Rod said.

"My gun is lighter because of the pearl handle. Yours is a swollen wood stock, and heavy. Try it again."

Matt turned and fired at a branch on a nearby tree knocking it down with one shot.

Rod drew Matt's pistol and fanned off three rounds, clipping the branch as it fell.

"Damn!" Matt said, as he stood there with his mouth wide open. "And with my gun. That I've gotta learn."

"A mite sticky on the hammer, Matt. Keep your sweetheart clean, and she'll never fail you."

"Rod knows about guns, Matt," Phil added, picking up some more tin cans. "What he says is true. I've seen him take out five, six men all at one time. Nobody believes me, but trust me, it's true."

"If your tie is loose anywhere, you lose again," Rod reminded Matt. "With my holster, one doesn't need it tied down."

The men returned each other's gun belts and strapped them back on. They sensed a strong bond, which went beyond explanation. Each knew that he had to play out the hand that was dealt to him, and each relied on helping the other. Matt sensed destiny's hand again.

Montgomery came to the fence with Suzan, ready for his first lesson as a fast draw.

"Mornin', gentlemen," he greeted them. "Heard you shooting earlier. Well, I'm ready."

"Watch us, Capt'n." Matt pointed to Montgomery to stay in back of them.

Phil had brought several bottles to the fence and set them on the posts some forty feet from where Montgomery would be firing.

When he returned from behind the fence, Rod turned, and fired at the bottles, breaking them with lightning speed.

"That's fast!" Montgomery exclaimed.

"Hamilton's almost that fast, Captain," Turner said as he walked up to the men. "Not quite, but he's fast."

"Want to call it quits, Capt'n?" Matt asked. "We can call Hamilton out."

"No, Matt, I don't. I think I have something that Hamilton doesn't have."

"What's that, Capt'n?" Rod asked, blowing the smoke away from his gun barrel.

"The element of surprise."

"What's this element of surprise?" Matt asked.

"The element of surprise is that he doesn't think I'll challenge him."

"Oh, that's gonna be a real surprise." Rod holstered his pistol.

"No sir," Matt added. "You're gonna make Rod and me convinced, or else we're not gonna let you go up agin' him. That's it."

"Then, gentlemen," Montgomery said, checking his revolver to make sure it's loaded. "Let's begin."

Matt looked at Montgomery's eyes and asked, "What are you looking at, Capt'n?"

"What do you mean, Matt?"

"That would have given me time to draw and fill you full of lead, Capt'n. Not to be disrespectful. But, a man can talk you into a sure death, just like I could have done if I drew down on you jest now."

"But I know you weren't going to draw down on me."

"Don't take that for granted when you're one on one with a killer, Capt'n. Keep your mind focused."

"Focused," Rod confirmed.

"I understand, boys," Montgomery said, and started to draw down on Matt.

Matt's pistol was out and cocked before Montgomery could clear leather.

"I see what you mean." Montgomery dropped his pistol back into its holster.

Throughout the day, before breakfast, after breakfast, and before supper, Matt and Rod stayed with Montgomery.

On the next day, Matt had secured his holster to his belt like Rod had taught him, and practiced with it. He found himself drawing faster than ever, and was pleased to have made a friend like Rod.

Montgomery was also pleased with his progress.

When Turner came out on the third day and watched Montgomery draw and shoot, he simply said, "You're ready, Capt'n. I've never seen a man learn as quickly."

"When you have a hate built up inside you, it helps, Turner."

Matt and Rod walked over to where Montgomery and Turner were standing. For the last exhibition, Phil took a tin can and walked out into the open field. The two men stood ready.

When Phil threw it in the air, Matt and Rod drew and fired their Colts, hit the can with every shot and kept it in the air until the twelfth bullet was spent.

"Think you're ready, Capt'n?" Rod asked, turning back to him after firing his last shot.

As the can descended, Montgomery drew his Colt and fired five more rounds at it, keeping the can in the air by spinning it. Then with the last round, he sent the smashed can flying out into the open field.

"Yeah," Matt said. "I think he's ready."

"You want Turner to ride back and warn Hamilton what he's up against?" Matt asked.

Montgomery supplied the three men with fresh cigars, and they all lit up together and laughed. He looked over at Turner's startled face and smirked. He knew that Turner had never in all his years seen such a demonstration of gun power.

"No," Montgomery answered, twirling his cigar between his fingers. "I want this to be a complete surprise. Turner, you'll accompany us when we ride into Fort Scott. Any objections?"

Turner shook his head. "Not from me."

When they turned around, Sandi and Suzan were standing there to cheer them.

"Sounded like the Fourth of July, so we had to come out and watch," Suzan said.

"Impressed?" Rod asked. He exhaled a stream of smoke, and smiled. "We're jest getting' ready for the Fifth of June."

The girls stood with a puzzled look on their faces. The men smiled and walked back towards the house. Turner followed.

# CHAPTER 14

## THE BURNING OF FORT SCOTT

June, 1858

I t took several nights of planning and making sure that the timing was just right. Then on the fifth of June, at eight in the morning, the men began to saddle up.

"Think it'll work?" one of the men asked.

"Stupid," said another, "he wouldn't have spelled it out like that if he thought it would fail."

"It'll work," Matt said, grinning from ear to ear. Like Montgomery, he never liked to use his gun for killing either, and success would make him an even bigger hero. He'd be known as the man who cleaned up Fort Scott.

"By gawd," Rod said, "Hamilton will have to come out into the open and we'll get him. I'm for it."

It was mid-morning when Matt, Rod, and Phil rode into Fort Scott ahead of the rest, caught the sentries off guard, and tied them up. Making certain that no women or children were on the streets, they gave the all-clear sign for Ben.

Ben took a small crew of men and rode quietly in so as not to disturb anyone. They dismounted at the rear of the Western Hotel and took coal oil from their saddlebags, which they spilled around the base of the hotel when they heard Montgomery's gang charge into Fort Scott.

Montgomery wore his best attire for this occasion, and led his men like a general in command. A nervous Turner rode with him. He was not afraid of Hamilton seeing him, but he was concerned that other members of the gang who were not privy to Hamilton's plan might.

The gang reached the Western Hotel where they saw people on the streets running to put out the fire. Many, including some soldiers, got to the hotel and began throwing buckets of water onto the fire.

Hamilton's men ran through the doors of the Western Hotel and joined in the effort.

Ben and his crew had not perfected their arson attack, ran, and within minutes, the fire was out. They mounted their horses, rode into the confusion with the rest of their gang, and hid behind the hotel across the parade grounds.

Montgomery dismounted in front of the hotel, knowing Hamilton would see him. Turner dismounted with him, took the reins of both horses and tied them to the hitching rail. They waited nervously in the middle of the street.

"Capt'n Montgomery is standing in front of the hotel with that turncoat," Homer said as he saw him from his window. Homer had taken Turner's place as Hamilton's right hand man.

"Turner?" Hamilton ran out of his room and down the hallway and Homer followed him. "Any one else with them?"

"Nope."

"Cover me."

Hamilton checked his revolver as he approached the top of the stairs, and then holstered it.

Two lone figures came out of the shadows and the sound of cocking guns made Hamilton turn around. Matt and Rod stood with their guns drawn.

"Stand easy, Hamilton," Rod ordered. "I don't miss."

"Who are you? What d'ya want?" Hamilton's hand quivered over his gun grip.

"A fair fight," Rod said. "That's all." He backed Hamilton to his room, flung the door open wide and saw Homer propped up against the window. "Drop it, or you're dead."

Homer quickly dropped his pistol and moved away from the window. His eyes followed the barrel of Rod's Colt pointed at him.

Rod picked up Homer's gun and lead him out into the hallway. "Now, Hamilton," Rod said with one gun under Homer's chin and the other aimed at Hamilton, "Capt'n Montgomery is waitin' for you outside. Said he's gonna kill you."

"How? In the back?" Hamilton asked nervously. "What's in this for you guys? Money?"

Matt closed the gap and stuck his Colt in Hamilton's belly. "Vengeance!" Matt said. "I saw those men you murdered."

"Hamilton!" Montgomery's voice sounded from the street. It was a loud and stern voice. Montgomery was angry. He was also nervous, but determined he was going to kill Hamilton in a fair fight. It was the first time in his life he knew he had to go against his principles and kill a man, and he felt ready.

"Hamilton!" he called out again. "I know you're still in there."

A crowd gathered around the front of the building watching a well-dressed man with a badge pinned on the lapel of his coat stand in front of the Western Hotel. Deputy Marshal Samuel Walker had been alerted to Matt's presence in town with the Montgomery gang, and watched from a distance at what was happening.

The marshal walked up to Montgomery whose hand rested against his gun grip. "Who are you, mister?" He knew full well who Montgomery was, just as he knew who Hamilton was.

"Just waiting for a friend to come out," Montgomery said.

"You set this fire?"

"Do I look like someone who enjoys setting fire, Marshal?"

The marshal peered at Montgomery. "What're you doin' here?"

"You know me, Marshal," Turner interrupted as he walked up to the marshal. "We have an appointment with the Captain." He referred to Captain Hamilton as he had just up until recently been his right hand man, and he knew Walker would connect him with Hamilton's gang.

The marshal recognized Turner and continued, "Sorry, Mr. Turner. I'm looking for some troublemakers. Someone set fire to the building around back. We got it put out though." He turned and walked up the street back to his office. He had a gut feeling that the moment had arrived for a showdown between these two magnates, and knew all he had to do was wait.

Montgomery motioned for Turner to get the people off the street. It was beginning to be too long a wait for him, and his palms began to sweat. But he stayed put with his hand on his pistol grip and waited for Hamilton to come out shooting.

Sure he was nervous, but he was also a proud man. This was the first time he ever stood up against anyone and called the fight himself.

He had never fired a gun at anyone, and he hoped he never would have had since he was in command of such a large organization. To him, Hamilton was an evil man that had to be done away with. It turned out to be a personal fight between the two of them, and now, he stood alone, and waited.

Turner kept the people off the street, and at the same time anticipated that he would also have to use his gun to protect himself. But he hoped he could stay out of the fight until Montgomery was down.

"So you're Hamilton?" Matt identified him, looking him up and down as he and Rod held him hostage in the hallway. "You're not a giant," he said sarcastically. "Everyone told me you were a giant in these here parts." In reality, Hamilton stood almost Matt's height, and even had some weight on him.

Matt was never one to hold back his anger, and the wrath that had been building up inside him since the massacre reached its peak at seeing Hamilton. With the back of his hand, he smacked him hard across his face bringing blood from his nose.

Hamilton fell against the banister and rolled down the staircase with Matt and Rod following him. Once at the bottom, he stood up, dazed, but conscious enough to see Matt's fist as it connected to his face. Hamilton hit the wall and bounced back into Matt's arms.

Matt took him up by his shirt and, as Rod opened the front doors to the hotel, threw him bodily out into the street and slammed the doors.

In the meantime, Homer had escaped out his bedroom window and down the back stairs where he alerted Hamilton's gang about what was happening.

"What d'ya think?" Rod asked as he watched through the glass door at Hamilton scrambling to his feet.

"You're a bettin' man, Rod," Matt acknowledged.

"I'll take Montgomery in thirty seconds," Rod replied looking at his pocket watch he pulled out of his vest pocket.

"Hunnert says he'll go the minute."

Both men put their noses on the door and waited.

"Now," Matt said, as Rod looked at the second hand.

Hamilton got his bearings back once he was on his feet, and saw a man whom he had never met before standing in front of him.

"Who are you?" he asked walking close to him.

"Your executioner," Montgomery replied, knowing that Hamilton was buying time by walking towards him.

"You're Montgomery?" Hamilton asked.

"Captain James Montgomery, and today you're gonna die."

147

"I heard you're a filthy polecat that hides behind someone else's gun." Hamilton inched his way towards Montgomery. "That right?"

"Not today," Montgomery answered without moving, keeping his eyes fixed on Hamilton's gun hand.

Hamilton's gang whipped around the corner fast and fierce, one of the men had an extra horse in tow for Hamilton. Some of the men rode up on the sidewalk causing Matt and Rod to leap farther back into the doorway for cover.

Hamilton took advantage of the distraction, his hand went for his pistol and drew it fast. His first bullet hit Montgomery in the shoulder. His second one caught him in the chest, and sent him backwards face down into the dirt.

Hamilton emptied his pistol at the hotel doorway where Matt and Rod stood, sending Matt and Rod again ducking for cover. He did a Pony Express leap into the saddle and rode hell-bent for leather with his gang. He was out of range and protected by the gang's backsides by the time Matt and Rod reached clearance and took aim.

Ben and Eli brought up Montgomery's gang from behind the other hotel from across the parade grounds. Eli kept the men riding after Hamilton's gang while Ben and another rider stopped at the hotel with horses for Matt and Rod.

Matt and Rod ran to the side of Montgomery as he lay in the street bleeding from the two bullet holes.

"Get a buckboard, Ben," Matt called out.

"Where?"

"Steal one, if you have to, damn it!" Rod shot back. "You," he pointed to the other rider who held onto the reins of the two horses as Ben took off for the buckboard, "ride for a doctor. Move!"

The rider dropped the reins of the two horses and rode hard in search of a doctor.

Matt gently turned Montgomery's body over and placed his hat under his head. While Rod brought a canteen of water from his horse's side and applied a few drops to the wounded man's lips, Matt applied his bandanna to the wound to stop the bleeding.

Marshal Walker rushed to the scene. "What happened here?" he asked looking down at Montgomery.

"He's alive," Matt said looking at Rod, "barely."

"Which one is he?" Walker asked.

"Captain James Montgomery, Marshal," Matt said through gritted teeth. "A friend of ours."

"I wouldn't advise gettin' any ideas with that shotgun, Marshal," Rod warned as he glared at him.

"I see Hamilton got him. It's all right fellas," Walker said. "For right now let's concentrate in getting' him fixed up. I want to talk to you boys later."

Doc Kramer rode up in his buggy and relieved Matt and Rod.

"Once we get the bleeding stopped, gentlemen," he said, "we'll move him over to my office."

Ben had the help of two other men in bringing a buckboard over for Montgomery. When the bleeding had stopped, they moved him to the Doc's office.

It was a heavy day in Fort Scott. Montgomery's men returned without success capturing any of Hamilton's gang. Government soldiers milled around in groups in hope of keeping the peace, while curious citizens gathered in front of the Western Hotel and Doc's office to get a view of anything or anybody. Marshal Walker stayed with the wounded Montgomery.

"I've been worrying about these two coming to blows for some time," Walker said, standing in Doc's doorway watching him tend to Montgomery's wounds.

"How about it, Doc?" Matt asked, standing next to the marshal.

"He's breathing," Doc said.

"Will he make it?" Rod asked, standing next to Matt.

"Let me do my job, men," Doc said. "I'll let you know."

The day turned into night, and Matt, Rod, and Ben stayed with Montgomery.

Matt and Rod watched Eli return with a few of the men. They rode by with their hands up to show that they came back empty handed.

"Go on home, Matt said. "The capt'n's holdin' his own. We'll let you know how he makes out."

Ben went to his horse, mounted up to go with the rest back to the farm and to Sandi. "I'll be back in the mornin'," he called as he rode off.

"Well, we can't do anymore harm here," Walker said, motioning to Matt and Rod. "Like to see you two in my office though."

Walker made his office at the Fort Scott Hotel, which was across the street kitty-corner to Doc's office, so the walk didn't take long. Once inside, the marshal offered the two men some coffee that was left on the stove from the morning.

"Still hot," he said as he poured himself a cup.

"No thanks, Marshal," Matt said, waving his hand and visiting the empty rooms.

"I'll pass, too, if you don't mind," Rod added, sitting on the edge of the desk.

"Hamilton got away?" Walker asked.

"Yeah," Matt answered, pushing his hat up.

Walker took a sip of coffee, and after a hard swallow, said, "you both know U. S. Marshal Whittaker, I presume."

Rod dropped his jaw and almost fell off the desk.

Marshal Walker's blunt statement opened Matt's eyes a little, leaving him with a dumb expression on his face.

"Who's Marshal Whittaker?" he asked.

"For your information, gentlemen, he is our boss. Oh, hell, it's about time you both knew about the other. Why did you think I didn't arrest you? "

Matt looked at Rod, and Rod looked at Matt, both pointing their fingers at each other.

"You, too?" Matt asked.

"I guess so," Rod replied. "And you?"

Matt nodded his head. "Would you believe it? I wonder who else is working for Whittaker."

"Just us three," Marshal said. "Now, you know why I came to you."

"Well, Matt," Rod said throwing up his arms, "it looks like we've been found out."

"Looks like."

"Your men came back empty-handed," Walker said. "Montgomery's gang knows the territory better than any one. Why wouldn't they be able to find them?"

"Same reason they never found us, Marshal," Matt replied.

"Well?"

"When we finished a raid, each farmer went to his own home," Rod answered. "A hunnert farmers, a hunnert different directions."

"They put sentries out throughout the trail where the farmers split off," Matt continued. "These sentries alert the farmers of a posse, and these men will hide until the posse rides by. Then they'll double back and go to their separate homes."

"Flat land makes hiding difficult," Rod said, sitting back down on the edge of the desk. "They had to come up with a good plan to make it work."

"We do the same thing," Matt said, sitting behind the desk and plopping his large boots on top. "What makes it difficult is, sometimes, we have some of their men ride with us."

"And they have some of ours," Rod related taking his gun out twirling it.

"So you spy on each other?"

"Not all the time," Matt replied taking his Colt from its holster and spinning it. "Just sometimes."

"What do you want us to do, Marshal?" Matt holstered his Colt and took a cigar out of his vest.

"Your call. All I know is, we've got to get Hamilton before he gets us," Matt said, "now that he knows the capt'n is shot up badly."

"You've got two men in front of you, Marshal," Rod added. "Two men should be able to slip by their sentries and find Hamilton."

"Now that we know what he looks like, it should be easy," Rod said.

"That must be why Marshal Whittaker chose you two." Sam said. "Something I forgot to tell you, boys," he added, putting his weapon back into its holster. The sheriff is our Free-State sheriff. He knows about you, but doesn't know what you look like. He's determined to bring Hamilton in, too."

"How many men does he have?" Matt asked.

"At most, around twenty."

"Hasn't done it by now, he probably never will," Rod threw out. "You saw part of Hamilton's gang ride in and ride out." He motioned with the palms of his hands. "Four or five men to the sheriff's one. I hope you're gonna tell the sheriff what we look like. I don't want him shootin' at us."

"Can't. You're still working for Whittaker, remember?"

Matt and Rod left Walker and headed back up to the Doc's office to check on Montgomery.

Rod opened the door to the office. "How's he doin'?"

Turner was sitting in a chair, and rose when the men entered. "He's asleep. Doc's in the other room."

Doc came from his bedroom drying his hands. "I got him patched up the best I can. The rest is up to the good Man upstairs."

"Wanna join Rod and me over at the hotel?" Matt asked Turner. "We're gonna bunk down there for the night."

"Why not. Been dozing off here."

Matt and Rod went over to the other hotel and took Turner with them. On the way over, Matt said, "Got a favor to ask of you, Turner."

"Sure. What is it?" Turner replied keeping his smaller frame in step with the two big men on the way to the hotel.

"You know where Hamilton is holed up," Rod matter-of-factly said.

"Been his right-hand man for a while," Turner replied. "I ought to know."

"Wanna lead us to him in the morning?" Matt asked.

"It's risky," Rod added, "but we're gonna bring him back, one way or t'other."

"A man could get killed, or wounded." Matt put his hands in his hip pockets as they strode together.

"He sees you with us, he'll want to kill you, I'm figurin'. We want you to make your own choice."

"I'll tell you how to get there," Turner said, as they entered the hotel. "I wouldn't want to go near him. I don't know what I'd do if I saw him again. He'd probably kill me. It's best you go alone."

"Have a ceegar, Mr. Turner," Rod said as he whipped one out for him with a smile. "I knew we could count on you."

# CHAPTER 15

## THE SHOWDOWN

**D**uring the night, the rains came, and sometimes in Kansas, they would not let up quickly. This was one of those times. Matt and Rod donned their rain slicks, saddled their steeds, and rode out after Hamilton before the sun came up. The trail led them to the border of Kansas and Missouri in Linn County.

By mid-afternoon, the two gunmen had afterthoughts. "You think we should come back when the weather's better?" Rod mused.

"You're joking, but right now I'd give anything for a nice dry bed, and a hot meal."

Kansas was a vast, rolling prairie with grass tall as a man's head when he's standing in a hole, and treeless except for some cottonwoods, ash, elm and hackberries in the creek bottoms.

On their second day out, the boys were soaked even wearing the slickers.

"We're close, according to Turner's directions, and any one of these farms could be his hideout," Rod said, as the rain poured down the crease of his hat.

"Turner said it was located on Sugar Crick in Linn County," Matt wanted to take the map out but didn't out of fear that the rain would disintegrate it.

"Well, this here is suppose to be Sugar Crick, and another day of rain is gonna turn the crick into a full-blown river."

"There's suppose to be some Cottonwoods lined up down by the crick and up a small gorge, that's what we're supposed to be lookin' for," Matt remembered.

Towards the end of the second day, it seemed to be a waste of time, and so the boys found a farmhouse and rode over to its warm and friendly looks. Light from the windows, and smoke from the chimney told them someone was home. As they rode closer, they could see the farm being over-run with the deluge of rain. Rain was good for the farmer, but when it came down hard and lasted more than two days, it could spell danger. A cow could be heard from inside the barn.

They reined up and began to dismount when the front door opened and an elderly woman with a shotgun greeted them on the porch. She looked to be in her early sixties, muscularly built, with her long hair rolled up in a bun. She chewed on an unlit corncob pipe.

"Friends or foes?" she asked holding tight to her shotgun.

"Friends, Ma'am," Matt said. "Damn good friends, too."

"We'll see about that," she replied lowering her shotgun. "Never can tell nowadays. Light down and set a spell. 'Spect you're hungry, tired, and wet."

"You reckoned jest about right," Rod said. "Can we barn our animals?"

"Nothin' in there but a cow," she responded. "If'n they can get along with her, go ahead. Some old rags in there, too. Come on in when you dried off."

The boys finished bedding down their horses, dried them off, and fed them some hay. They dodged the raindrops as they dashed over to the house where the lady had the side door open.

"What's your names?"

"I'm Matt. He's Rod," Matt answered shaking the rain off his hat outside the door.

"Jest got corn bread, tomatoes, beans, and buttermilk. Not much, but you're welcome to eat all you can."

"I must have jest died and gone to heaven." Rod smelled the aroma of hot food.

"Ma'am," Matt said, "we are two of the starvenest boys you've ever met. Thank you kindly."

The kitchen was large, with a huge wood-carved table and six chairs. A wood stove, newer than most and decorated with white porcelain and black iron, stood against the left wall with a full kindling box beside it. Matt and Rod looked around to see where the others were.

"Jest me and Minerva," she said, pointing to her cat on the kitchen counter. "My husband passed away ten year ago. Lost my two boys up in Leavenworth in a bawdyhouse."

"A bawdyhouse, Ma'am?" Rod asked, with a frown on his face as he went for the cornbread on the table.

With a switch, she came down hard on the back of his hand, not to bruise or cut it, but simply to make it smart."

"We say grace in this house, mister," she said quite seriously. "Where's your manners?"

The boys waited for her to sit, and then they sat down at the table. They closed their eyes and waited for her to say grace.

"You gonna say it?" she asked with her eyes wide open.

Matt looked up at her, then over to Rod. He nodded and began saying grace.

"Lord, we thank you for the food, for the house, for this lady. Amen."

She picked up the corn bread and passed it to Rod.

"That was real pretty," she said with a tear in her eye. "Now you can have some food."

"You said you lost your two sons in a bawdyhouse," Matt reminded her as he swallowed down his first glass of cold buttermilk.

"Younger than you boys, they were." She passed a plate of canned tomatoes. "Seemed they were experiencing their manliness, as you call it, when some cowboys came in shootin' up the place."

"They shot your boys?" Rod took a good size chunk of corn bread with his hands.

"No, no," she replied. "They thought they were coming to get their girls, so they jumped out the window and ran."

"And the cattle stampeded over them?" Matt said, stretching the story with his hands to get her to finish it.

"Nothin' like that, boys," she continued. "I lost them."

"How'd they die then?" Rod spooned some hot beans onto his cornbread.

"They never come home," she said wiping a tear from her eye with her apron. "After all these twenty year, they never came home."

"You heard they were killed somewhere?" Matt made himself a tomato sandwich with his cornbread.

"No, no," she said again. "They jest never come home. So ... I lost them."

Rod and Matt looked at each other, raised their eyebrows and shrugged their shoulders.

"You lost your boys?" Rod asked again. "You mean you never found them again?"

"Yes, yes," she said with a slight smile. "I lost them. It was twenty year ago. I thought you might be them, but then I saw you weren't so I took my shotgun and was gonna shoot cha."

"Real glad you didn't, Ma'am." Matt added beans to his plate. "Got any more buttermilk, Ma'am?"

"Reach behind you, son," she answered. "What you boys ridin' in this rain fer anyway? Where're ya headed?"

"We're lookin' for a man."

"So am I," she said wryly. "Who you lookin' for? Maybe I know him."

"Doubtful, Ma'am," Rod said. "He's a killer."

"You're right, young man," she returned. "Don't know any killers. If I did, I wouldn't know them, I suppose. What's his name anyway?"

"Hamilton," a voice said, coming from the darkened front room.

Matt and Rod abruptly stopped eating, looked towards the voice and saw a shadow of a man behind a pair of Colt's.

"Captain Charles Hamilton at your service, gentlemen," the voice said as he appeared into view walking into the kitchen. "Would you like to stand and drop your gun belts? I know how handy you two are with guns."

They stood and obeyed Hamilton, dropping their gun belts as they rose.

"I'll be go to hell," Rod said dumbfounded.

"This is the man we're lookin' for, Ma'am," Matt said with a worried look on his face.

She picked up the gun belts and put them on the counter against the far wall. "Gentlemen, I want you to meet my brother, Charles."

"Brother?" they both asked simultaneously.

"I didn't see any horse in the barn," Matt said, as he looked around for more surprises.

"One of the reasons no one found me." Hamilton confessed. "I never kept a horse. It's a sign of betrayal. You see, Maggie here lives by herself. Everyone knows that, except for my right hand man. Turner told you where I lived, but he didn't tell you about Maggie, ya know why?"

"No," Rod answered. "But I'm beginning to suspect."

"Hello, gentlemen," Turner said as he came into the light from the front room. "Sorry about my little masquerade, but you can understand my situation. A man can only be loyal to one man."

"Turner!" Matt exclaimed. "Why?"

Hamilton slid a chair away from the table, turned it around and straddled the seat, dropping his arms over the back. "We knew someone was working with the marshal. We didn't know who. The government was against us. Montgomery was against us. And the sheriff was against us. How were we to win against those odds? Well, gentlemen, we had to use deceit to defeat deceit." His east Georgia roots echoed in his words. "Turner was our Trojan horse. Making everyone think he had gone soft, he lit out and joined your group."

Hamilton rose, walked over to the window and peered out at an imaginary world through the rain as it poured down,

"Then, after I shot Montgomery, and the marshal evidently confided in you as he did, Turner saw a good chance of getting you two out of our way for good."

Swiftly he turned away from the window and slammed his hand down on the table.

"Now, gentlemen, we have Kansas!"

Walking around the backs of the men, he picked Rod's gun belt off of the counter, leaving Matt's.

"That's a nice pearl-handled Colt you've got here. Nice gun belt, too. Never saw one like it."

"I made it special," Rod retorted.

Slipping his gun belt off he handed it to Maggie.

"Here, Maggie," he said as he gave his .36 to Maggie to hold. "You keep this one as a souvenir. I'm going to use this from now on."

He fitted Rod's gun belt around his waist and tightened it. He was a little awkward taking them out of their holsters because of the way it sat on his waist.

"It don't like you," Rod said.

Hamilton twirled it as he felt its smooth and even balance. He examined the cylinder to make sure it was loaded.

"Real nice," he said, and ran the cylinder up and down his arm. "Good feel to it."

Rod tightened his thin lips, letting his drooping moustache betray his disgust at Hamilton. He turned to Maggie and angrily said, "Our last supper, I take it, Maggie."

"Sorry I couldn't have made it a lamb, gentlemen," she returned. "But you know how hard it is to get lamb in Kansas, it being a cattle state and all."

"Excuse us if we don't laugh," Rod came back bitterly.

"What next?" Matt asked.

"We're Southern gentlemen," Hamilton said. "We believe in giving our enemy a chance to escape."

"You tend on shooting us in the back with our hands tied?" Rod asked, looking at the rain through the window.

Maggie listened, but the words bounced off her like rain off a tin roof. She didn't connect her brother with the Marais des Cygnes Massacre. She had been led to believe that the Montgomery's gang did it, and Matt and Rod were part of it.

"No," Hamilton answered rubbing his jaw where Matt before had hit him, feeling a little more uncomfortable with Rod's insinuations. Taking the poker iron standing beside the stove, he brought it across Rod's back. "I owe you that and more, but that's not what I have in mind. I don't want any blood spilled on my sister's land. Now get outside"

Rod's body fell limp as he doubled over catching himself on the wall. He didn't fall, but grimaced in pain. Hamilton shoved him out the door, kicking him as he fell off the porch.

"Get their horses, Turner," he ordered. "Bring them around."

"You're not going to let us ride out?" Matt asked, going to Rod's assistance.

"You must be kidding," Hamilton said. "Move out."

The rain came down harder, and Matt and Rod had difficulty understanding what Hamilton was saying because of it and the thunder, but they got the message when he pointed his gun their way.

Turner brought the saddled sorrels around and held the reins for Hamilton's next move.

"I'm a sporting man," Hamilton said. "I'm gambling that you can't outride a bullet. I'm going to let you try to ride out of here, gentlemen. Now Turner here is an excellent marksman with the Sharps. I'll get at least one of you. If I should happen to miss the other, trust me, he won't."

"So you're going to let us ride out and shoot us?" Rod surmised still holding his hands in the air. "You're not gonna tie our hands behind our backs like you did with those farmers?"

Maggie cringed again at hearing Rod recount part of what happened at the Massacre.

"Shut up!"

"What happens if one of us gets away?" Matt asked.

"You won't. I'm an excellent marksman with the pistol."

"Yes, we know," Matt returned. "We saw you kill those defenseless farmers."

Matt saw a strange look creep on Maggie's face when she heard what he just said as she stood on the porch.

"You're not going to shoot them now, are you, Charles?" she asked still holding on to his gun belt.

"Don't listen to them, Maggie. They're liars. They're the ones who shot those farmers in the back."

Turning to Rod, Hamilton brought his fist to his jaw, knocking him out into the mud. "I told you to shut up! Get up on your horses. Hold those reins tight, Maggie."

Maggie came around and took the reins from Turner as he took his Sharps, walked down the road and took position to shoot the boys as they rode towards him.

Hamilton followed him with Rod's Colt.

"I'm going to stand here at the end of the road," Hamilton told them. "Like I said, I'll get one of you at least. Hopefully both. If one of you gets by, Turner will blast you to Kingdom come. Now get up on your horses."

Rod looked daggers at Hamilton aiming his own Colt at him.

"You told me Montgomery killed those farmers," Maggie yelled, loud and clear for Hamilton to hear as he walked to the end of the road. She still had his .36 in her hand.

"They're lying, Maggie, to save their hides," Hamilton returned. "Ask Turner. He was there."

"Tell her Turner," Matt yelled out as he mounted Skeeter. "Did you leave the scene because Hamilton told you to, or did you leave because you couldn't shoot a farmer in cold blood?"

"He left because I ordered him to," Hamilton said. "Now ride."

"Turner left because he couldn't pull the trigger himself, Maggie. None of his men could kill those farmers in cold blood. Your brother pulled the trigger. He killed five innocent farmers in the back, with their hands tied. They never had a chance."

"You killed Jeannie's husband? Him only a father two weeks?" Maggie asked with anger building up in her insides. "You said the Montgomery's men killed them and I believed you. You said the soldiers were on their side and keeping you from making something of yourself. You lied, Charlie. You lied to me."

"Put my gun down, Maggie," Hamilton yelled out over the rain. He stood there sopping wet and Maggie looked at him as if blood was dripping down his face.

She saw the blood of the farmers who were once her neighbors. She saw Jeannie's husband as he once sat at her table showing off his new baby to her just weeks before.

"We'll talk about it later, Maggie," Hamilton yelled again. "I swear to you, I didn't do those things. Montgomery did, I swear to God. Turner will tell you."

Rod mounted his sorrel and watched for a chance to spur him to safety as Maggie kept arguing with her brother.

"Turner!" Maggie called out into the night. "What really happened?"

"It's like he said, Maggie," Turner returned at the top of his lungs for her to hear over the rain falling.

Rod sat his horse quietly without motioning for it to move, he figured it was time he said something more.

"I rode up to the site, Maggie," Rod said. "I was the first one there. I saw your brother shooting eleven innocent farmers with their hands tied behind their backs. On the Holy Bible, I swear, he shot at every one of them."

A shot rang out. Rod felt a sting across his leg. The bullet missed entering his leg but ripped his pant leg.

"Your horse moved," Hamilton yelled out. I won't miss next time. Now shut up!"

Rod gripped his leg, and seeing he was only scratched, continued. "His men turned and ran when they saw me shooting down at them. I was too far away; else, I would have done some damage to your brother. He got his ass out of there with the rest."

"Shut up," Hamilton yelled, firing again but missing him.

Rod threw himself off his horse and rolled in the mud to safety of the shot.

Matt saw the chance to spur Skeeter while Hamilton's focus was on Rod, and took it.

Rod ran to his horse and quickly mounted him on the run, pulled his body down close to the shank and held onto the mane. Both men rode fast and hard towards Hamilton while the jolt pulled the reins from Maggie's grip, leaving them dangling in front of them. They hoped to distract his fire, and through the confusion, Hamilton and Turner would miss both of them. Whatever the outcome, they knew they had to ride; there was no other choice.

A sudden peel of lightning and thunder added to the confusion and caused Hamilton to miss both men as he fired at them riding straight at him.

Maggie's gun went off, and the sudden discharge caused Hamilton to look toward her for a brief second as Skeeter collided hard against him, shoving him to the ground.

Turner watched Hamilton go down hard in the mud. He decided quickly that he would only get one at best, and then the other would come after him, so he threw his rifle away and stood defenseless with his hands in the air.

Matt dismounted, grabbed Turner's .36 out of its holster and belted him across his head with it. He turned sharply and ran after Hamilton.

Hamilton rose, positioned Rod's Colt again, and fired at Matt running across the road in the heavy downpour.

Matt dove into the ground with his pistol leveled at Hamilton and fired his Colt.

Hamilton was hit in the chest. He stood with the Colt high in the air, and as he fell he fired into the mud. His body lay silent, and the blood oozed onto his sister's land. He had met his match in gunplay. Matt was faster and more accurate.

Maggie fell twice in the muddy ruts as she dropped her brother's gun and ran to his side. She knelt down beside him as the rain soaked her body.

"Help me get him inside," she cried as she tried to lift his heavy body. "Please."

Matt bent down, picked Hamilton up, and carried him towards the house, while Rod brought Turner, picking up the rifle on his way.

"I'm sorry, Ma'am," Matt said. "I didn't mean for this to happen."

"It could have been you, son. I didn't do a thing to stop it. I should have. God forgive me, I didn't."

She opened the door and led Matt into the bedroom adjacent to the kitchen.

"This is his room." She helped Matt lie him down on it for the last time. It was a large bed and matched the large kitchen table with the six chairs in the kitchen.

Rod brought Turner in, and they both gazed at the corpse of the once infamous guerilla leader.

"I couldn't shoot him," Maggie said, still crying. "He was my brother. I just wanted him not to shoot either of you. I jest tried to scare him. Hell, I ain't no shot."

"We'll have the sheriff come out and claim the body, Maggie," Rod said. "We'll turn Turner over to the marshal."

The night was long and dark. The rain came down harder and soaked Hamilton's blood back into the earth. No one slept that night, lightning flashed all night, causing its thunder to roar throughout the rolling plains of Kansas.

The rains eased up the next morning, but the trek back to Fort Scott was still slow. The boys had hoped to bring Hamilton back alive. Instead, Hamilton was dead; his widowed sister grieved alone, and the man once thought to be their friend, turned out to be a double turncoat. No, that day in Kansas was not a happy one, even though the rain stopped, and the sun had come out.

"Kinda funny, ain't it?" Matt said riding high on Skeeter.

"How's that?" Rod asked, spurring his sorrel ahead while holding onto the reins of a horse with Turner riding him behind.

"How Hamilton got killed with Turner's gun, the gun he wouldn't use to kill those innocent farmers."

"Yeah!"

Turner never said a word all the way back to Fort Scott.

# CHAPTER 16

## THE ARREST OF BEN PRICE

**M**arshal Walker sent a wire off to U. S. Deputy Marshal Whittaker in Topeka reporting Captain Charles Hamilton's death, and that the rest of his gang would probably seek out revenge for his killing.

At Walker's request, Judge Gerald T. Bartley sent another wire asking Governor John Geary that troops be sent in to intervene as an all-out gang war was bound to happen. He wrote in the wire that it also would be an opportune time to rid Fort Scott of all of Hamilton's gang and clean the territory of Pro-slavers once and for all.

Within twenty-four hours, the marshal received word back that government troops were on their way to Fort Scott as he had requested. The governor added that, "this was the greatest news he'd heard since he's taken office."

When the judge saw the wire, he figured it was time to finish the game.

Turner sat locked in a room at the Fort Scott Hotel awaiting trial, and only Hamilton himself knew that Turner had not turned against him, and he had carried the secret to his grave. The rest of the members of his gang believed that he was one of Montgomery's leaders now.

Sheriff Bull, a large, robust man with a long moustache, and squinting eyes, kept riding Turner about his loyalty to Hamilton since the day of his capture.

It was a cold night when the judge chose to visit Turner. Walking over to the hotel, he met Bull sitting outside the hotel, and greeted him. "Nice night, Bull."

"Yeah. What brings the judge out at a time like this?"

"You kinda know me, after all these years, don't you, Bull? How long you been sheriff now, ten, twelve years?"

"More like fifteen."

"Ever see it get this tough?"

"About to blow its lid, Judge," Bull said. "We gonna get any help?"

"Soldiers? They're on their way. Governor Geary assured me."

"I'll believe it when I see it. If they don't, we're in for it, Judge."

"I'm inclined to agree with you. Scared?"

"Ain't you?"

"Well, yeah. But don't go telling anyone, you hear?"

"How's our prisoner, Bull?"

"Same. Not talkin'."

"Maybe something I have will help him to be more friendly."

The two of them walked inside, and down a long corridor to the room that housed the prisoner. The sheriff unlocked the door, and the two men entered Turner's room where they found him pacing.

Showing Turner the latest wire from the governor's office, the judge said, "Governor Geary is sending troops here to clean the rest of you out of Kansas, Turner. You'll probably swing, unless you help us, and you know it."

"I'll swing anyway," Turner said while reading the wire.

"Maybe not if you cooperate. Hamilton's dead. What will happen to the gang now?"

"They'll stay together. Select a new leader."

"You?"

"No. Unfortunately, they think I deserted them. Only Hamilton knew about our arrangement."

"When they find you, they'll kill you, won't they?"

"More'n likely, I suppose."

"Worried?"

"Who wouldn't be?" Reading the wire again, Turner asked, "What will happen if I don't cooperate?"

"To you? You'll probably do time in Leavenworth. We'll have more of them going with you to Leavenworth real soon. Think about it, Turner. These are men you worked with, and now they think you betrayed them. Especially with Hamilton dead, you know they know you helped Montgomery. How are they going to feel with a traitor in their midst?"

Turner thought about what the judge said, and made him think more seriously about his situation.

The judge took out a cigar and offered it to Turner. Taking it, Turner bit off the end. "How many are there in your gang, Turner?" The judge lit it for him, looked him in the eye and waited for an answer.

"Two hundred or more," Turner said. He took a deep drag from his cigar and let it all out.

"Tell us everything you know about their activities, and I'll see that you get across the border, a free man."

"Me? A free man? What do you want to know?"

Bull leaned in to listen.

"How do they determine when and where to raid?"

"Hamilton always did that."

"He's dead. How will they plan their next raid?"

"You want me to tell you that?"

"Your choice, Turner. You can go a free man."

"All right. I have your word?"

"This is the judge, Turner," Bull interrupted.

"They only raid when the moon is full. They do that so they can make sure of their get-away, and also because it helps scare the farmers when we ride down on them. You know, a full moon and a bunch of noisy riders wearing masks and shooting off guns."

"The moon is full right now," Bull said, looking out the window.

"Have you heard of any raids being pulled off lately, Bull?" the judge asked.

"Not for about a month, now."

"They'll make a raid. You can bet on it," Turner added.

"Where?"

"That's determined by the leader. Hamilton's gone, so the next leader will have to decide."

"You know how they pick it," the judge argued glaring directly into Turner's eyes.

"They stay within an hour's ride on a night like tonight"

"An hour from where?"

"From close to Hamilton's sister's house, where we were. Hamilton would meet them at the fork in the road, a mile north where a grove of oak trees stand. We would leave from there and ride for about an hour. That way our horses wouldn't be tired. If we were chased, we'd split up, and meet back there once we outran our pursuers."

"I know where the place is, Judge," Bull said.

"Good. Then he's telling the truth?"

"I'd say so. Everything makes sense."

"Tell me, Turner," the judge said, lighting his own cigar. "Did you try to kill those farmers in the ravine?"

"No sir," Turner answered. "I swear. I thought he was going to just scare them. That was our original plan, to simply scare them. What happened after I left, I can't explain."

"What were your plans at that time?"

"We had planned that I would defect from Hamilton's camp and go over to Montgomery's side as a protester, like I did. I was to shout and protest Hamilton's command at shooting the farmers like he was really going through with it. But, when I saw he was dead serious about killing them, I tried to stop him. I swear to God, I tried."

"Why didn't you?"

"He would have killed me," Turner said, sobbing. "Something went wrong. I never saw him like that before. He was a mad man. Up till then, we had put up with his tantrums. Oh, he had them from time to time, but not like this one. Now it seemed that, because nobody was going along with his plan and the other men disobeyed him, he went over the edge. Don't ask me why. I ran. I didn't hear the gun fire then. It was when I brought Montgomery's gang to the ravine that we found the bodies already shot."

The judge turned and walked to the window. "With the troops on their way, we'll have all of you out of the country in a few days. We'll check your story. If what you say is true, I'll release you, and you can go across the border and stay there. If not, we'll see you on the gallows. God help you if you're lying."

The judge opened the door to leave, stopped and said, "Get the marshal and come up to my quarters."

Within the hour, Bull rapped on the judge's door in the hotel.

"It's open, Bull. Come on in."

Bull took off his hat and threw the cold from his body with his huge arms, as he and the marshal entered.

"I hear you're going to release Turner," Walker said, taking his hat off and sitting down.

"Bull, I want you to take a well-armed posse and ride out tomorrow night to the grove of oaks that Turner talked about. If you find anything, take care of it.

"You're right, Walker. I'm going to release Turner, if his story bears out. He's always appeared to be a good man to me. Getting mixed up with Hamilton was his doing, but killing, I don't think he had the stomach."

"What if he goes back to the Hamilton gang?"

"They'll probably fry him and have him for breakfast. He knows that, too."

"Our sending that wire out getting the governor to send in the troops was a smart move, Walker. I'm certain we'll be seeing Hamilton's gang soon enough. The way I figure it, they'll want to know more about Hamilton's death and they'll come after Matt and Rod. Getting them all in the open will be the best break we've ever had."

Matt and Rod were back at the Montgomery's Farm while Doc had made another call to check on Montgomery's condition. Eli had brought Doc from town that day, and was sitting in the buckboard ready to take him back.

"I don't know, Matt," Doc Johnson said climbing up into the buckboard, planting his medicine bag on the floor. "It's the bullet that I took out of his chest that did the most harm. He's got a deflated lung, and that's not good. Infection could set in."

"Thanks, Doc. We'll see to it he pulls through."

"You do and it'll be a miracle. I'll be back in a couple of days."

"Sorry we have to blindfold you, Doc," Eli said as he pulled a bandanna back over Doc's eyes. "Don't want anyone to know our whereabouts."

"That's fine, Eli," he came back. "Your shoulder giving you any more trouble?"

"None, Doc. You did a damn fine job. Thanks."

"You're a strong man. Lucky your muscle kept it from going deeper. You might have been like the capt'n here.

"You still there, Matt?"

"Still here, Doc. All of us. Have a safe trip back."

Ben Rice had other plans, which couldn't wait while Montgomery was laid up. It had been a while since the Montgomery gang last raided any farmers. "We've got to get away from the Capt'n, honey,"

Ben said as he lay with Sandi that night. "It's not right for two women to be under the same roof."

"I've been tellin' ya, Ben," Sandi opined, nibbling on his ear. "Suzan and I can't agree on everythin', and well, it is her house, and we're jest sharin' a room."

"I'll ride out in the mornin' and contact some of the boys for another raid. It'll help get us some money to get out of here," Ben said, kissing her over and over again. "When it's all over, we'll tell the Capt'n we're leavin' and head on out for the west coast, like we always planned."

"Oh, Ben, not another raid. You'll wind up dead somewhere, I jest know it."

"Not Ben, honey. Not Ben Rice. I'm invincible, you know that."

He rode out early the next morning without telling anyone where he was headed. He found some of his gang and asked them to join him in one more raid together. He knew some of the members were poor farmers and extra loot from homes in other counties could help them. They just needed a little encouragement. After all, "they would only raid the rich slave-owning farmers," he told them.

He knew he would not be able to get Eli to ride with them, because he was back in Fort Scott being a blacksmith and a family man.

Eli knew his days of riding with Montgomery were much in the past. The purpose for which he rode was completed, now that Hamilton was out of the way.

Ben rode the circuit, rounding up some members of the old gang. "One last raid, men," he said, sitting high on his stallion, "that's all. It'll be a long summer, and we'll be all set for the rest of the year."

Ben had always been a smooth talker, and figured he knew how to convince some of the men in following him. He had had a few years experience working with Montgomery. Now, he applied it for his own use. However, by the time it was all over, he had less than twenty following him, which was all right by him because it meant less to share the loot with.

He also talked it over with a handful of men working the Montgomery farm when he returned, and got a few of them. The others agreed to keep quiet about it.

When he was ready, thirty men were willing to meet with him. Ben was not interested in the fair maids on this ride, and left them alone because he was now a married man.

The men met at their designated spot, a fork in the road leading from Linn to Bourbon County. As usual, they wore masks so as not to be recognized.

Sheriff Bull was confident that his posse would come across some action that night as they cantered their horses towards the grove of oaks Turner had told them about. It happened sooner than he thought, for in the distance on the way to the grove, while the sun was yet in the sky, he saw a group of men riding hard and fast away from the Jackson farm.

"Take some men and find out what happened at the Jackson's," he ordered the rider next to him.

The rider took off with five other men. Bull spurred his horse forward, and with a motion of his arm signaled the rest of the posse to follow him. Their horses were already tired from the trek from Fort Scott. The men ahead of them started to out distance them in the chase.

The group was not Ben's gang, but a segment of Hamilton's gang. But like Ben would have done, they planned better than the sheriff and walked their horses to their destination so they would be fresh for the raid and the get-away.

It was while Ben's gang was getting organized at the fork that they saw the small segment of raiders who were riding fast and hard towards them, fleeing the sheriff's posse.

Seeing Ben's gang, the raiders reined up and veered off in separate directions.

"Now there goes a pack of fools," Ben said ready to ride after them. "They're up to something. Probably coming back from a raid, I'll betcha. Choose your own, men. We'll meet you back here."

Sure enough, Ben's gang found that the other gang had been on a raid, and had their saddlebags and dusters full of stolen items.

Ben's gang, with fresher horses, out ran the raiders. They quickly relieved them of their loot after they caught them, and sent the small band of raiders on their way, frustrated and with their pride hurt.

Ben awaited the return of his men back at the fork. When they all hooked back up, Ben addressed them. "Well, gentlemen, looks like the Lord has been good to us tonight," he said as they dismounted and examined their saddlebags of the newly acquired loot. "Our treasures have been dumped right into our own laps."

His attitude at receiving the Lord's blessings was interrupted with the sound of horses heading in their direction. As the sound got louder, the men closed their saddlebags, swung back into their saddles, and rode like the wind back to their farms.

Sheriff Bull and his posse were still in hot pursuit after the small gang who left the Jackson Farm, but lost them. Following their fresh tracks at dusk was easy but slow. However, when they saw riders scattering ahead of them, confusion reigned supreme. They were more riders and they weren't wearing masks. When they saw the dispersion of riders in various directions, Sheriff Bull's men, still outnumbering Ben's gang, started riding down on them and began firing their weapons as they rode.

Because the men were quite a distance away, and Bull's horses were tired from cantering the distance from Fort Scott, they got away.

Ben and six others were not so lucky, they were surrounded and captured with out too much of a chase, and taken to Fort Scott, and incarcerated in the Fort Scott Hotel.

Word of what happened got back to Montgomery on his farm, and without a moment's hesitation, he yelled out to Suzan, "Have them get the buckboard out, Suzan. We're going into Fort Scott."

"You can't go into Fort Scott after Ben, Capt'n," Matt warned Montgomery. He was amazed at how quickly he responded to Ben's capture even in his bad condition.

"Matt," Montgomery coughed out. "Get them the hell out of Fort Scott. Bring them back."

Out of range of Montgomery's hearing, one of the farm hands said, "They never raided any farm, Matt. They were going to, but they met up with another gang who had already raided a farm and was making away with their loot. I rode with them, and we all saw fit jest to take the loot away from them. It was as easy as takin' candy from a baby, Matt. They saw us comin', and with their horses a rippin' and a snortin' they skeedaddled out of there and ran for home. We gave chase with our fresh horses, caught up with them, and three to one, we jest laid into them. They never gave us a fight, jest gave us the loot and rode on home."

Matt knew his place, and saddled up Skeeter. "We'll bring Ben back, Capt'n? You comin', Rod?"

Rod threw the blanket and saddle on the mare and bridled her. He planted his left boot into the stirrup, and, with the grace of an eagle, swung his long, lanky leg across the saddle and into the other stirrup, and holding loosely onto the reins, allowed the mare to swiftly go into a gallop.

At the request of Suzan, the men on the farm followed suit, saddled up, rode out, and joined them. Loyalty within the Montgomery gang was like that of a family.

Other farmers who rode with them saw them coming. Not one of them failed to drop what he was doing, and reined in with the gang after finding out what was happening.

The ten men of the Hamilton gang also spread word that the Montgomery gang had attacked them, mercilessly beat them, and stole their loot from them. This infuriated the other members because of the fact that some of their own had been taken advantage of and robbed of their own takings. Their pride had to be avenged.

When word reached the Hamilton gang that the Montgomery gang was headed to Fort Scott to get Ben Rice out of incarceration, they began to gather their members for a ride to Fort Scott, it was time for a show down.

Over two hundred men rode together, including some of the ones who were on the raid with Ben that night by the time the Montgomery gang reached Fort Scott.

Rod and Matt rode point with men who some would call ruffians, while others would simply call them dirt farmers with a mission. When they got to Fort Scott, every man was armed to the teeth with his Sharps rifle, Colt revolver and ready for battle.

Sheriff Bull walked out to meet them.

Matt reined the gang to a halt and did the talking.

"Release Ben, and we'll go home, Sheriff," he said with a look that could have condemned Satan himself.

"Can't do that, Matt," Bull answered, cradling his shotgun. "They raided a farm, and

I just learned they killed a man."

Matt dismounted and took the shotgun away from Bull as easy as a frog would zap a fly with his tongue. Rod joined Matt, and the two walked into the Fort Scott Hotel to find Ben.

"Where're the keys?" Matt asked looking on the walls as he walked inside.

"On the rack behind the door," Bull answered.

"Okay Bull, show us where they are."

Bull led them to a room where Ben sat waiting.

"He's got to go to trial," Bull said. "It'll be a fair trial."

"They'll string him up, Bull. String up Turner, Sheriff," Rod said looking in at Turner cowering in his corner. "He tried to kill Matt and me, or are you forgettin' that?"

Once Matt and Rod got the couple outside, they noticed that the town folk began gathering to watch.

"Where's the judge?"

"Right up here," the judge replied from a window in the second floor of the hotel, "Judge Gerald T. Bartley at your service."

"You've got the wrong man this time, Judge," Matt said.

"That's for the court to decide. Not you. And who are you, may I ask?"

"My name's not important like yours at this point. Just say I'm a friend of these two and have their best interests at heart."

"Well, mister, if you want what is best for them, you'll leave them incarcerated. If they're innocent like you say, the court will find that out and you'll have them home in time for dinner. Take it or leave it."

"Judge. As I see it, I've got them out already," Matt said, showing the more than two hundred men armed and sitting their horses.

"These are the two men who killed Hamilton, Judge," Bull pointed at Matt and Rod.

"You take them by force, and you'll take their place," the judge warned. "Mark my word. Government troops are on their way as we speak. On the other hand, leave them for the court to decide, and if they're innocent as you contend they are, they'll be set free according to law. That is my offer, and like I said, take it or leave it."

Bartley was a firm man, and one who didn't like arguing from a window. His hand went up to shut it at the next dissonant sound coming from Matt or anyone else standing next to him. This would mean that Matt and his men would be forced to fight right then and there, and if they escaped, they would be considered outlaws, something that Matt and Rod didn't want.

"So, you're the two men who shot it out with Hamilton? I'd like to shake your hand sometime, but right now is not the time."

"Yes, sir," Matt answered with a smile. "Thank you."

Rod grabbed Matt by the arm and pulled him aside.

"As I see it, the judge is making sense, Matt," Rod said, rubbing his chin and looking at the town folk gathering.

"I'm thinkin' the same."

Matt looked up at the judge still standing with his hand ready to close the window.

"When you aimin' to try them?"

"As soon as I've had my breakfast. They deserve a speedy trial, and I've scheduled it for this morning at ten."

"It's almost that now."

"We got a deal, Mister whatever?"

"I'm Matt Jorgensen, Judge. This here is Rod Best," Matt said, tilting back his hat to scratch his head. Looking over at Rod, he continued, "Shouldn't take long, Rod. Let's put 'em back."

Then in a whisper he added, "If it goes agin' them, then we'll break them out."

They escorted Ben back inside the hotel to the relief of Sheriff Bull.

The sound of the judge's window was heard like lightning across the prairies before a big storm.

# CHAPTER 17

## THE TRIAL AND THE PARASOL

U ntil they were able to call a meeting together in the great hall of the Free-State building, the government kept tight security over the people of Fort Scott. Because of Montgomery's scare tactics in the past, more deputies were on hand than usual to keep the peace. The people were still shaken from the torching of the Western Hotel and the near jailbreak, so they kept on their guards to avert any more attacks. However, the fact that Montgomery was wounded and pretty much out of action, and the news that Hamilton was killed made the people feel more comfortable with holding trial in the meeting hall.

Over two hundred members of Montgomery's gang came to see Ben's trial, as more farmers came to town. Most stayed outside of the meeting hall on Matt's orders.

Four men attended the meeting incognito so that the trial would not be disturbed. Matt, Rod, Phil, and Eli were dressed in bib overalls and straw hats, and looked like good honest, hard-working dirt farmers. Of course, it was almost a disgrace for Rod, as it was unlike the well-groomed man that he was. Because of their apparel, no one paid any particular attention to them as the meeting hall was overflowing with people. Eli came out to help his good friend, Ben.

Sandi and Suzan came together. Sandi wore her best dress and shoes. She was in the company of Suzan who was always well-dressed.

Some of the people on the outside blocked the open windows by peering in.

Walker found Ben and the six other men tamed and willing to attend their trial when he and his deputies brought them into the meeting hall. They were seated in the front pew of the hall.

Just behind them sat the three men from South Carolina. In comparison to the rest of the crowd they stood out not only because of their quiet and obedient attitude in compliance with the rules of the meeting hall, but also because of the style of clothing they were wearing. They were men in their fifties dressed in custom-fitted clothes, the type one would get from the east coast. They appeared to be well-educated gentlemen.

Around them sat other notable gentlemen with their wives, blending well together since they belonged to the upper echelon. These people were here with great expectations that this segment of Montgomery's gang would swing for the killing of a farm hand. With their execution hung the way the rest of Kansas would go as to the issue of slavery, and decidedly a victory for the Pro-slavers.

With the announcement by one of the marshal's deputies of the judge's arrival, everyone rose as the judge walked to a table in front, which he used as his bench.

The chattering of conversation going on throughout the meeting hall made it difficult for Judge Bartley's gavel to be heard even as he continually banged it on his bench after he was seated. Finally, at the judge's request, a deputy took his gun out, aimed it straight up, and fired two quick rounds to get the people's attention.

"This court is now called to order," the judge said, looking down from his spectacles at the people settling down. "If you wish to sit in on this trial, I urge you to keep quiet. If you don't I'll have a deputy escort you out. You people looking in through the windows will have to keep the noise down, or we'll be forced to close the windows. And you folks know how hot it'll get in here after that. You may be seated."

He turned toward Ben and the six other men. "Now, being absent a prosecutor, I'm allowing Sheriff Bull here to handle the matter at hand. And, I don't suppose you people have an attorney to defend you?" Ben shook his head. He looked at the others. "And you men, the same?"

"In that case, Marshal Walker will act as your defense attorney." Looking over at the sheriff and the marshal, he asked, "Is that all right with you gentlemen?"

"Yes, sir," the marshal responded and walked over to the empty chair by the defendants and sat down.

"Yes, sir," the sheriff responded in like manner.

Then, looking over his spectacles again, he summoned the two gentlemen to the bench. "Bad news, Sheriff. Marshal just received a wire saying the troops had to go to Fort Riley. Some type of emergency elsewhere. They won't be coming." Then, as matter-of-factly, he said, "State your case, Sheriff."

This startled Sheriff Bull, still standing, as he never had time to sit while trying to keep order in the hall. He looked around and out the windows where Montgomery's gang were standing on the lawn, staying out of trouble. Then he looked back at the judge and, realizing he was on the spot, walked up to the bench.

"Not coming?" he mouthed. Perspiration began to bead up on his forehead as he opened his argument.

"These men and this woman, your honor," he stated loudly, "are on trial for raiding farms, terrorizing the people, and killing a man."

"And what about this killing?"

"Well, your Honor, it was out on the Jackson farm in Bourbon County "

"I see," the judge said. "Who was killed?

"A farm hand, your honor. Timothy Carlton."

"I knew Tim. Fine boy. Young. A little hot-headed at times, but good. Are all those charges true?" He leveled a gaze at Ben.

"We didn't raid any farm, your honor," Ben replied, "and we didn't kill no one."

"Is the Jackson family here?"

"Right here, your honor," the marshal said raising his arm.

"If Mr. Jackson's here, Marshal, bring him down and sit him beside me."

Mr. Jackson was a lean man in his forties, who looked like he could lose his temper at the drop of a hat. He wore bandages around his head from a wound. The marshal walked him to the front of the hall where he took the seat next to the judge.

"Tell us what happened, Mr. Jackson," the judge told him, peering at him over his spectacles.

"Well, your honor," he said, holding his head as if in pain, "we had jest come in from the fields, washed our hands and such when this gang of ruffians wearing masks came riding up. Well, sir, they knocked me down, and held guns on all of us. Next thing I know, a gun went off and my hired man was lying beside me, shot in the head."

"Do you recognize anyone here that was there that night, Mr. Jackson?"

"When I tried to get up, I was pistol whipped. No sir, I can't. But I'm bettin' they're part of the gang, right there." He pointed to Ben and the other defendants.

"What about your wife? Is she in the room?"

"Yes, sir."

"You can go sit down, Mr. Jackson. Bring Mrs. Jackson down, Marshal," the judge ordered as Jackson rose and went back to his seat.

One of the marshal's deputies escorted Mrs. Jackson to the front.

She was a small woman, and everyone watching her walk down the aisle showed that they had pity for her for having to go through such an ordeal.

Once she was seated, she put her hands together and stared at the floor in a dazed look.

"Mrs. Jackson," the judge began. "I know this is hard on you, but we must know the facts. Can you identify any of the men who killed your hired hand and stole your goods?"

She straightened up, looked around the room, and recognizing no one, said, "They wore masks over their faces, your honor. I'm sorry. I don't recognize any of them."

"All right, Mrs. Jackson," the judge said in a compassionate tone of voice. "Marshal, please escort her back to her seat."

When she returned to her seat, the sheriff approached the bench once more.

"We came to see a hanging today," Phil Taylor said. He was number one of the three rich men from South Carolina. "Let's get on with it."

"Mister Taylor," the judge addressed him peering again over the top of his spectacles. "There is only one judge here, and you are looking at him. I know who you are, you and Mr. McHenry, and Mr. Jones are who are sitting with you. And I know you are rich. But neither your money, nor your presence is going to hinder these defendants from getting a fair trial."

"I'm just thinking, Judge, that we're wasting valuable time," Taylor said, shaking his head. He was determined that Ben was going to hang. Knowing that Montgomery was near death, getting rid of Ben would almost assure him and the other two from South Carolina a sure victory for the Pro-slavers. He also knew that Hamilton's gang was riding in to avenge their leader's death by getting Matt and Rod. They had already paid a visit to them with good money.

"Time is what we have a lot of here in Kansas, Mr. Taylor. If you want time, I suggest you go back to South Carolina. Please continue, Sheriff."

"Well, they must have done it, your honor. I caught them trying to get away," Bull responded.

"Away from what, Sheriff?"

"Away … well, we came across them at this place, and when they ran we gave chase. Most of them got away, but we caught these," he said, pointing to the defendants in the front pew.

"And what were they doing?"

"Nothing, your honor."

"Nothing. Were they sitting on their horses? Were they standing? Were they playing games? They must have been doing something to have run away? Or did you start chasing them first?"

"Oh, no sir, your honor. When they saw us coming, they started to run, and then stopped and just let us arrest them."

"We didn't know it was the sheriff at first, Judge," Ben said from his seat. "When we did, naturally we stopped."

"That sounds logical. Did you ask why they were there?"

"We knew why they were there, your honor."

"For raiding a farm? "Did you see them actually raid the farm?"

"No, your honor, but their tracks led to their hiding place where we caught up with them."

"They made tracks?"

"Yes sir, your honor. Plenty of horse tracks."

"You know that for a fact, Sheriff? Why are you so positive the horse tracks were made by the horses belonging to these men?"

"'Cause they were there with a saddlebag of loot."

"A saddlebag of loot? What kind of 'loot'?

"Things taken from a farm."

"Do you know what this so-called 'loot' was that was taken from a farm?"

"Yes sir, your honor," the sheriff said beaming, thinking he finally scored a point for his side.

The judge looked at Ben and addressed him. "Son, the sheriff here said that he and his men were following some tracks. Is that right, Sheriff?"

The sheriff nodded his head.

"Were those your tracks he was following?"

"No sir, your honor."

"Now, son, he said they were. Who am I to believe? Would you like to sit up here?"

Ben nodded, rose, went to the front, and took a seat by the judge's table.

"For your sake, talk straight. Tell us what you were doing when the sheriff arrested you. The sheriff says he caught you with the loot."

Ben squirmed in his seat and fidgeted a little with his hands as he looked out to the crowd of people gathered. He saw Matt who gave him a wink, and Rod staring straight at him. Both men pulled their straw hats down over their eyes to keep from being recognized.

"We never raided any farm, and that's the truth, Judge."

"If you didn't raid any farms, then what were you doing in the area and what were you doing with the so-called 'loot'?"

Ben had a good look at the back of the room at some men standing with their arms folded. Like the rest of his gang, he never got a look at the men they robbed. They wore masks and it was nighttime. But, now he was feeling their presence in the meeting hall.

"We rode up as some others rode away. I guess they got scared of us coming and ran. We saw this saddlebag filled with stuff, so we began to help ourselves. We just thought they were throwing the things away."

"Is that the way you see it too, Sheriff?" the judge asked with a slight grin.

"May I show you what they thought was things being thrown away, your honor?"

"Well, first of all, Sheriff, let me ask you this. Are you saying that the things you are about to show me are things that they might have found?"

"Yes, sir. – No, sir. I mean, your honor. We have the loot they stole, can we begin with that?"

"It's what we consider evidence, Sheriff. And, yes you may begin with that. I've been curious to know what it is that we're talking about for some time now."

One of the sheriff's deputies brought the confiscated saddlebag to the judge's table and laid it in front of him. He opened it and showed the loot to be valuable items such as jewelry, money, and expensive heirlooms.

The judge stared with his eyes wide open as he examined some of the things within his reach.

"This is rather expensive for anyone to, how did you say it, 'throw away', Mr. Rice," the judge said after examining more.

"We didn't get a chance to see any of it, Judge," Ben came back. "These outlaws dropped them when we rode by and ran off. When we got off our horses, Sheriff Bull and his men chased us. What were we to do?"

"Sheriff," the judge began as he continued examining the evidence. "Is that what happened?"

"Well, we saw some men leave, your honor, but when we caught these men with the loot, we knew we had the leaders and arrested them. You know Ben Rice is considered to be Montgomery's right-hand man."

"This young man, Ben, is the leader? What about the other six men?"

"They're just our neighbors," Ben quickly added. "We were all just having an after-supper ride out on the hillside."

"Are you going to buy that story, Judge?" Phil Taylor asked.

Pounding his gavel, the judge continued, "I will not tolerate any outbursts from anyone here in my court this day. I trust I make myself clear."

He paused. "And Sheriff, you say you saw some other men ride away. Why didn't you go after them as well? Didn't you have enough men?"

"Oh, we had enough men, all right, but his men were long gone, your honor. And like I said, we already had the leader."

The marshal stood up and said, "Sheriff, these people could have been there after the raid. Isn't that right?"

His remark made Sheriff Bull a little uncomfortable.

"Well, yes, sir, if you look at it that way, your honor," Sheriff Bull returned.

"And you arrested them because they just happened to be there?" the marshal asked.

"You hear what I heard, Rod?" Matt asked holding back his laughter. "The marshal is arguing pretty good for our side."

"Do you have witnesses for any of this, Sheriff?" The judge glared over his spectacles at the talking from the back row. He had not recognized Matt or Rod, but was beginning to be concerned with the buzz of talking. "Quiet. If I hear any more talking out of the back row, I'll have the marshal's deputies escort you out. Do you folks understand me?"

It was then that he recognized Matt with his bushy hair and moustache. He looked in Matt's direction and gave him a knowing look of recognition, then he slammed his gavel down to finish his remarks.

"Now, sheriff, I asked you a question. Do you have any witnesses?"

"No, your honor. I didn't think I needed any."

"Then why are we here, Sheriff?"

"Your Honor, I thought I had the right people," the sheriff whispered as he leaned over the table.

"You don't have to whisper to me, Sheriff, and keep your hands off my bench."

"Mr. Rice, gentlemen," the judge addressed Ben and the six members of his gang. "Even though the prosecutor, Sheriff Bull, doesn't seem to think he has a case, I'm afraid I have to disagree. Unless the marshal can argue otherwise, the court sees the overwhelming evidence is against you."

"Your honor," the marshal spoke up waving his arms. "Does not anything that has been said in their defense raise the slightest doubt about their guilt?"

"Marshal," the judge addressed him, "it seems to me to be too obvious. The sheriff's posse, as I see it, rode up and caught Ben Rice and the others in the area, while the rest of his men rode off. They were left with the goods. None of them has a solid enough alibi to help you win your case. Like I said, unless you can come up with something, I'm going to have to rule against them."

A loud yell came of enthusiasm from the back of the room from a man standing against the wall. It startled the people in the hall, and especially Mrs. Jackson.

When she heard it, she lifted her face and looked as if she had come alive for the first time in days.

"That's the man," she yelled out. "He's the one. He's the murderer who killed poor Tim."

"Marshal, find that man and bring him here," the judge ordered, slamming his gavel down on his bench.

The man turned, and with his nine other companions ran to the main door. They quickly discovered two deputies, on guard since the start of the trial, barred their exit..

Matt, Rod, and Eli, climbed over the pews and ran through the people as everyone talked and stood because of the commotion.

The rest of Montgomery's men could no longer stay out of the fight. When they heard the eruption inside, they joined in. But when they saw Hamilton's gang gallop into Fort Scott towards the meeting hall, they quickly turned and met them face on.

Several members of the Hamilton gang dove from their horses, while others dismounted and charged at the Montgomery gang. It was almost an even number of men on both sides as fists swung in every direction.

Inside the meeting hall, one of Hamilton's men turned to Eli and busted him in the mouth with his fist. Matt came over the top of a pew and grappled the attacker to the ground. Another man came from the other side of the pews and whacked Matt across the side of his face. Matt reeled backwards and released his grip on the other man. He returned with his fist, coming up and plowing it into the man's face.

Two more charged at Matt, but he caught them around their necks and butted their heads together.

Fists and arms flung with men fighting each other to the point where some never knew who they were fighting, or why they were fighting, but they kept on swinging anyway. It was one hellofa melee.

Out of the corner of one swollen eye, Rod caught sight of a whirling woman in red wielding her parasol like a weapon and about to slam it down on a friend's head. He grabbed her around the waist with one hand and snatched the parasol with the other.

"Now, now. Ladies should be ladies," he said.

What he thought was a lady kicked him in the shin, wriggled around him so fast he didn't even see how she resnatched her parasol. But he did feel the resounding smack alongside his head and the floor when it crashed up to meet him.

Matt stopped when he saw this and doubled over in laughter. She spun at the sound and charged after him with her parasol poised like a spear. Matt grabbed it before the sharp end pierced his gut and wrenched it out of her hands.

He ducked under flying fists and, still laughing, pulled Rod to his feet. "Who's your lady friend?"

Rod elbowed Matt in the ribs, and shook his head to clear his rapidly fading vision. Then he saw the lady in red, really saw her. His throat went dry. "Excuse me, Ma'am."

"You oaf," she said, and hit him again with her parasol.

He stopped her swinging arm, relieved her of her parasol, and sat her down in the pew. He let a smile creep across his face as he stared hypnotically into her beautiful gray eyes.

A man turned him around and planted his fist in Rod's face. Rod reeled backwards spread eagle across the pew and landed face down in the soft folds of her dress where it gathered in her lap.

Rod groaned and lifted his head. He could just see over the swell of her breasts. The top of her dress was unbuttoned almost to where his hair brushed against it. Her red hair tumbled around her face, pins hanging off the end. What a wonderful place to land after such a lousy beating. A great place to sleep, he dropped his head back into her lap.

Matt stepped over an unconscious bloodied man and yanked Rod up from his resting spot. With her sitting on the pew, Rod's head fit nicely in her lap facing downwards.

"Of all the idiotic, contemptible, imbecilic morons, you are the worst I have ever seen," she said with her hair messed up, and the top of her dress unbuttoned. "Get your head out of my lap."

"Sorry, Ma'am, my friend seems to be sleeping in your lap. I'll carry him away, if you don't mind."

"Mind?" the lady shot back. "Get him off me, now! And I'm not a ma'am. Not by a damn sight."

The fighting escalated. Bodies flew out windows and crashed through doors. People who'd come for the trial tripped over themselves and the brawlers in their hast to escape.

Matt scooped Rod up and plunked him down in a pew. He turned in time for his jaw to connect with a barreling fist that sent him flying over Rod in a heap on the floor.

A wiry man came charging at Matt's back but was stopped abruptly when Eli came across the man's head with his fist, and sent him reeling out the window.

The lady looked at Rod as he sat on a pew simply admiring her beauty, almost oblivious that a fight was going on.

"Well!" The lady blew a stream of hair up over her eye and sent a lock of hair over her forehead. She stared incredulously at Rod.

"What?" Rod asked with a smile and his arms outstretched.

"I have never seen such a coward in all my born days. Are you going to just sit there and stare at me without raising a hand to defend your poor friend there?" She pointed her parasol at Matt who had a muscularly built man in a headlock, and was about to give another one an uppercut.

When the man connected, she winced. "Oh, that must have hurt. That poor man," she cried out.

"Me, a coward?" Rod pushed himself up, unsteady in his boots. "Let it never be said that Rod Best is a coward. Not by any man. And certainly not by a lady as charming as you, my dear."

"Oooh!" she said, reeling around again swinging her parasol as hard as she could. Her weapon missed its target, Rod's head, and instead connected with one of three wealthy men worming his way out of the meeting hall with his two partners.

"If I were you, Miss, I'd run," Rod said, as a man shorter than the lady herself jumped on his back.

Rod twisted and knocked the man off and out the nearest window. When he spun back to his female companion, he saw the sheriff with a good grip on her arm. As another fist came his way, Rod shielded his face with his left arm, and brought his right fist square into the man's nose bringing blood. He then proceeded to take the muscularly built man off of Matt's neck with his strong right fist.

Two more strong men came towards Rod at the same time. He ducked the man's blow, came up with his fist at the other and knocked him over and down between two pews.

Rod plowed another man in his face with his left fist, and returned to his jaw again with his right.

The man twisted around, but instead of going down, came back swinging. Rod ducked again causing the man's swing to go wild. As he flipped onto Rod's back, Rod grabbed a firm hold of his head and legs, twirled him around and flung him out the window knocking down the three rich men trying to run past the window.

The man got up and, confused, swung his fists at them, causing them to hightail it in the opposite direction. They lit out in their two-horse carriage and drove down the road towards South Carolina.

The sheriff sat the lady down and rejoined the fight with his deputies.

Rod made his way over to her, avoiding the sheriff and his deputies, and wiped his forehead wound with his bandana. "May I introduce myself, Miss?" he asked. "My name is . . ."

He was interrupted by the press of a shotgun placed against the back of his head.

"Rod Best," the man holding the shotgun said, "You're a dead man."

The fighting came to an abrupt halt when the sheriff took his Colt and fired off a round in the air.

Rod turned around and faced his accuser, a heavy-set man who appeared to be somewhere in his thirties, with a black beard and moustache and a mean look on his face.

"Drop the shotgun, or you're dead where you stand."

"Hold it, Sheriff!" the man ordered. "Look around you."

It didn't take much to convince Bull that something went awry. Slowly he turned. At every door and window was a man from Hamilton's gang with a Sharps at each opening, aimed at him.

"Throw your gun down, you're outnumbered."

"Well," Rod said, "it looks to me like you have me at a disadvantage. Mind taking the shotgun from my face?"

"You! I spotted you right off when I came in," the man said pulling back on the shotgun. "You were the one shooting at us down at the ravine. You killed Capt'n Hamilton, too, I hear."

"No," Matt said behind him.

What echoed next were sounds no man ever wanted to hear in his life. They were the repeated clicks from shotguns, from rifles, and from pistols all aimed at him. Men who had come a long way to fight with Matt and Rod saw that other members of their gang were being overrun. They advanced from behind and relieved Hamilton's gang of their weapons, and gave them to their own men.

"I killed Hamilton, jest like I'm gonna kill you if you as much as twitch," Matt yelled out. "Drop the shotgun!"

The black-bearded man froze with his hand on the trigger.

Rod turned, smiled, and put his arms down, but never moved from his spot while the shotgun was still in his face.

"Well, Rod," Matt said, "take the shotgun."

The black bearded man was persistent, and knew he had to face what was happening. Holding his shotgun on Rod, he moved his eyes as far as he could to see who was confronting him in this standoff situation. He saw his men at the windows being relieved of their weapons by Montgomery's men.

"I do believe you can take over now, Matt," Eli said with a grin that stretched from one side of the room to the other while he held his shotgun in the face of the black-bearded man.

"I'll jest take your shotgun to add to our collection," Rod said.

The man still didn't readily comply, and Eli pushed the barrel of his shotgun harder into his gut. It was a standoff, all right.

After some long seconds where the black-bearded man sweated profusely through his heavy coat, he realized he was a thin hair close to meeting the Grim Reaper. He finally brought his shotgun down and turned it over to Eli.

"Thank you," Eli said taking the shotgun. "Now ain't you forgettin' somethin'?"

"What's that?" the man asked with his head bent low almost as if he were ready to crawl away with his tail between his legs.

"You owe this man an apology, attackin' him that away, when he's jest been interduced to a pretty little filly."

Eli waited, but the man remained quiet.

"Apologize, damn it," Eli poked his shotgun into the black-bearded man's ribs.

"All right, I apologize. Now get that iron away from me before it goes off."

Matt escorted the black-bearded man to the front and stood at the bench.

"Well, Judge," Matt said, "looks to me like you jest incarcerated the gang's new leader. And he's already confessed to taking part in the Massacre."

With the help of other members of their gang, Rod and Eli brought the ten men who started the ruckus in the beginning up to the front.

"These men here are the ones you want too, Sheriff," Rod said with a wry grin.

"This one here is the one who yelled," Eli said, as he shoved a young man forward. "Right pretty yell, too. He kinda felt the trial was over a little too soon and decided to give out a victory yell. I think Mrs. Jackson can identify him for you, Sheriff."

Judge Bartley hammered his gavel and continued hammering it again and again and again, until finally the courtroom quieted.

"Sheriff Bull, take these men into custody and jail them." Looking at the man who yelled, he added, "It's going to be a pleasure to see you before me real soon. I find the defendants not guilty. Court dismissed."

The judge joined Matt and Rod out on the parade grounds where Montgomery's gang had the rest of Hamilton's gang lying on the ground and disarmed.

The deputies for both the marshal and the sheriff learned that the Montgomery's gang had held down a near riot when the people heard the confession of the men involved in the Massacre.

The people still stood around with clinched fists as the Hamilton gang was rounded up.

"It's just a good thing you men were here," Judge Bartley said.

"They thought we were just plain folk standin' around, Matt," one of the men said as he held his rifle on the men on the ground. "We backed away letting them think that, and when they weren't lookin', and more of us came in, we took them all by surprise."

"What now, your honor?" Bull asked, watching Walker and his men walk over to join them.

"Any one killed?"

"Not a one, your honor," Bull responded.

"Where are those three men from South Carolina, Marshal?"

"If they were those fat dudes dressed like sissies, we seen them high tailing it south, Judge," one of the farmers spoke up slapping his leg and laughing loudly. Many others of the gang, including Matt and Rod, joined him in laughing.

"Guns and saddles, gentlemen," the judge ordered. "They can have their horses, but keep their guns and saddles. They will help pay your fines for disturbing the peace, and my courtroom."

He walked among the men as they lay in their prone position, and addressed them. "You men are to ride out of here, and join your kind across the border. My name is Judge Gerald T. Bartley. I want you to remember that name, for as long as I am the judge here in this district, you will not set foot again in Kansas. See to it, Bull that they get the hell out of my sight."

Sheriff Bull and his deputies took charge, and let the Montgomery men disperse in an orderly manner.

Ben stood beside the judge as he started to walk away.

Looking at the couple still standing in front of him, he said, "You can go home, now, too. You're cleared."

Sandi approached the judge, stood on her tiptoes and kissed him on the cheek.

"What's that for?" he asked with a smile.

"For marryin' us."

"Oh, yeah. Well. I've never had one come back on me, yet. Now get outa here and enjoy your lives together."

Ben shook the judge's hand, put his arm around Sandi and walked towards the back of the hall through the midst of a smiling crowd, the same crowd that earlier had almost become a mob.

"And kids," the judge added, making Ben and Sandi stop and turn around, "no more raids! Not in my district."

Ben winked at the judge, and with Sandi, watched him walk to his hotel.

It was a welcome sight, watching over two hundred members of the now defunct Hamilton gang ride bareback out of Fort Scott to the jeering of the people. The pistols and rifles resounded along the route to salute their departure.

The judge watched from his window across the parade grounds until the last man rode through the gate and the sun set behind him. He looked down at Matt, Rod, Ben, Sandi, and a certain lady, smiled, and walked away from the window.

Rod took the certain lady with the broken parasol by the arm and walked her towards her carriage. Matt went back to the meeting hall, found and picked up his hat from the floor. Dusting it off, he smiled at the couple as he walked out of the hall alone. "It's my good luck hat," he said.

It was a good day in Fort Scott, for the Montgomery gang had won a decisive victory. With nearly three hundred men, they brought justice to the small town, and created a sense of security for the people for the first time in years.

Most of the Pro-slavers had vanished, and Fort Scott was almost totally free of the Hamilton gang.

The next afternoon, the government troops arrived at Fort Scott and spent the next several days assuring Fort Scott of safety.

The old meeting hall was in the process of transformation as several men and women with hammers, nails, and paint, tackled the job of restoring it.

"Well," Rod said as he walked the lovely young lady to her handsome one-horse carriage. The horse was a black Tennessee Walker and straight-eared all the way. She was a fine specimen of an animal, with a neatly combed mane and tail and polished tack.

"Yes, Rod?" she responded waiting for him to help her up into her carriage.

Obliging her, he offered his arm and gently assisted her into the driver's seat.

"May I call on you sometime, Miss ---?"

"Agnes Bartley," she informed Rod. "And yes, you may call on me."

"Agnes Bartley," Rod said softly as he looked her in her beautiful eyes. "Agnes Bartley. What a nice name. It seems like I've always known you, Miss Agnes Bartley."

Then out of the blue, he gulped and said, "Bartley?"

"Yes, Rod. Agnes Bartley, Judge Bartley's daughter."

With that alarming discovery, Rod never again felt uncomfortable in the presence of a fine lady as Agnes Bartley, for he escorted her daily in her elegant one-horse carriage, and dined elegantly with her father from time to time. He had come into a family of his liking and choosing, and savored every moment of it.

# CHAPTER 18

## AMNESTY

**W**hen Captain James Montgomery healed up to where he could rely on crutches to get around, he and Suzan Martin were married in Fort Scott, Kansas, with Judge Gerald T. Bartley officiating. It was a large wedding, with most of the townsfolk attending, and all of the farmers of Linn and Bourbon Counties. Ben acted as best man, but Matt and Rod got to stand with him

Marshal Walker and Sheriff Bull were among the invitees to the wedding. It was no longer a secret that the real Captain Montgomery was uncovered, for they had all become friends.

"Have a ceegar, gentlemen," Montgomery offered the men at his wedding.

"You havin' one, Capt'n?" Matt asked, lighting his.

"I'm afraid his ceegar smoking days are gone for a while," Suzan retorted in the men's style as she escorted her husband to a lounge chair. "His lung has healed, but Doc told him to stay off cigars."

"I'm glad someone pays attention to what I tell them," Doc said, lighting up his.

The party had waned and many of the guests had gone home when Montgomery took the opportunity to whisper something in Suzan's ear. She smiled and sauntered to his office. She returned in a few minutes with two books from his collection and gave them to him.

"Matt and Rod," Montgomery said, handing them each a book, "may you cherish these pages for a long time. Finish your drinks. You can read them in your spare time."

Suzan walked over to Matt and Rod and said, "Be sure to read chapter one before you go to bed tonight."

Sure enough, the men turned to chapter one before they turned out the light back in their bunks. Each of them found his money in the full amount Montgomery had agreed upon at the beginning of their employ. The sight of it brought a yell that could be heard in both counties.

For the next few weeks, Rod enjoyed escorting his new lady Agnes in her carriage around Linn and Bourbon Counties, showing the people his refined style of living.

Tim's murderer was later found guilty and sentenced to hang at Leavenworth. The men who were with him were also sentenced to Leavenworth at hard labor.

"Brother Rod," Phil said while saddling his horse. "You've found your place. Now, I've got to find mine."

"Hope you're as happy a man as I am," Rod returned.

"You didn't have to split your money down the middle," Phil said mounting his horse.

"Told you before, we're a team. A team don't mean one man is better than other, big brother. Stay in touch."

"Always." Phil spurred his sorrel and road north waving his Stetson.

"We'll see him again, won't we?" Agnes asked slipping her arm around Rod and waving to Phil.

"He'll always be around," Rod replied and waved goodbye to his brother.

On a cold December morning, Judge Gerald T. Bartley summoned Marshal Walker and Sheriff Bull to his chambers.

Both men thought the world was going to come down on them when they stepped into the judge's chambers, for it was only on such dire matters that he would call them into his chambers.

"Your honor," Walker addressed the judge nervously, for he knew he was in for an admonishment from the judge. It seemed the judge enjoyed picking on him at times.

"Sit down, Walker, and you, too Bull," the judge said as he sat at his table with his back turned to the gentlemen. He was writing something in his book, and when he was through, he turned around to face them.

"I have here a decree from Governor Geary's office," he said, giving the paper to the marshal. The Governor had wired the judge that such a decree was forthcoming, but for now it was a simple piece of paper with no official writing on it at all, but one that the judge thought he'd entrust to the marshal right away. It was his way of keeping Rod a little longer, in case he and Agnes decided to get married. He didn't want Rod to leave the state any too soon, figuring Rod and Agnes, who were prone to roam, would not want to make Fort Scott their home.

"What's it say, your Honor?" Bull asked as he looked at the paper in Walker's hand.

"In layman's' language, it simply says, 'let bygones be bygones'."

"Yes, your Honor," Walker said again, attempting to read the decree. "What's that mean?"

"It means that Montgomery and all the Free-Staters are to go free."

The judge looked over his spectacles at the marshal and continued. "You are not to go after Captain Montgomery or any of his gang ever again. They are to be free of any and all charges. That, Marshal Walker, is what it says. And I wholeheartedly agree. I want you to take it out to Captain Montgomery and inform him."

"Yes, your Honor," Walker said. Then repressing his excitement, he stood up. "If we may be excused, your Honor."

"You may, gentlemen."

The two men turned, and walked proudly out of the hall. Walker was certain that U. S. Marshal Whittaker had a lot to do with it, and he was proud to be serving under him.

Bull walked back to his office shaking his head, while Walker rode out to Montgomery's farm.

When Walker reached Montgomery's Farm to tell them the good news, he did so cautiously, for fear that he could still be shot if anyone mistook the intent of his visit.

"Capt'n!" he yelled a hundred feet from the house, waving a white flag of truce.

Motioning for him to come in, Matt and Rod walked out to greet him.

"What is it, Marshal?" Matt asked. "Did we do something wrong again?"

"Hell, no," Marshal replied taking his flag down. "Where's the capt'n?"

"Right where I should be, Marshal," Montgomery said yelling from the porch where a couple of farm hands helped him outside after seeing Walker ride up. He sat down in a large chair and rested his leg over a block of wood, and kept his Sharps close by.

"Say your piece."

"The Governor granted a pardon for all of you. You're free." He waved the piece of paper the judge had given him. "Captain Montgomery," Walker said, "you're free of any and all charges brought agin' you. You and your men are free."

"Is there a hitch?" Matt asked as he and Rod walked up to Walker.

"It's true," he said, turning to them with excitement in his eyes. "They're holding nothing against you. I came all the way out here to tell you."

Matt looked back at everyone watching him and Walker conversing together. He could not keep his eyes off Ben until he saw him disappear with Sandi behind the house. He knew this also meant a pardon for him and his crimes.

Walker turned his horse to head out, stopped, and looked back at Montgomery. "Jest don't ever set my building on fire again, or I'll come down your throat so fast, you'll wish you ain't never been born." He turned again and rode away.

Montgomery and the rest knew the marshal for who he was, a man just living out his job until retirement, and enjoying setting more than two hundred men free from any prosecution by the government.

Matt and Rod threw up their arms, gave out a victory yell, and drew and fired their pistols in rapid succession. Ben and Sandi came from around the back of the house, as did some of the men who heard the commotion from out in the fields.

"Amnesty, my dear brothers," Rod yelled out. "Amnesty!"

Ben and Sandi smiled a moment of relief. "Does that mean we are free to stay, now that no one wants to hang us?" Ben asked Montgomery.

"That it does, Ben," Montgomery smiled. "That it does."

With the pardon, Ben and Sandi knew they were free to stay, and that pleased everyone.

"Why, Ben," Montgomery answered hitting the stump of wood with his cane, "you're going to be my assistant in Topeka."

Matt and Rod had just been biding time, with no hurry to leave. But, now it gave them a reason.

"Does this mean we earned our money, Capt'n?" Rod asked.

"And more," Montgomery agreed.

"Guess we're no longer needed then Capt'n," Matt said. "We've done all the good we can do. You and Ben can head up Kansas and somehow pay back the judge, the marshal and our friend the sheriff for all their help and support. And you can run for Governor, like you wanted."

Montgomery watched as the good news spread among his people. He saw the faces on Matt and Rod, and knew they would be leaving now.

Early the next morning, as frost lay on the ground, and crisp dew was in the air, Matt, Rod and Agnes said their good-byes to Ben and Sandi and to the rest of the farmers who dropped by. Montgomery was dressed smartly and standing on the lawn with Suzan to say farewell to their good friends.

"Well, Capt'n," Matt said," since we're no longer needed, you'll become governor some day, and with Ben as your aide, it's time to light out."

"Like I said at the beginning, Matt," Montgomery reminded him, with laughter he could not contain. "You're free to go anytime you want."

Montgomery's laugh was contagious, for Matt and Rod caught on to what he meant as he said this so many times before. So did the rest of the men standing around, including some of the ladies.

With a serious note, Montgomery added, "You're free to come back any time you'd like, too. All three of you."

The truth of the matter hit them hardest when Matt saddled up Skeeter for the last time on Montgomery's Farm.

Rod had already hitched up a new one-horse buggy rig for him and Agnes, and with his sorrel tied to the back, they waited for Matt.

"Where're you folks goin?" Matt asked, mounting Skeeter.

"Up to a place called Mud Creek," Rod said. "Ever hear of it?"

"Yeah," Matt answered, "I have. There's a man and his family who own a farm up that way. They'd put you up, if you've a mind.

Their name's Hansen, you'll see their name on a post on the main road. Got a little girl, too. Her name's Lori. Their farm hand is a good friend of mine, too."

"You gonna find yourself a 'filly'?" Agnes asked.

"Maybe, some day, if I can find one as beautiful as you.

"All right, Rod. See you two around some time."

The Montgomery hands waved to their three friends as they rode off together.

Eli waved his big muscular arm at them as they rode past his farm, and yelled out, "Ye be stayin' out of trouble, now!"

At the fork two miles up past the farm, Rod Best and his lady friend, Agnes Bartley rode west to Mud Creek, while Matt rode on to Texas.

# PART TWO

# ABILENE, KANSAS

# CHAPTER 19

## ROD BEST'S WIDOW

February 10, 1871

**T**hirteen years didn't make the travel up to Abilene by train any easier. When the Missouri, Kansas & Texas Railway drew up to a stop, Matt stepped out with his luggage in hand.

"Mr. Jorgensen?" a driver asked, taking Matt's bag. "I'm to drive you to the hotel."

Agnes had made the arrangements for Matt to be picked up and taken to the Main Street Hotel to meet Agnes Best, Rod's widow. Arrangements for the meeting were made earlier by telegram.

When they reached the hotel, Matt climbed out and handed the driver some coins. "Thanks, I can manage from here."

Matt walked up to the desk and inquired about Agnes' where-abouts.

"She's in the dining room having something to eat, I reckon," the desk clerk pointed out to Matt. "Down the hall on the left through the glass doors."

Matt took his bag and walked into the dining room. It was an impressive hotel, rails and banisters, ferns, and waiters in uniforms with gold braiding on them.

Seated at the far end of the dining room was one of the most beautiful women Matt had ever seen. It wasn't too difficult to recognize her, she wore a wide-plumed hat and expensive clothes. She sat with a man who appeared to Matt to be her bodyguard. He had a tranquil nature, tall and slim, young, and looked to be slightly handsome to Matt and in his late teens. He had sandy curly hair, blue eyes and stood medium height, a clean face with a shadow of a moustache.

Matt sauntered over to her, taking in her beauty. He remembered her riding out with Rod thirteen years earlier, wearing a similar outfit and carrying a parasol.

"Agnes," he said, in a somber voice, setting his bag down.

Her eyes complemented her face, which was still young and radiant. "Matt," she replied, extending her hand to meet his.

"May I?" he asked, and kissed her hand.

She motioned for him to take a seat. "This is my brother, Ian."

"Agnes told me about you in her letters." Matt extended the welcome. "I'm glad to know you, Ian."

"Under different circumstances, Mr. Jorgensen," Ian returned.

"Did you enjoy your trip?" Agnes asked. "I had my driver pick you up."

"Yes, I guess," Matt replied. "It was an experience. Treated me like a gentleman. Even took my bags."

Ian looked at Matt's gun. "You're from Texas?"

"A ranch, just south of Waco."

"What do you do?"

"I help run the spread, you might say," Matt returned, tongue in cheek.

"You knew Mr. Best quite well, from what Agnes tells me."

"Well, we sort of grew up together."

"They were hired guns," Agnes interrupted. "Don't be modest, Matt."

"Yes, you told me. He's the famous Brazos Kid. I just wanted him to tell me."

"The name's, Matt. You may call me Brazos, if you like."

"He didn't mean to be curt," Agnes continued. "It's just that he's from Ohio, and they really don't have gun play there like they do here. I rather think he is fancying your getup and gun."

"It seems to be the sport here," Ian said, "and I don't care for it at all. It's the reason for Marshal Best's demise."

"So, where's your abode?"

"I live here in town, Matt. Judge Bartley left me a nice size house, and I stay pretty busy, if I say so my self."

"I'm sorry about your father."

"Hard to believe it's been five years."

"You two would like some time to get reacquainted. Why don't I take your bag? We already have you checked in," Ian volunteered. "Room 221 at the top of the stairs."

Ian left and went to the lobby. A waiter came to the table.

"What would you like, Matt?" Agnes asked.

"Bourbon," Matt replied.

"I'll have the same, thank you," she told the waiter, "and you can take my champagne away."

The waiter smiled, picked up the two glasses, and left with a bow.

"Why are you smiling?" Matt asked.

"Because you, Rod, and I always drank bourbon together back at Montgomery's."

"Those were the days," Matt laughed.

He sat still for a moment and reflected on the past. Unsure of how he should ask her about Rod, he held his glass for the longest time and looked out into emptiness.

"What are you thinking, Matt?"

"About Rod, and the good times. I don't know how to talk about him."

"You want to know how it happened?"

"Yes. Yes I do," Matt answered, putting his glass down. "How did it happen, Agnes? You don't have to talk about this if you don't feel up to it."

"You're the only person I feel I can talk to, Matt," she confided. "It was awful. He was always a very cautious man. When he walked in to the saloon, he'd scan the crowd, and after stepping up to the bar, he'd look back at them again through the bar mirror."

"I still do. Learned it from Rod."

"This one time, he apparently forgot, and, well, this weasel," she continued, "snuck up behind him and stood there, out of his line of sight. When he knew Rod couldn't see him, he called him out and drew."

"I read about some of it in the papers."

"Well, he and some cowpokes were laughing, and it gave that weasel the opportunity to take his gun out, and pull the trigger. Had Rod not been laughing so hard, he would have seen the man with the gun."

"You just answered two questions that have been running through my mind," Matt said. "Why he didn't use the mirror right away, and why he didn't know someone was pulling a gun on him. Hell, Rod could smell someone pulling a gun on him a mile off."

"Well, I'm told everyone at the bar was laughing because he was drunk, Matt. They claimed he had a woman with him. If they didn't want him as marshal, why didn't they just tell him? Vote him out or something. They didn't have to get him drunk and kill him."

"You're sayin' it was all a plan to get rid of Rod?" Matt asked.

The waiter came and set their glasses down. Matt kept still and looked around the room until he left. Matt sensed the world was listening at that moment.

He raised his glass of bourbon slightly and clicked it with Agnes' glass. "To Rod. May he always be remembered."

"And may his killer be hung and rot in hell," she added, and sipped her drink.

"Let's get out of this place, Agnes, and go someplace where we can be alone."

Matt stopped her hand as she opened her purse to pay for her meal. "Keep your money, Agnes," he said, laying some bills on the table as he stood up. "A lady in my company never pays."

Agnes took another sip, put the glass down and stood up.

Matt quickly noticed her condition when he took her by the hand and helped her to her feet. He could only smile through his surprise.

"Matt," she said, wiping a tear from her eye. "I'm carrying Rod's child."

"That's wonderful, Agnes!" Matt exclaimed with excitement. "I'm happy for you."

"Think it's a boy?" Matt mused.

"It's wishful, Matt. I'm starting to carry him high. Oh, he'll be a wild one just like his dad, I know. But, if she's a girl, she'll be the best damn looking girl in town. Makes no difference. Now can we leave because it feels like everyone's eyes are on me?"

She left the dining room and allowed herself to be escorted by Matt to the hotel.

Ian met the couple in the lobby. "I waited to see what you would like to do next," Ian said.

"I want to take Matt to see Rod." She stopped at the door and waited for Matt to open it. "Don't be too far off."

Matt and Agnes walked over to her one-horse carriage just outside the hotel while Ian went back into the dining room.

"The same type of carriage you had in Fort Scott," Matt said.

"You remembered."

"You always had class. Where are we headed?" Matt asked as he lifted her up into her carriage.

"To visit Mr. Best, of course."

"Of course."

The ride outside of town with a lovely lady on his arm in an open carriage was good for Matt's soul and ego. He remembered the good times when the three of them would get together. Wherever they went together, they seemed to forget their worries, and instead concentrated on being together.

He also remembered the warm feelings he had for her. She was the prettiest lady in town. But, he kept his distance from her at all times, out of respect for the one man he admired, Rod Best. Had it been the other way around, and he had been the one who fell in her lap, Rod would have given the same respect to him.

The sound of the horse's hooves beating on the roadway seemed to keep time with the couple's thoughts as they headed out to the cemetery where Rod laid buried.

"He had many friends, Matt. Seemed the whole town came out for this funeral. Oh, Matt, he was laid out in an elegant coffin. I had him dressed in his finest Prince Albert frock coat, riding breeches, and dark blue flannel shirt with a sash around his waste. I kept his pearl-handled revolver, but he kept his Sharps. He always told me he'd never be without it. I know he would have been pleased."

"I wish I could have been here."

"You are now. That's what counts. We didn't have a hearse, so they made a litter and a fine stallion of a horse pulled it slowly down the street for all to see. Our friend, Wichita, who owns the saloon in town where Rod got shot, had the coffin decorated with silver, and draped in the black. It seemed the whole town followed him. When we crossed the creek, most of the people stayed on the other side, while a few of his friends crossed over. It was so sweet and beautiful. The preacher said just the right words, and Rod was laid to rest."

The grave had been prepared on the mountainside toward the east. They found it and Matt saw that the grave marker was a tree stump. Matt got out first, went to Agnes' side of the carriage and, taking her hand, escorted her to the gravesite. Dusting some snow away from the wood stump, Matt read the inscription.

*"Rod Best*

*A brave man murdered by a coward*

*Age 37 years*

*February 1, 1871"*

Standing at the foot of the grave, Agnes reflected the writing on the stump. Wichita had a woodcarver cut the words deep into the stump.

"Isn't it beautiful?"

"Yes, it is beautiful."

"I'd like to replace it, though, with a more permanent one later."

"You were sayin' you thought it was a conspiracy, Agnes," Matt reminded her as he watched her lovely smile turn into tears.

"It had to have been. The killer said Rod was messing around with his girl. When Rod turned and drew on him, he said he had to defend himself."

"That's what the papers reported," Matt said, taking her hand in his. "Rod wasn't a woman chaser. He didn't need to, he had you."

"And he could out drink the best of us when he wanted to, remember?" Agnes added. "But not on the job. He was too dedicated a marshal."

Embracing her to give her comfort, he was comforted himself. The two stood in each other's arms for a moment, relaxing and letting the tension of the moment pass by. When Agnes finished sobbing, she looked up into Matt's blue eyes, and then looked around the cemetery.

"What a hell of a place to feel like I do right now," she said, breaking her grief-stricken face with a smile.

"Friendship is sometimes unexplainable, Agnes," Matt returned with a smile. "We all had a great love for one another. That won't ever go away."

"Thanks, Matt," she said, taking her dainty hanky from her sleeve and dotting her nose with it. "I believe more people were involved other than that son-of-a-bitch. You saw Abilene. It's just becoming a town. But a lot of dishonest folk don't want the town cleaned up. Rod did, and he kept it clean so that decent folk could live here."

Matt was concerned for Agnes' safety and security in Abilene.

She walked a few feet away from the gravesite, stopped and turned back. She looked at the other gravesites around and kicked a clod of dirt with her boot. She turned, took off her wide-plumed hat, and held it in her hands while she put her hands on her hips.

"Damn you, Rod Best!" she shouted to the wind. "Why'd you have to go and die?"

Matt stood and watched her, and said nothing.

"He came here to be the marshal of Abilene. Judge Bartley got him the job, and we developed friends. Matt, my life is here with him," she reflected. "I'll raise our child in the town he loved."

"Is your father buried here?"

"Over there beside my mother," she said, pointing down the path from where Rod laid. "Mud Creek . . . Abilene has been my home all my life," she mused. "I've got good friends here."

Matt walked over to Agnes, took her hat from her hand and placed it clumsily back on her head. She took a pin out and secured it neatly back on her head, and smiled.

He took her gently in his arms, held her tenderly, and they stood there for what felt like an eternity, allowing Rod's spirit to intertwine them and the grass, the trees, and the cold gray Kansas sky.

The couple stood at Rod's grave and held hands, and then slipped their arms ever so gently around each other's waists and watched the sun set in Abilene, Kansas, February 10, 1871.

# CHAPTER 20

## MEETING THE KILLER

**M**att and Agnes entered the dining room of the Abilene Hotel and were escorted to a table by the headwaiter. Once seated, the waiter offered his services.

"We'll both have bourbon, thank you," Matt ordered and watched the waiter walk away. He and Agnes stayed focused on the circumstances surrounding Rod's death. Matt leaned back in his chair against the dining room wall and looked over at Agnes while he took out a cigar.

"Mind?"

"I've always loved the smell of a good cigar," Agnes answered.

Matt lit up his cigar. "Those were the days," he said, exhaling a stream of cigar smoke. "I've always thought about Fort Scott, Captain Montgomery, and Suzan. How are they doing?"

"Suzan and I stay in touch. They moved back to Ohio. James gave up his run for governor here, but he's still in politics. They've got two children, a boy and a girl."

"Wonderful. And Ben. How's he doing?"

The waiter interrupted their conversation, set their drinks down and left.

"Sandi's a widow. Ben was caught and hung. He said it would be his last raid. It was."

"Sorry to hear that. Very sorry." He thought back on the day he saw Ben shoot the soldier in the back at Paint Creek. *Justice caught up with you Ben.*

"Sandi's remarried. A dirt farmer. They live just outside of town, pretty close to Martha's place."

"Martha? I haven't heard from her, well since I left."

"I knew you'd get around to that. We've talked about you ever since Frank died. She's never forgotten you, Matt."

"Remarried by now, I suppose?"

"No. She and Lori run the farm quite well with the help of some hired hands. Oh, she's been at socials, and from time to time I see her with a beau, but nothing serious." Agnes looked into his blue eyes and saw compassion. "Would you like to see her?"

"I'm sorry about Frank," Matt answered. He looked back at her, and sensed that she suspected something. "Did you tell her anything about me?"

"Oh, how well you were, and how you went through the Civil War, unscathed, and all that. I told her you came out a Captain, and got a job down in Texas. She knew about you through me all these years."

"What does she say?"

"She wanted to hear from you, I suppose. Like me, she was brought up waiting for the boy to ask."

"How could I ask if I didn't know?"

Agnes took another sip of her bourbon slowly, laid the glass down and said, "You never answered my question."

"Yes, Agnes. I would like to see her."

She looked at Matt with a frown, and then smiled. "She's in town. I'll let her know." She looked at Matt again and said, "I'll settle my father's estate, and carry on the Bartley name with Rod's child. God, I hope it's a son."

"What?" Matt asked, his mind still on wanting to see Martha. "I'm sorry." Matt saw the hurt look in her eye when he was talking about Martha. Maybe Agnes wanted him to take up the void in her life. He looked at her and chuckled. "I remember the day you swung at everyone with your parasol during Ben's trial."

"That's when I first met Rod."

"You two fell in love right then, as if your were made for each other."

Agnes looked into his eyes. "If Martha isn't the one, Matt," she said biting her lip, and blotting her eyes to keep from crying.

Matt sat and watched her, and took hold of her hand. He knew what she meant, even though she didn't finish what she was saying. "I'm not the marryin' kind, Agnes. I doubt if Martha would have me after all these years. I'm thirty-five, single, and have no girlfriends. If there's no spark between Martha and me, and I decide I want to get hitched, I'd climb a mountain to ask for your hand. But I must say in all sincerity, I do not intend on gettin' hooked by anyone."

Ian ran into the dining room, composed himself, and finding them, walked up to their table.

"Sit down, Ian," Matt said, as he rose and offered him a chair. "Dinner's on me."

"I'm not hungry at the moment, thank you, Matt," he returned, drawing the cushioned-chair out and sitting down.

"Where have you been all day?" Agnes inquired, sipping her bourbon.

"These people think we're spying on them," Ian said looking around.

"I wonder where they got that idea," Matt said, rather tongue-in-cheek.

"We found our man," Ian said in a whisper.

"We're through here," Agnes replied, rising. "Let's go up to your room where we can talk."

When they reached his room, Matt opened the door with a key and allowed Agnes to enter, and he and Ian followed her. He closed the door and offered a chair to Agnes.

"He's back at the Main Street Saloon," Ian said. "I'll point him out to you."

"Thanks, Ian, but I won't need anyone to point him out. Jest tell me what the varmint looks like."

"He's in his thirties, dark black hair, clean shaven, and well dressed. He's also got a woman in a red dress on his arm, and it ain't the same woman who he claimed was his wife. I saw his so-called wife before, and it ain't her," Ian said fidgeting with his fingers. "Sure you don't want me along?"

"You stay here at the hotel, both of you. I don't want to attend any more funerals," Matt said.

He checked his Colt to make sure it was loaded with six rounds. He also felt the ease from which his Colt slid out of its holster. He was ready. He left and headed for the Abilene Saloon. "Be careful Matt," he heard Agnes say.

When he threw back the swinging doors of the saloon and entered, heads turned to examine the tall cowboy. His height and the way he carried himself made eyes shift towards him. He was no ordinary cowpoke in for a drink or for a hand of cards for the evening. They could tell he was a man bent for trouble.

Four men were playing cards at the table near the door, but neither man fit the description of the killer, Paul Windsor. Matt walked past the second table. Finally, at the last table, a man sat with his back to the wall who did fit the description. A woman in a red dress stood beside him.

Matt took a hold of an empty chair and threw it aside, freeing space around him, which he needed to draw. Everyone's attention was immediately drawn to him, and the crowd hushed.

"Your name Paul Windsor?" Matt watched the man's hands as they held onto the cards.

The woman in the red dress quickly moved away.

"Who're you?" the man asked.

"If you're Paul Windsor, I'm calling you out."

"What for? I don't know you."

"You'll have a short time to get to know me. Stand up and draw."

"Don't let him push you around like that, Paul," the woman in the red dress yelled out to him.

"Thanks, lady," Matt replied, keeping his eyes fixed on Paul.

"I'm not in the habit of getting' myself killed over nothin', stranger," the man said nervously. He looked around at others at the table.

"What do you want him for?" the dealer asked, rising and slowly backing away from the table. The other two card players followed suit.

"Jest want to see what color his back is," Matt returned.

"Anyone know who he is?" Paul asked.

"The Brazos Kid," Wichita said from behind the bar. "He's a friend of the marshal you killed."

Wichita was tall like Matt, but not too handsome. He wore expensive-looking clothes to give him an air of dignity. He was blond and wore a moustache and goatee.

Matt glared at the man's eyes as they widened at what he had just heard.

"You killed him! Now, tell your wife to go home."

"I'm not his wife, and he ain't married," the woman corrected Matt. "So, leave him alone."

"Get up, mister!" Matt listened for the clicking of any guns around him, or for any movement towards him. There was none.

Paul laid his cards face down and placed his hands on top of the table. "I ain't got no beef with you."

"You killed a good friend of mine." Matt said, waiting for Paul to make his first mistake. "You told everyone he was drunk and making out with your woman."

"So? He was." Paul laughed loudly, and then looked at the people around him.

"Your woman? You mean like her?" Matt pointed at the woman in red.

"You can leave her out of it, Brazos," Wichita said. "She works for me. Some other woman came in with him. I didn't see her but a few minutes before Paul threatened the marshal at the bar."

"You're lyin'!" Paul shouted back at Wichita.

"Was she reason enough to kill a man? Get up!" Matt ordered and pushed the table into his gut.

"It was a fair fight. Ask Wichita. Ask the rest here." Paul nervously rose and put his hands up high. "Hell, I'm not stupid enough to draw agin' you." He turned and faced the wall. "Here, you can see the color of my back."

"We knew the marshal had a drink," Wichita added, "but I don't know if he was drunk. He could have been, and Paul here accused him of it. He told him that he was messing with his woman."

"Shut up!" Paul shouted and turned back around. He dropped his hand to draw, and stopped.

"Do it! Draw! I'll turn my back like the Marshal Best had his back turned." Matt turned his back on Paul and peered at him through the bar room mirror. He waited for Paul to make his move.

Wichita moved between the two men and blocked Matt's vision long enough for Paul to take advantage.

Paul drew his pistol, but Matt, hearing him slap leather, whipped his Colt out with lightning speed, fanned it, and put three bullets in Paul's chest before Paul could cock the hammer on his gun.

Paul's body fell backwards and hit the wall with a loud thud, bounced and fell forward onto the saloon floor, dead. His blood spilled and flowed from his body and covered a stain where Rod's body had lain nine days earlier. It was as if Rod had swallowed him up whole.

"I'll attest that this man drew first." Wichita walked from behind the bar and stood over Paul's lifeless body. "Someone call the mortician."

"Never saw anything like it afore in my life," a voice said from the back.

Matt looked angrily at Wichita for blocking his view. He said nothing but walked away, throwing the saloon doors wide open as he left.

Agnes and Ian ran across the street from the hotel to meet Matt.

"Was he in there?" Agnes said, putting her arm around Matt.

"Still is."

The mortician came walking down the sidewalk towards the saloon escorted by a couple of men from the saloon.

"Hungry?" Matt walked back to the hotel with Agnes, "We've never finished our dinner."

"I'm really not hungry," Agnes said walking to her carriage where her brother was standing waiting for them. "Seems that I've lost my appetite for some reason. Why don't we postpone our dinner until tomorrow evening? They'll have the Saturday night dance in the ball room."

Before the night was through, the whole town knew the Brazos Kid was in town and had avenged the death of Marshal Rod Best. The story of Paul's blood spilling onto the same floor as Rod's made interesting reading the next day in the *Abilene Journal*.

Two men who read about it were Jim Brandy and Blacky Farnsworth. Both were young men in their twenties, hard drinking cahoots whose gambling and fighting had already built them a bad reputation in Abilene. Word of a stranger in town avenging the murder of the previous marshal was of interest to them. They were the men at the bar laughing with Marshal Best the night he was murdered, and their thoughts of making some extra money filled their greedy minds as they saddled up and rode to Abilene.

# CHAPTER 21

## *Three Ladies and a gent*

Matt walked slowly down the stairs to the lobby of the hotel. He was dressed in a dark suit with a string tie, and a fancy brocaded waistcoat under his suit jacket. A cigar added to the picture of sartorial perfection as his presence graced the curved staircase of the hotel.

He noticed a young lady sitting in the lobby. She appeared to be in her late teens. He stopped in the middle of the stairs and gazed upon her beauty, feeling he was certain he had seen her before.

He continued down the stairs at a slower pace, took the cigar from his lips, approached her and stopped. He did recognize her, he thought, *but she's much younger. Much, much younger.*

"Martha?" he asked as he stood there in a complete trance almost dropping his cigar. *Of course it was her,* he thought. *But how could she have possibly kept her youthful and trimmed figure, and beautiful looks?*

The young lady rose to greet him and politely said, "No. I'm Lori, Martha's daughter. And you must be Matt Jorgensen. My mother has talked about you often. I'm sorry, but I only vaguely remember you."

Matt saw in her all the elegant beauty of Martha. He was completely dumbfounded with delight as he continued feasting his eyes on her beauty. She appeared to be so well mannered and proper as if she had graduated from the finest school for girls.

"Lori?" he addressed her.

How quickly his mind went to the day he set eyes on her as a five year old girl.

Matt took her gloved-hand and politely kissed it. You have grown into a beautiful young lady."

"You say that to every lady you see?" a light feminine voice sounded behind him.

He turned, still holding onto Lori's hand and recognized Martha standing in the doorway with the sunlight silhouetting her slim figure.

"Martha!" He ran over to her and clutched her in his arms.

They broke away and looked into each other's eyes.

He gained his composure, looked around and said, "You're more beautiful than ever. My God, it's good to see you. Please, sit down." Matt escorted the ladies back to the hotel divan where Lori had been sitting.

"I heard about Frank, Martha. I'm sorry," Matt continued, sitting in a chair next to the ladies. "It must have been pretty hard on you."

"It was just after Toothless passed away."

"Toothless gone, too? Damn. I sure liked that ol' coot." In his excitement of seeing Lori and Martha, he felt a sadness as well about the loss of two good friends.

"It was difficult for a while. When Frank died, I had to refocus on my life. It was called Mud Creek when you were there. Remember?"

"Yeah."

"Agnes has us staying at her house while we're in town. She and Rod have been friends of ours ever since you had them drop by after you left for Texas."

"Remember? You told Rod and Agnes to drop by and visit with us when you left." Lori said. "He told some good stories about you and him."

"Agnes is supposed to be stopping by for dinner. You've got to join us," Matt said taking her hand as he stood.

"She's the reason we're here, Matt," Martha said with a smile. "She invited us, too."

"Well," Agnes' voice broke in as she entered the hotel lobby, "what are we all waiting for? Let's eat."

She was dressed in a long flowing gown with opened chiffon, decorated with little blue ribbons, and flowing in the cold breeze from the doorway. She wore a jacket around her shoulders, and had gloves on.

"Ladies," Matt said, taking Agnes' hand. "Shall we?"

"Ian is tending to the carriage," Agnes informed them. "He'll be along in a moment."

Matt led the ladies into the dining room.

The headwaiter escorted them to a table, seated them and left them to assign a waiter to their table.

"Ladies," Matt said with a grin, "we'll have a drink, if we can find a waiter."

No sooner had he said that than one appeared, pouring cool water, and then waited for their order.

"We're goin' to have the best meal possible. Let's start with a drink. There will be five of us, and we're goin' to enjoy this evening."

The waiter took their order for drinks and bumped into Ian on his way out.

Ian was late in joining, but when he saw them, he walked over.

"Someone is stirring up the people in the street, Brazos," he said sitting down. "Rumor is that you're going to kill everyone who didn't like Rod."

Matt sat back, put his hand to his chin, and pondered what Ian had said.

The ladies looked worried and wondered what Matt was thinking.

He looked at Ian, and then at the ladies, grinned and said, "let's eat. I'm famished."

The evening's festivities were capped by the dance held in the ballroom of the hotel. When the five of them entered the room, he had the uncomfortable feeling that eyes were staring at him.

Matt had always loved dancing, and when he saw them playing the merriest of dance numbers, he just had to get out there and dance. His first choice of course was with the lovely Agnes.

"Agnes," he said, bowing to her politely, "may I have this waltz?"

The two stepped out onto the dance floor and began to dance. The other couples on the floor stopped and walked off the floor. Matt and Agnes watched them as they left, and kept on dancing. After awhile, the music came to a halt, and everyone stood listening.

"Beautiful music they're playing, isn't it?" Matt asked as he continued dancing with her, cautious with her delicate condition.

"Oh, Matt, shouldn't we stop dancing?"

"Are you tired, m'lady?"

"The music has stopped, and the people are staring at us."

"And what does Rod say, m'lady?"

"Rod says, to hell with them. Let's dance."

And they continued dancing until Agnes felt a little weary and Matt took her back to her table.

"Ah, Martha," he said, putting his hand to his ear pretending to hear the band play, which had still remained silent. "The band has started up again. Marvelous music. Would you do me the honor, Ma'am?"

She took his arm, and waltzed onto the floor just like she did at Fort Scott, Kansas thirteen years earlier. He reeled her out, brought her back, twirled her around, and marched with her side-by-side, and back again with the rhythm of the imaginary waltz.

"You dance just as you did then," Matt said softly in her ear. "And you're more radiantly beautiful tonight than you were then."

"And you are as handsome as ever, decked in your neat suit, and silk vest," she said smiling, oblivious to the fact that no music was playing, and that people began chattering about them.

He accompanied Martha back to her table and sat her down.

He looked at Ian, and shook his head. "Don't you dance, Ian?" he asked. "I'm sure Lori here would love to dance with you."

"No, sir," Ian answered sheepishly. "I never learned."

"In that case, may I have this dance with a princess?" He bowed to Lori and offered his hand. "The waltz or the reel. Ah, it is the reel that they are playing. Too fast for you?"

Lori giggled and took his hand, and the two began doing a faster dance than before. The faster their feet kept in rhythm to the imaginary band, the louder their laughter became. Even the ladies and gentlemen at the other tables were beginning to have a good time and joined in the laughter.

The band started up again with the downbeat of the conductor's baton, and some of the others joined in the dance. They began playing the reel, and Matt and Lori were already in step. They laughed and danced together until the music stopped.

Matt looked over at Agnes and Martha, and knew he could not last the night without one of them feeling slighted, and when the music stopped, he took Lori back to the table.

"Ladies," he said, "it's gettin' late."

"And I am very tired," Agnes interrupted. "I'm sorry. I must be getting home. Ian, would you bring the carriage around for me.

Matt rose and helped Agnes get up while Ian left for the carriage.

Martha and Lori gathered their belongings. "We must be getting back too, Matt," Martha said.

"No, no," Agnes said quickly. "You two stay and have a good time. Besides, here comes a stranger. I'm sure the gentleman will want to dance with Lori."

"I'm sure he would, too," Martha said, watching the man come to the table, "but we'll go with you, Agnes, if you don't mind."

Matt saw the look in Martha's eyes like that of a protective mother.

"Ladies," the cowboy said doffing his hat. "I hope you're not leavin."

"Yes, we are," Agnes said. "We're sorry, but I'm rather tired."

"Does that mean the whole party has to leave?" the man asked, standing with a look of dismay on his face. He was tall, in his mid-twenties, with sandy curly hair and blue eyes. He wore a suit and string tie with a black Stetson. His gun belt was tied low on his thigh like he was a fast draw.

Matt saw no threat in him at the moment, maybe because of his friendly attitude and winsome smile.

"We'll see you tomorrow, gentlemen," Martha said gripping Lori's elbow and leading her out. Her eyes stayed on Matt's eyes for a while, and then she turned and left with Lori, following Agnes and Ian.

"Did I come at the wrong time?" the man asked

"There never seems to be a right time," Matt answered.

The gentlemen sat down and summoned the waiter to their table.

"Beer!" he called out, "and keep 'em comin'."

"I'm Tex Barnett," the stranger introduced himself to Matt. "I was at Rod's funeral."

"From Texas?"

"San Antone."

"Nice meetin' you, Tex. You know mine by now?"

"I heard them call you, Brazos. I know the Brazos down Texas way."

"A ranch South of Waco."

"Rod talked about you once or twice. You and he wiped out fifty of the Hamilton gang down in Fort Scott, all by yourself."

"That's Rod," Matt said with a smile. "Always exaggerating."

"Sorry about disruptin' your party, but I thought, one guy with three gals ... well you know," Tex said taking out a cigar. "Want one?"

"Now you're talking."

Matt felt comfortable having another man around to talk with, and talk they did until early morning.

# CHAPTER 22

## THE SHOWDOWN

I n town that night Brandy and Blacky agreed on a high price for the head of the Brazos Kid. They were informed that he was staying in room 221 at the Abilene Hotel.

When they got to Matt's room, they kicked down the door and fired their .44's into the darkened room, mostly at the bed, but they also peppered the wall. They turned up the gaslight and found the room to be empty.

Matt stood at the end of the dim-lit hallway with his legs straddled, and his .45 aimed at the would-be killers.

"Gentlemen, you missed," Matt said with his cigar clinched tight in his jaw.

Blacky and Brandy realized their mistake too late, for as they turned to meet Matt's Colt, their last thought was how foolish they were for anteing up in the first place. Flashes of fire from Matt's Colt were the last things they saw as they fell dead in front of Matt's room.

Matt slipped back inside his room and waited for the crowd to gather.

The hotel clerk was the first of many who came cautiously up the stairs. When half-a-dozen men reached the hallway, they saw the two bodies in front of room 221.

Matt opened the door and watched them examining the bodies. He had quickly undressed to make it appear that he hadn't been involved in the shootout, and stood there in his union suit with his cigar between his teeth, and said, "Hard place for a man to get some sleep. Might have to move out."

No one witnessed what happened, and the incident looked like just another gunfight between two men in a hallway. Nothing was said about the attempt on Matt's life, or the holes in his room, no one bothered to look inside. Besides, Matt looked innocent as he stood in front of everyone in just his long underwear.

The mortician came and, with the help of some of the men milling around, removed the bodies. Matt went back into the room, dressed and with his gun strapped on, went back to sleep.

The loud bang on the door made Matt jump out of bed.

"Door's unlocked," Matt said. He stood on the far side of the bed.

Several men entered the dimly lit room and faced Matt "You're coming with us, mister," the sheriff said, pointing a shotgun at him. A group of men had formed a posse to arrest Matt.

The sheriff was a big bruiser, weighing in around three hundred pounds on a five-foot ten frame. He looked menacing enough to pull the trigger at the slightest provocation. Actually, Willie's real job was farming, but he was elected as temporary sheriff because of his size. Behind Sheriff Willie was another man in the group dangling a rope with a hangman's knot in it.

Matt pulled his Colt, cocked it, and had in Willie's face faster than Willie could cock his held weapon.

"Tell them to drop their guns, Sheriff, now!" Matt barked. He pushed his .45 against Willie's cheekbones demonstrating he meant what he said.

"Don't shoot, anyone," Willie shouted in his high tenor range. "Drop your weapons boys, or he'll kill me."

Matt took the shotgun away from him, turned the big man around, and put its barrel to his back.

"What are the charges, Sheriff?" Matt stopped carefully scrutinizing the man with the rope.

"You murdered two of my friends," Sheriff Willie said.

"Your friends? Not that I murdered anyone, but they jest happened to be your friends? Sheriff, have one of your men turn up the lantern. Your 'friends' shot up my bedroom, including my bed; they were tryin' to kill me."

"That ain't the way I heard it," the man shot back with saliva dripping from his lips. "You'd be dead if they did that. Them men were good shots."

One of the men turned up the lantern. The sheriff and the rest saw bullet holes across the wall.

"Mister, they missed me because I wasn't in bed. But I didn't. I was out in the hallway defending myself. Some of your men are standing in the blood stains where they fell."

Some of the other men who were standing at the doorway jumped back.

He kept the shotgun on the sheriff and his .45 on the rest of his admirers, especially the one with the rope.

"Put the rope down, friend, or you'll be wearin' it." Tex stepped into the room and relieved the man of the rope. He stood with his .44 in hand. "Need any help, Brazos?" he asked.

The rest of the men stood gazing at Tex's demanding presence.

Tex cocked his .44, held it high for all to see, and yelled, "Now everybody calm down!"

Matt welcomed his presence and continued talking with the sheriff.

"It sure looks like self defense from where I stand," the stranger said. "You see any different, Willie?"

"Somebody said you killed them in cold blood," Willie nervously shot back.

"Yeah, and their guns were in their holsters when the desk clerk came up," another man yelled outside the door.

"Well, where is the desk clerk now?" Matt asked.

"I'm back here," he said, cowering behind the rest of the group. "We were talking and I told them I thought their guns were in their holsters, and I really thought they were."

Matt gave the shotgun to Tex.

"Stay there," Matt said moving through the crowd. "You still with me, Tex?"

"I've got them covered," Tex said with a grin.

"You saw them, one on top the other just like they laid," Matt said pointing with his .45 to the place where the men fell. "Think. All I want you to do is tell them where you saw their guns."

The desk clerk remained silent.

"Marv," Tex said keeping Willie and the others at bay with his Colt. "I was here and I saw how they laid. Their guns were completely out of their holsters, mister. I put them back in when I helped moved the bodies."

"Then that's maybe what I saw," the desk clerk added with a sigh of relief.

"Try getting a better pair of glasses," Matt said, and walked over to Tex.

"Thanks for coming forward," Matt said, shaking his hand.

"Don't like a railroading and this had all the earmarks of one."

"Good thing you came along when you did and had a few beers, else I coulda been killed. Just got up the back stairs when it all happened."

The group of men dispersed and Willie came out of Matt's room with the man who had the rope.

Matt took the shotgun from Tex and gave it back to Willie. "Am I free to go, Sheriff?"

"I'm sorry, Brazos," Willie said. "I only moved on what I was told."

"Jest who told you?"

"Someone at the saloon," Willie returned.

"Who at the saloon?"

"You know?" Willie answered nervously. "This person you know said he heard these two men were just walking down the hallway when you shot them for no reason."

"Saloon, huh?" Matt started down the stairs with Tex following him. "I wonder why."

"It's a small town," Willie added following them out of the hotel. "Go back to Texas, if you want my advice."

"Can I guy you a beer?" Matt walked down the hall, and Tex followed.

"Just thinking about having one, Brazos," Tex said. They turned and walked down stairs while Willie and the rest of the group disbanded. "And I know just where to get the best beer in town," Tex said.

"Well, what are we waitin' for?"

The two men headed down the middle of the street towards the Abilene saloon.

A shot rang out, and the sound of a rifle bullet whizzed past Matt's ear, piercing a man's head walking behind him, and killing him instantly.

Matt turned and saw a rider in the far distance put his rifle back into its scabbard and ride off.

Willie saw Matt's vain attempt to get a horse and ran to his own horse tied on the other side of the street. "Take my horse. He's right here." He untied his sorrel and gave the reins to Matt. "He's fast as hell, Brazos."

Matt mounted up quickly and chased after the killer.

The killer knew the town better than Matt, and attempted to elude him by going through back streets where the laundry was still hanging low on the lines.

Matt stayed with him through the streets and out of town, through mud holes and across gullies.

The ride went through camps, up one side of a hill and across the creek close to where Rod was buried. The rider reined up, took his rifle and, taking a bead, yanked the trigger and, because he did, missed.

Matt flew off his horse and rolled for cover, brought his .45 up and fired. A bullet busted the man's rifle to splinters. A second bullet went through the man's shoulder and knocked him to the ground.

"Don't shoot!" he yelled. "I'm hit already."

Matt walked over to him and noticed that he was a well-dressed gent.

"Get up, mister," Matt ordered, picking him up under his good arm. He took the killer's .44 and stuck it inside his belt.

"I got you real good," he said examining the killer's shoulder wound. "If you're lucky, you'll die before we get back to town. Save you from havin' to hang."

He tore the man's shirt and used part of it for a bandage, which he stuck in the bullet hole to stop the bleeding. "Why did you shoot at us, mister?"

"Tried to kill you," the killer coughed out.

"I figured. Why?"

"You would have found out."

"About what?"

The killer coughed and his eyes rolled back into their sockets, and he passed out.

The ride back to town took much longer with the wounded killer draped over his horse and tied to the saddle. Matt paraded the man down Main Street towards the jail where Willie and his deputies met them.

"Why that's Red," Willie cried out, pulling the man's head by his hair to take a good look. "It's Red all right. Still alive, barely."

"Who's Red?" Matt asked, giving the reins back to Willie.

"He and Wichita own the saloon. Figure they must do a ton of business the way they spend money in town. Did he say why he tried to kill you?"

"Wichita," Matt repeated.

Willie took off his hat and scratched his head. He gave the reins to his deputy standing beside him. "Take him down the street to Doc's. You bled on my saddle, Red. That'll cost ya."

"You got lucky, Brazos. He coulda killed you. He's a good shot."

"I'm goin' after Wichita, Willie," Matt reloaded his Colt. "Care to come along?"

"You figure he's behind all this? I'll wait down by my office. I've got a wife and four kids to care for."

"You've got my gun," Tex said, walking up to him.

"Much obliged," Matt said.

Tex replied with a grin, "I was waitin' for you to come back."

"You've got a whole saloon of his friends inside, Brazos," Willie said as he sauntered back to his office.

Matt and Tex continued their stroll down the street towards the Abilene Saloon while a crowd of followers got bigger.

"What's they gonna do?" one of the men in the crowd asked, stumbling his way along with the others.

"Why that's the Brazos Kid," another man said. "I'd hate to have to go up agin' him. He's fast. He's already killed three men in town, and in one day."

"Where were you when I needed you before?" Matt asked Tex.

"The good Lord musta planted me here when He thought you'd need me most," Tex replied. "You've done one hell of a job so far."

"Hang in there, Tex," Matt said, walking slow and carefully towards the saloon. "I'm hopin' there ain't no more, but if there is, I jest might need your gun for sure. Back my play."

One man was stationed on top of the roof of the millinery shop across the street, and shot at Matt, nicking him across his shoulder.

Tex drew and fired at the flash and brought the man down with a single shot. Matt looked at the man fall, and kept walking, holding his shoulder.

"Thanks," Matt said, keeping his eyes fixed on the saloon.

Two men, who had seen Red draped across the sorrel with his hands tied, ran inside and informed Wichita that Matt and Tex were coming towards the saloon.

"Get outside and kill that son-of-a-bitch!" Wichita pushed the men out the door and kicked them with his boot.

They positioned themselves outside on opposite sides of the street and watched Matt and Tex head towards them. One of the men stepped out of the shadows on the left side of the street and fired at Matt. He missed.

Matt brought out his Colt and answered the fire. He hit him dead center with one shot.

The other stepped out from across the street and fired, hitting Matt's hat.

Tex took him out with two shots.

"Took you two that time," Matt said picking up his hat.

"The wind picked up," Tex answered.

From then on, both men kept their hardware out of their holsters.

Wichita pushed the swinging doors to his saloon out and walked slowly to the middle of the street, his right hand on his gun grip.

"You're shootin' up the town, Brazos and my men said you shot my partner, Red. Makes me want to know why."

Matt and Tex stopped walking. "It's my fight now, Tex," Matt said, holstering his Colt. "Cover me from the side."

Some of Wichita's friends started out the door and stood on the sidewalk.

Tex kept his .45 on them. "It's their fight, gentlemen. I'll shoot the first one who even thinks about drawin' his gun."

Matt stood facing Wichita. He knew again he had to draw against a man to kill him or be killed. He briefly thought about Rod being shot without a chance to defend himself just feet away from where he now stood.

"You paid that son-of-a-bitch to kill Rod!" Matt said with gritted teeth. "Why?"

"Who said that? Red? He's my partner. He wouldn't lie about a thing like that."

"You killed a good friend of mine. Before you die, I want to know why."

"You're gonna be an old man, then, because I didn't kill him."

"I'm goin' for my gun in five seconds. Give me the satisfaction to know why you killed him."

"I'm fast, Brazos. Maybe faster than you."

"Four seconds."

Sweat trickled down the sides of Wichita's face, and his hand shook over his gun handle. "I had no cause to have your friend killed. Go look for the real killer."

"Three seconds. You're sayin' someone else paid him?"

"Maybe."

"Two seconds."

Wichita turned and ran, but Matt aimed his .45 from his hip and made the dirt kick up around his boots and stopped him. "One more step and you'll buy the property," Matt warned him.

Wichita stopped and turned back around

"He's crazy," Wichita yelled, holding his left hand out with his right hand wavering above his gun. "I need help."

Tex walked towards the saloon with his .45 aimed at the men. "Everyone stay low and you'll live longer. Let's stay out of it."

"We're backing your play, Tex," said one of two deputies that walked up behind Tex, each carried a shotgun.

The rest of Wichita's men were on the sidewalk watching motionless.

"I'm a businessman," Wichita said as the sweat ran down his nose. "You're the Brazos Kid?" He laughed. "Hell, you're supposed to be in Texas. What're you doin' here?"

Matt stood ready. He remembered the extra second that Rod taught him. "Watch his gun hand, Matt," he could hear Rod saying. *Don't listen to his words. He's tryin' to divert your attention.*

"I'm looking at garbage," Matt challenged him. He knew he was facing Rod's real killer, the man who paid Windsor to pull the trigger. The question that remained in his mind was, *Why?*

"Time's up. Draw, or go to jail!"

Willie caught up to Matt, and seeing Wichita, walked to the other side of the street out of the line of fire, telling others to do the same.

"I'm not drawing against you, Brazos." Wichita turned and walked away. "I know your reputation."

"Your partner knew my reputation, too. Didn't stop him from tryin' to kill me."

"He's a hot head. He probably thought you were someone else. You've got him, if he's still alive, ask him."

"I said, draw or go to jail!"

Wichita kept walking. Willie realized he was heading his way, and again quickly moved. He waved his arms and motioned for the rest to get out of the line of fire.

"Go to hell!" Wichita yelled with his hands up as he continued walking away.

"You're on your way, mister," Matt said. "Tell Satan hello for me."

"You can't shoot me in the back," Wichita said quivering as he kept walking, and letting his arms drop a little at a time until he thought Matt wouldn't see him draw.

He went for his gun and turned, but Matt's pearl-handled .45 barked first, putting two bullets through Wichita's mid-section.

Matt stood still with his smoking Colt hanging by his side. The crowd milled around the bodies of the three men in the street.

Doc had his hands full with patching up Red at the jailhouse.

Willie walked slowly over to Wichita, bouncing every ounce of fat in his body as he moved. He stopped next to Matt and looked down at Wichita.

"Why?" Matt asked.

Wichita's eyes fluttered as blood spilled from his mouth. "I'm – the --father," he coughed out and died.

"What'd he say?" Willie asked. "I couldn't hear him."

Matt heard Wichita, but kept his secret. "Something about Rod getting close to finding out something shady in his business," Matt said. "Something like that."

"Who'd a thought?" Willie said.

Willie walked back to his deputies and ordered them to pick up the bodies.

Matt put a fresh cigar between his teeth, offered one to Tex, and gave one to Willie.

Matt and Tex lit their cigars together, turned and gave each other a nod, then walked away back to the hotel.

A band of trail riders rode around the hotel and down Main Street shouting and firing off their weapons in the air as a signal that they had just brought a load of cattle into Abilene.

They reined up at the saloon, looked at the deputies hauling the bodies away, and dismounted.

"Great to be back in Abilene," one of the cowboys said. He shook the dirt off his duster, and walked in the saloon with the rest of the cowboys.

# CHAPTER 23

## GOING HOME TO TEXAS

T he next morning, Agnes' driver pulled the carriage to the front of the hotel. Martha and Agnes sat in the back seat while Lori sat up front with the driver.

"I wonder where Matt is," Martha asked Agnes. "He must still be in the hotel. I'll go find out."

When Martha got to Matt's room, she found the door ajar and saw he was having difficulty trying to get his bag closed with his left arm in a sling.

"Need a hand?" She walked in and stood next to the bed.

He closed it tightly, strapped it down, and then proceeded to pick it up when he saw an inviting look in Martha's gray eyes. He took the bag to the doorway, set it down, turned back to Martha, and kicked the door shut.

She reached out and took hold of his hand with her gloved-hand, and thanked him.

"For what?"

"For shutting the door."

He leaned forward, grabbed her like he had wanted to do for so long, and kissed her tenderly on her moistened lips. They let go of their hands, put their arms around each other and experienced a moment of long awaited ecstasy. Even through her thick clothing, he could feel the throbbing of her body as she pressed hard against his.

Their mouths fashioned a tight union of their spirits as his hands reached under her hair and stroked the back of her smooth neck. He brought his hand down across her shoulder and felt her soft rosy cheeks. He continued with his hand down her smooth throat, cupping it, and brought her lips in harder against his. Finally, the moment was theirs to share.

She whispered in his ear, "Remember under the shade tree when I brought some cold water to you?" She was referring to their first moment of flirtation on her farm, when he plowed the fields for her and her late husband.

"You were desirable then, and much more now," he murmured.

"Did you want me then?"

"More than you'll know," he answered, bringing his lips back to hers.

"Do you still want me?" she asked, speaking from lips close to his, with her two fingers pressed against his lips.

He looked into her gray eyes and kissed them softly. Then he kissed her nose lightly, and slid his lips down to her lips and kissed her hard again. They allowed their lips to mesh.

Her hands unbuttoned the middle of his shirt and found their way inside to feel and rub his hairy chest as their mouths met again.

He broke from her for a parting moment, looked at her corseted bosom and stroked her with his fingers.

"You didn't answer me," she said breathing deeply.

A knock on the door interrupted their moment like a stone hurled through a window.

"The driver is waiting, Mother," Lori said softly from outside the door. Her manners taught her never to enter a closed door without knocking first, even if she had the key. She was an obedient daughter.

"Oh, damn," Martha whispered.

Matt gave her a look of astonishment.

"Yes, dear," she responded as she broke from Matt's grip and wistfully straightened herself up.

When once she knew that she and Matt were properly prepared to meet the world together once more, she looked at him, smiled, and said, "Ready!"

He grabbed the bag, tucked it under his arm, opened the door and let Martha precede him out the door. Lori was already down the stairs and waiting by the carriage with Ian.

Agnes was sitting in the back of the carriage waiting. "It's going to be a dull day in Abilene without you, Matt."

"Mornin' Agnes," Matt greeted her. "Yes, it is a fine day."

"Good bye, Ian," he said, shaking his hand. "Take care of your sister for me."

"Good bye, Brazos. I'll do that." Then he lauged. "It's been, may I say, one hell of an experience."

He gave Lori a kiss on the cheek. "You're as beautiful as your mother."

"Well, thank you," she replied, and curtsied.

"Goin' back to Texas, Brazos?" Tex's voice sounded in Matt's ear from behind him.

"Mornin', Tex," Matt replied. "Yep."

"Sure gonna miss you."

"Thanks Tex. Now if you don't mind." Matt took hold of Martha's hand, looked into her eyes and saw again that welcome look he had been joyfully experiencing for the past few minutes in his room. He wanted to take her in his arms again and kiss her one more time. Instead, he shook her hand.

She stared into his eyes and asked, "No kiss?"

He removed his Stetson, embraced her and kissed her passionately. He felt the warmth and sweetness in her kiss that told him to hurry back. "Texas is a mighty big state," he whispered. "A man can get lonely down there."

"I know where to find you," she replied in a wispy tone of voice.

Agnes closed her eyes for a moment, opened them, and then smiled as she watched Matt climb on board and sit beside her.

"Sorry you're not staying?" she asked, twirling her parasol.

Matt returned her smile and sat down next to her. The whistle of the train sounded a warning for its passengers to get on board, and the rider's horse whinnied.

"We best get going, driver," Agnes told the driver, taking hold of Matt's hand.

"I'm sure you'll be back," Tex said, doffing his hat to the ladies.

Lori's eyes opened wide while a smile appeared on her face at the sight of the handsome man named, Tex. She remembered him as the stranger at the dance, but didn't get too close a look at him then. She did now, and liked what she saw.

Martha caught the gleam in her daughter's eyes, and turned to Matt who had a startled look on his face.

Sheriff Willie bounced down the sidewalk, and took off his hat as a gesture to the ladies. "We're jest happy that you came and brought justice for Rod, and peace back to Abilene," Willie added trying to catch his breath.

"Driver," Agnes called out.

The train whistle blew again, and the carriage turned and headed for the depot. Matt stood up, took off his hat and waved it to Martha and Lori, and to all of Abilene.

Agnes held onto his hand and squeezed it hard.

## EPILOGUE

April, 1871.

**M**att, and Steve had just rode across the range and reined up at the banks of the Brazos. The sun was barely straight up, but the day was already warm.

"Agnes carried Wichita's child, you say?" Steve dismounted and took his horse down the bank of the Brazos for a drink. "Why would he have Rod killed if that were his child?"

"The whole ugly mess, Steve." Matt joined him at the edge of the river. He took out a letter he had carried in his vest pocket and read it again to himself. "Agnes said that he had raped her, and she didn't tell Rod for fear Rod would kill him. She carried the baby hoping Rod would think it was his."

"And Wichita wanted the baby?"

"I don't think so. I think Wichita wanted Agnes, the mansion and the wealth that came with it. The judge had accumulated a fortune from his years of practice, on top of what he had inherited from his father. He was worth a sizeable sum of money when he died. He left it all to his only heir, Agnes."

"Why didn't Rod just accept that style of living instead of risking his neck as a marshal for a few dollars a month?" Steve brought his horse back up the bank and tied him to a branch.

"Rod was his own man. He lived for the gun and excitement. He couldn't accept a life of leisure." Matt folded the letter and put it back in his vest pocket. He brought Skeeter back up the bank and secured him, also.

The two men sat on the bank of the Brazos and skipped stones across its surface.

"I suppose Wichita thought by bringing shame and disgrace to Rod by getting him drunk and accuse him of messing around with some guy's woman, and then having him killed, Agnes would have no other recourse but to go to him."

"But, how did he accomplish all that, Matt?"

"It was all a frame-up, Steve. Rod wasn't drunk any more than Wichita was that night. He had a drink, which he did on occasion, but they all put on a show with that phony laughter, loud enough to distract Rod from knowin' another man was standin' behind him with a gun."

"And his number one rule about using the bar-room mirror?" Steve stood up, took some makings, and rolled a cigarette. "Why didn't he see the man in the mirror?"

"Same way I didn't see the man when he tried to shoot me in the back. Wichita knew I always used the mirror, and he stood between the man and me, and blocked his view. Lucky for me, I heard him slap leather so I could draw on him. He did the same with Rod."

"Rod didn't hear anything, not even the click of the gun?" Steve offered his cigarette to Matt and rolled himself another.

"The man had already taken his gun out of his holster and had it cocked when he challenged Rod." Matt lit his cigarette and blew a smoke ring that wafted out over the Brazos and disappeared. With the same match, he lit Steve's cigarette.

"And everyone said it was a fair fight?" Steve exhaled a ring of smoke above the Brazos like Matt's, and smiled. "One thing still bothers me."

"What's that?"

"Why did Wichita want you killed? He could have let you ride out."

"Competition. He thought I was horning in on his property, and that I would have found out about him soon enough from Agnes. He was already afraid that Agnes might have said somethin' about it. Figured he would have lost out completely after all he had done."

"Pretty nasty set up," Steve surmised. "I guess that's Abilene. Someday, someone will come along, clean it up, and make it a decent place to live. What about Martha and Lori?"

"Agnes needed them, and, because they became such good friends, she had them move in with her. Couldn't ask for a better arrangement. They're good for each other. Understand Lori's going to finishing school in Boston."

"And Tex?

"Handsome dude. Seemed he had eyes on Lori. Have to wait and see."

"That's it, Matt?" Steve mounted his horse and waited for Matt.

"Oh, I figure we'll visit them on our next cattle drive. Abilene is the place for long horns, let me tell ya."

"You gonna go on a cattle drive? That I've gotta see."

"Just one more thing," Matt said climbing up on Skeeter. "Abilene has herself a new marshal. Willie turned in his badge."

"Anyone I know?" Steve spurred his horse into a gallop and headed back to the ranch.

"Fella by the name of Wild Bill Hickock." Matt spurred Skeeter and joined up with him.

Matt was home again, on the Brazos.

He received another letter from Agnes a few months later. She had a boy.

www.ermal.com

duke@ermal.com

www.johnwayneshow.com

An excerpt from the next thrilling story in the Brazos series

# CALL OF THE BRAZOS

### PART ONE
### BOZEMAN, MONTANA
### 1882

# CHAPTER 1

## Ghosts

"**C**hange" is a word not found in many a cowboy's vocabulary, especially one Matt Jorgensen, a cowboy from Montana. A cowboy's way of living can take many turns along life's trail before he finds his ultimate calling. One never knows from where the calling comes or, in most instances, how to best answer it. A cowboy only knows that he's got to trust what he's got to trust, and some of the time it's difficult to understand, especially when one is torn between right and wrong, place of birth, and color of skin, and then change becomes all important to get one's perspectives in order.

Matt Jorgensen's call was to a ranch in Texas, south of Waco, across the Brazos where he earned the nickname, "The Brazos Kid." The reverberating echo of his calling and the continuing plague of his southern culture against his northern heritage was his birthplace in Montana. Although many Montanans were sympathetic to the South, Matt had been reared twenty-one years without being prejudiced, mostly because he had never encountered a race or slavery situation. He left Montana clean of any racial biases and came back a different man. His life had again changed and taken on a different perspective when he met beautiful but rugged Ginny McBride, whom he lost soon after the mortar struck at Fort Sumter. He vowed to the wind that he would never fall in love again.

Twenty-one years and a Civil War later, he returned to Montana following his mother's funeral. He found himself about to make another major change in his life when he met Mary Beth Paterson, a refined attorney with many frills and laces, the complete opposite of Ginny. She preferred to be called by her middle name.

From an eagle's eye view, two figures silhouetted by the pale pink Montana sunset appeared on the Ruby River Ranch. It was late afternoon of Thanksgiving, 1882.

Matt's arm cradled Beth's back as they stood in the stillness of the evening. She was a lovely young woman, with long flowing brunette hair to match her sparkling brown eyes. She was thin, and to Matt's liking, just a little too thin. She had come to Virginia City as an attorney from Richmond, Virginia, and in setting up her practice, took Matt's mother on as a client to put her property in order in her last will and testament.

The cowboys on her ranch had laid Mrs. Andersen in her grave before Matt made it back from Texas, a place he called home for over twenty years. He was a cowboy in his forties who stood six-feet-four-inches tall with a rugged look and scars he earned through the Civil War and various battles in Texas. At his mother's request, he had returned to his birthplace to see her before she died, but she succumbed before he could reach her. Being her only surviving heir, he was the new owner of the Ruby River Ranch.

The faint sound of a rifle echoed through the woods, causing the forest creatures to take shelter out of fright. Matt turned his face towards the sound, listened to the wind as it whistled through the treetops and, hearing nothing else, settled his eyes back on Beth.

"What was that?" Beth asked, turning her head quickly and looking into the tall timbers on the hillside.

Matt looked intently into the northern wind. "Monty cleanin' out his rifle, I s'pose." He knew different, but for the moment, he let it pass as he looked at Beth's curious face.

The first snow of the season fell softly around them. Matt had not seen snow for some time having lived in Texas for so many years.

Beth looked around, and seeing nothing unusual, said, "You're looking puzzled about something."

Matt felt something evil in the wind, but the quietness of the moment and the excitement he felt being with Beth left him with the task of assuring her that nothing was wrong. He rationalized to himself that certainly Monty, the foreman of his ranch, or any of his cowboys riding the range could simply be shooting at something. But he thought, "Not likely, though, because they know that the noise will disturb the cattle." He sensed it, but as the herd remained undisturbed, he put it behind him, hoping that nothing was wrong.

He brushed the snow from Beth's coat and said, "There's white stuff all over us."

Beth laughed. "Snow, silly. Pure, unadulterated snow." She wiped the few drops from his face and kissed him. "Like it?"

He shrugged his shoulders, feeling like a kid as he watched her face beam with happiness.

The snow was wet and stuck to their faces and clothes until they soon became whitened with it. A Montana snow comes up suddenly and stays for a great while. The temperature having dropped into the single digits, this was the first one of the season.

"Don't you remember what snow is?" she asked with a slight giggle as she pulled her woolen scarf tight around her neck, locking in her coat's collar.

"Sure. Just haven't seen it for awhile. Gotta get used to it agin." He took his bandanna and wiped the snow from Beth's face. "You sure do look pretty."

She received his kiss with increased passion, sliding her arms through his jacket and around his back.

"Wanna go back inside?"

"Later. Let's enjoy our first snow alone together." Reflecting quietly, he added, "I'm glad Dan brought me back."

The Wrisleys were long-standing friends and neighbors of the Andersens for many years. It was their son, Danny who had brought Matt back to Montana from Texas.

Beth looked at him lovingly, took her arms out of his coat and walked with him down the path to a clearing in the trees where they stood to watch the wind blow the snow around in gentle swirls. She knew she was in love and was waiting for him to give her the chance to show it.

A cow lay dead on the outlying slopes of the ranch from a bullet wound through its head.

"We got meat, boys!" a mean-looking cuss yelled out as he rode with his men down the side of the mountain to pick up their game, one of Matt's cattle.

They were six of the worst-looking, worst-smelling men anyone could ever come up against. Men of no morals. Each of them looked mean and ornery enough to strangle a rattler with his bare hands.

Biggun was their leader, a large grizzly of a man who appeared to have never gone without a meal. He stood about six-foot seven inches tall and looked meaner than sin. His beard had the look of a mop dragged through a pigsty, gray like his long dirty curls and moustache. His clothing, with food stains up and down his vest, had never been cleaned. His coat was long and shabby-looking, torn at the hem.

"Cut it up and cook it now," he barked at his men. "I don't aim to go a day without good food, and I'm hungry."

He let out a mountain yell that would send shivers down the gullets of the nearby coyotes and scared the hawks out of their tree nests. He pulled his Bowie out of his belt before the others, and slid it into the belly of the beast, carving it upwards.

Three of the men joined in with their knives while the other two started building a fire.

Matt watched the snow as it continued to fall, and tried to lick it as it stuck to his face. "Isn't this kinda early for snow, even in Montana?" he asked. "I mean, this is Thanksgiving."

"Looking at how it's coming down, it's good that the Wrisleys and I will be leaving for home in the morning." Beth slipped her arm through his. "I'm happy you asked me to visit you here on the Double R. Having spent so much time with your mother before she passed on, it's almost like home to me."

Home to Beth was now a single-story dwelling behind her office in Virginia City, Montana, where she hung a shingle to advertise her services as an attorney-at-law.

"I'm glad you accepted my invitation. Out here with a bunch of rowdy boys is not my idea of a good Thanksgiving. Down in Texas, we had several ladies in the household who could cook up the finest dinner this side of heaven."

They turned back and walked down the long trail leading to the main road and watched the sun become engulfed by a dark sky. The wind picked up and the temperature dropped a little. They made fresh tracks in the snow that painted the land and forest surrounding the Ruby River Ranch.

"The way the sky looks," Beth said, "it wouldn't surprise me any if an early blizzard might be moving in."

"You lookin' for a fight?"

"Hmm?"

"*Bluster.* That means someone lookin' for a fight down in Texas."

"Oh, no. I said, *blizzard.* It's when the snow falls fast and furious like sand in a windstorm. We call that a *blizzard.*"

"Well, I've seen many of them up here when I was a kid. Never called them *blizzard*s, though, jest snowstorms. New lingo, I 'spose."

The sun slipped silently behind the ridge of trees and darkness quickly engulfed the land, and yet, it was still early in the evening. The wind howled through the treetops, and the full moon lit upon the new fallen snow lighting the way as they walked down the gutted road.

"Don't know if it's safe for you to go anytime soon with a blizzard comin'." Beth said. "I've got a lot of catching up to do with some of my other clients in Virginia City."

"How many clients you 'spose you have?"

"I've got some. Enough to keep me busy anyway."

They turned and walked back to the ranch in a slow rhythmic pace.

The cowboys' singing and guitar strumming drifted from the wranglers' quarters, but the lovers were oblivious of everything except each other.

When they reached the corral just past the bunkhouse, Matt climbed the orchestra seat and pulled Beth up alongside him. In the full light of the moon, they viewed the mountains surrounding them.

"I'll be all right. We'll stop at the Wrisleys' along the way before they take me to Virginia City. They'll see to it that I'm looked after." Matt was shivering. "Didn't Texas ever get this cold?"

"If it did, I wasn't there to feel it. I plumb forgot how cold it could get here in the mountains."

They caught the sound of the animals of the forest scattering through the brush.

"The animals running is a sign that a winter storm is heading our way," Beth said, looking into the hills.

As a hired gun from Texas, Matt knew the smell of death and sensed that their running was caused by something far more serious than merely a winter storm.

As they watched the windblown snow  drop against the north side of the trees and fence posts, they continued to listen to the gentle music playing from the bunkhouse behind them. For a long time, neither said anything.  Unaware of the gunshot that Matt and Beth had heard, the cowboys continued talking, singing, and playing cards within the close confined of the bunkhouse.

"I'm supposing you're thinking about Texas, aren't you, Matt?"

Matt said nothing but looked out into the hills.

"She must have been a real pretty girl," Beth continued.

Matt reflected, showing he was a little amused, then began reminiscing. "My pa and the others fought Injuns on that hill there as they'd come whoopin' down upon us. The fightin' didn't seem to last long.  We'd shoot some, I remember that.  Later, most of them were jest young bucks seeking some fun, scarin' us and stealin' one of our cows to take back with 'em. Pa'd let 'em jest to keep the peace. He knew they needed food."

"Was she real pretty?"

He ignored her question, although not intentionally. He was just completely lost in thought about his youth. "Lukas and I came ridin' bareback down that slope yonder, chased by a couple of Sioux right about there." He pointed to a wide trail leading from the top of the hill to the bottom that had become a natural trail over the years leading to Bozeman. "We were ridin' bareback, jest like them. Never thought my horse could run so fast. I looked back at Lukas, who was right on my heels, when a stupid branch stood out and swatted me in the face. Knocked me off Skeeter and I tumbled all the way down. See? The tree is still a standin'. Busted my arm up. Had to write left-handed in school for awhile."

"You got away, naturally?"

"Wull, I'm here, ain't I?"

"How do you know it's the same tree?" She watched him for awhile as he stared out into the distance.

"Are you thinking of going back to Texas?"

Matt sat silent for the moment and then turned to look at her. "Looking at you just now reminds me of how little I really know about you."

"A lot about you I don't yet know either."

"You will, my darlin'," he answered. "It'll just take time."

He climbed down and stood for a moment, looking out to the hills as he closed his coat tighter.

"Lukas was wild, but I was a hell of a lot wilder. I could out drink him, out cuss him and out shoot him anytime. But he had a crazy way about him I couldn't tame. He was like a mustang. You know what I mean?"

"Well, mister," Beth said. "Are you going to give a lady a hand?"

He reached up and brought her gently down.

She clasped his hand in hers as they walked into the night, away from the ranch house and the singing of the cowboys. "As openers, I'm a graduate of William and Mary College, received my law degree there. I have a family of two brothers and a sister living in Virginia. Mom and Dad passed away. I left home and came to Virginia City to set up practice. I'm single, never been married. Not that I haven't had the opportunity. There have been plenty, I must tell you. Just never met a man I could love, or really liked, for that matter. Been here for almost a whole year, and then your mother came in one day and hired me. And, now. . ."

"Now?"

She let go his hand and ran away, then stopped and bent down to roll a snowball and throw it at Matt. She laughed as it splattered in his face.

Wiping it away, he scooped up a handful of snow and ran after her. Their shadows moved in the moonlight as they ran toward the hill where his parents were buried.

Matt caught up with Beth and brought her down laughing in his arms.

He rose just as quickly and helped her up. Looking back at the hills he began to reminisce again.

"He's like a ghost up there, Beth."

"Your brother?" She followed his gaze. "Then let him be a ghost. You're not."

"I feel like I don't belong here."

Beth slipped her arms around Matt to console him. "Don't think about it."

He was thinking about the day his pa made him leave his father's ranch, the Double O. He never liked the name, so, when he inherited it, he renamed it the Ruby River Ranch, then shortened it to the Double R.

"Your father had that boy removed and buried somewhere else," Beth said. Matt looked at her. "I never thought about telling you until now."

Matt gazed into her eyes as if searching for something deep within his spirit. Looking at her made him search deeper.

"I spent the better part of my life in the South running from my past. Those ghosts made me fight a war against my own people." He said, referring to the part he had played in the Civil War when he served as a captain with Terry's Rangers.

Beth put her head on his chest.

"Just before that," he said, almost inaudibly, "I fell in love for the first time."

Beth looked up into his eyes and saw the pain.

"My people took her from me." A long pause stretched seemingly throughout the night while she waited for him to continue. "She was lovely."

Beth bit her lip, closed her eyes, and buried her face deep into Matt's coat. She wanted to hear, but was afraid to listen.

"My land here, these hills, this ranch, these people were taken from me." He pulled away and gazed off into the distance as if looking beyond the hills.

"I came back, and it's like I'm a stranger. The townsfolk remembered. They remembered that I was a murderer who killed their minister in a botched-up robbery."

"You proved you weren't involved. They believed you."

"But they were waiting, Beth. They were waiting. It was like the ghosts from twenty-four years ago were all waiting for me to come back."

"Are you going to let the ghosts beat you, now that you've won your freedom and proven yourself?"

"They 'spected who I was, Wil and Anne Andersen's surviving son, the one who ran away."

"You did not run away, Mr. Jorgensen." Beth stood firm before him, her fists clenched at her side. "You weren't going to run. Your father made you leave. The townsfolk would have lynched you had they known you were at the robbery. Instead, the law gunned down one Jeff Manning, mistaking him for you. You had to run to stay alive."

"And now I'm supposed to accept this ranch as if I had never left?"

"You're home." She caressed him again. The snow fell harder and the wind picked up.

"Want to talk about her?" she asked, pulling away and looking him straight on.

"Someday, maybe," Matt answered, grabbing her hands and holding them gently. "You've no cause to worry."

"Oh, hell, Mr. Jorgensen, I know that. I only want you to know that *you* don't have to worry."

He felt an aching disturbance, much like one feels without any apparent explanation for it. He couldn't put a finger on why he felt that way. It had nothing to do with his first love. He just knew something was gnawing at him, and that he had to get a grip on it.

When looking at the cemetery, the hills, the ranch house, the corral, and even in Beth's eyes. He could only see ghosts.

Matt turned, faced the cemetery, and pulled his coat tighter for warmth. He gripped her hand, and they walked toward the cemetery on the north side of the ranch. "There's no one in my grave?"

They stopped by the fence and stared at the crosses.

"It's just an empty grave." She looked at his face and saw a curled smile appear. "Feel better?"

Matt stared at the markers and affixed his eyes on one that read

Charlie Nightlinger
? – 1882
Trail Cook

"Charlie's a nigger, ain't he?" Matt asked without taking his eyes from the marker.

A couple of wranglers, Danny Wrisley and Cookie Benson, walked out of the bunkhouse after having watched the couple walk up to the gravesite. Danny was a young cowboy, barely twenty, lean, clean, and good-looking. Cookie was the oldest man on the ranch with a set of store-bought teeth and a bald head that he kept covered with a well-seasoned Stetson. He looked underfed, in the face as well as his belly, and wore a rope around his pants to keep them up. His beard was long enough to catch snow and make it appear white, though most of it was still black. He had been with the ranch ever since Nightlinger passed away.

"Mr. Nightlinger?" Beth asked.

"Mr. Nightlinger," Matt answered, with his hands on his hips, almost defensively.

"He's a Negro," Beth answered. "You knew that from the moment you arrived on the ranch."

"Point I'm makin' is, shouldn't he be buried in another field somewhere?" Matt looked around at the men staring at him, and then at Beth. "Just askin', mind ya."

"Ordinarily, yes," Beth replied. "But your mother and the boys saw it fittin' to bury him here."

"That's what's been botherin' me all day yesterday and last night."

"Surely you aren't having second thoughts about Mr. Nightlinger? He was a kindly old man."

"Never gave it first thoughts, I guess." He rubbed his gloved hand under his chin, looked around, then pointed to the north. "What about the other side of the hill?"

"You mean to dig him up, boss?" Cookie asked, handing Matt a tin of coffee.

"And move him?" Danny looked sternly into Matt's face, then took his hat and brushed it on his pants.

"That don't make sense."

"It does if you're a Reb," Beth reminded him. "You can send four men to their graves and not bat an eye. Now you intend to dig up a dead man and inter him in a piece of ground away from his friends. What is it about you that makes you so callous?"

"Callous? Yeah, guess I am." Matt nodded to the hill behind the ranch. "Right about over there would do nicely."

Other wranglers gathered around them with their plates in their hands, enjoying leftovers from the dinner.

"We havin' a meetin' or sumpin'?" one of them asked, smiling broadly from ear to ear, thinking nothing was wrong.

"Gentlemen," Beth addressed them, holding back her anger. "Your boss wants Mr. Nightlinger dug up and interred behind the ranch house."

The men looked at one another and chattered amongst themselves.

"That's right," Matt assured them. "I looked out back and saw a nice place where he would be all by himself. Cozy and warm, so to speak."

Danny spoke up, "You talk like he's still alive,".

"No. No, just dead. But he needs a new home, away from my parents."

"Why?" Beth asked annoyingly.

"Jest because I said so, Miss Paterson."

The men sensed a little orneriness in Matt's tone.

"'Spose he's right," one of the older wranglers said, picking pieces of food out of his teeth. "His land, and he's the boss."

"He's the boss?" Beth repeated. "Yes. Do what he says."

"Wait a minute," Matt interrupted. "You don't have to tell 'em again. I already told 'em."

"Yes, you did. I'm sorry," Beth replied and stomped away, packing the snow hard with her boots.

"You don't have to do it this very minute," Matt said.

Beth stopped, turned, and asked, "Just when do you want the men to do this?"

"They're my men. I'll tell 'em."

"Well, Mr. Jorgensen. Tell them!"

"He's a nigger," Matt yelled out to her. "He's no right to be by my parents in their restin' place."

"Oh!" Beth walked back and stopped within a few feet of Matt. With a stern look of seriousness about her, she said smartly, "He's a Negro. And just because you came from Texas and fought on the side of the South doesn't cut it with me, Mister."

"That's right," Matt came back angrily, swinging his fist into empty space. "I fought, and now I demand my rights--I want him removed!"

"I was born and raised in the South," Beth retorted.

The wranglers were enjoying this argument. Some sat down in the snow to watch, while others leaned up against a tree or sat on a nearby stump.

Beth noticed the group and gathered her senses about her. In a more calm fashion, she continued. "If anyone has a prejudicial right to hate the Negroes, it could be me, but I don't. I take pride in living here in Montana, and in helping you get back your ranch. But I don't take pride, Mr. Jorgensen, in watching a mean man take vengeance against someone who never did anything but good for your folks."

Matt also sensed the group watching them but went ahead and stuck his chin out. "You through?"

Beth turned and continued her trod to the house without looking back. Once in the house, she slammed the door hard enough to cause snow to fall from the roof.

Matt cringed and said, "What bee's up her bloomers?"

"She's got a good point," Danny said.

"But it's my land, and I'll damn well do as I please with it."

"When?" Danny asked, watching the house for Beth to return.

"Why not wait 'til spring, I'm thinkin'," Monty said with a smile. Monty was a man who always obeyed orders without putting much thought to it, but he pondered well this time. "The sod will have been thawed by then," he thought aloud to himself. He took out his makings and rolled himself a cigarette.

"Damn if she don't remind me of someone," Matt said, gritting his teeth.

Monty smiled and said, "Yeah. You."

Matt looked at Monty, took the rolled cigarette from him, and said, "Thanks."

"No bother," Monty said, throwing an empty tobacco sac away and licking his lips. "Want a match?"

"Yeah," Matt answered. He lit his cigarette, and stared at the house. He took a drag and then, as Monty watched in consternation, threw the cigarette to the wind. "You ever want something so bad you hurt deep down inside?" he asked, his eyes fixed on the warm-lit ranch house. Monty reached down for the cigarette and said, "Yep. Know jest whatcha mean."